Sherlock Holmes and the Seven Deadly Sins

Envy, Pride, Wrath, Greed, Lust, Gluttony & Sloth

From the Notes of
John H. Watson M.D.

Edited by

Roger Riccard

First published in 2024 by
The Irregular Special Press
for Baker Street Studios Ltd
Endeavour House
170 Woodland Road, Sawston
Cambridge, CB22 3DX, UK

ISBN: 978 1 901091 93 9

Cover Illustration: Hieronymus Bosch's *The Seven Deadly Sins*.

Typeset in 8/11/20pt Palatino

About the Author

Roger Riccard has Scottish roots, which trace his lineage back to the Roses of Highland, Scotland. This ancestry encouraged his interest in the writings of Sir Arthur Conan Doyle. With this volume, Roger now joins that select group of Holmes storytellers whose works surpass the number of original Sherlock Holmes stories published by Sir Arthur Conan Doyle.

He lives in a suburb of Los Angeles with two cats named Bela (after Bela Lugosi who played Dracula, because he likes to bite) and Amanda (after Amanda Blake who played Miss Kitty on the old television western series, *Gunsmoke*) When not editing Watson's notes of Sherlock Holmes adventures, he is singing with a group which entertains senior citizens in retirement homes, serving his church, or watching baseball, crime dramas, musicals, old movies, and British mysteries on BBC America.

To the Memory of My Rosilyn,
My forever Inspiration

&

To My Support Team:

Kendra, Kathy and Miss Nute

Thanks for your continued
encouragement and assistance

Review by Michelle Stanley

Each short case is distinctive with its described sin and is well played out with good character development. Sherlock Holmes displays an indifferent, aloof, but smart personality in all the tales. Dr. Watson offers the strong support and sage advice that is needed by Holmes and his clients. Inspector Lestrade is one of my favourite characters, as well as Holmes's landlady.

Sherlock Holmes and the Seven Deadly Sins is an anthology where Sherlock Holmes and Dr. Watson are kept busy with cases that are based on the seven deadly sins. These sins are envy, pride, wrath, greed, lust, gluttony, and sloth. Envy rears its ugly head when a judge is murdered in *A Perpetrator in a Pear Tree*. Pride is the mask we wear to hide our weaknesses in *The Etheridge Escapade*. In wrath, Holmes finds the security for the Prime Minister too deadly for comfort. A food critic makes enemies after writing bad restaurant reviews in gluttony. True love cannot be bought as evident in lust. For sloth, a young woman becomes concerned when her fiancé is missing. Greed is the motive when a kidnapped man is found dead.

The stories are moderately paced, interesting, and amusing at times whenever Holmes goes into deep thinking mode or Dr. Watson subtly describes Sherlock Holmes so that readers can get to know him better as I did.

Contents

Prologue

How did 'The Seven Deadly Sins' come about? To go back to the roots of this list, it started out as 'The Eight Evil Thoughts' by a 4th century monk named Evagrious Ponticus. His list included: Gluttony, Lust, Avarice, Anger, Sloth, Sadness, Vainglory and Pride. In the 6th century, St. Gregory the Great (Later Pope Gregory I) replaced Sloth with Envy and named Pride as their overriding sin. Later still in the 13th century, St. Thomas Aquinas brought back Sloth, eliminated Sadness, and decided that Vainglory was already covered under Pride, bringing the total down to the seven that we recognise today.

Envy

A Perpetrator in a Pear Tree

Chapter One

As we sat in our rooms at 221B Baker Street on a cold winter's day in London, Sherlock Holmes lit his churchwarden pipe with a lump of hot coal that he had retrieved with the fireplace tongs. The city had been snowbound for several days, a condition which curtailed my friend's profession as the world's first consulting detective.

Having finished the breakfast provided by our landlady, Mrs. Hudson, we were indulging in our pipes and reading the morning papers when there came to our ears the sound of heavy footsteps on the stairs.

Before the knock came to our door, my companion cried out, "Come in, Inspector Lestrade!"

Slowly the door opened and the Scotland Yard Inspector entered with a quizzical look upon his face. "How'd you know …" he started to ask, then changed his mind, remembering that Holmes had done this to him before. "It's the footsteps again, isn't it? It's devilish I say! I don't know how you can distinguish mine from those of anyone else."

Holmes smiled and waved the man to a seat by the fire, for his coat was quite damp and snow still clung to his bowler.

"Your footsteps were heavier this morning," Holmes admitted. "However, the sound was its usual pattern. Combining that with this headline from *The Times*, I was able to logically expect a visit from one of our friends at the Yard."

He held up the front page with his finger pointed at the first column, which read:

IMPOSSIBLE MURDER IN MUSWELL HILL

The Honourable Justice Jameson Mason of Fortis Keep in Muswell Hill was found dead yesterday under mysterious circumstances. Upon receiving no answer when called upon for breakfast, Sir Jameson's son, Edgar Mason, sent for assistance. Servants were required to force open the tower room where the retired judge had retreated the night before to work on his memoirs.

Initial investigations indicate that he appears to have died from a wound to his heart. However, no weapon has been identified and no trace of an intruder has presented itself.

Inspector Mossgarden of Scotland Yard has ordered an exhaustive search of the area.

The story went on with more details and some speculation as to the possibility of former convicts who may have sought revenge upon Sir Jameson, who was known for his harsh sentencing.

"Yes," replied the Inspector. "The reports from Mossgarden indicate that there are some unusual aspects to the murder that I believe you would find to be of interest."

Holmes leaned back in his chair and steepled his fingers in front of his chin, gazing intently at our visitor.

"I shall be happy to accompany you, Lestrade," he responded after a few moments. "But only if you will explain to me the *real* reason you wish my presence on this case."

The Scotland Yard official feigned ignorance and started to protest, but Holmes cut him off.

"No, no, my friend. Do not deny it. You have another motive for wanting me along."

Lestrade's shoulders sagged in defeat. Finally, he cast his eyes down and made his admission.

"Mossgarden is a very formidable individual, Mr. Holmes. He is stubborn and bitter that he has not yet received the credit he feels that he deserves at Scotland Yard. He will do what he can to push this case through to trial and conviction. Unfortunately, I have reason to believe that he is rushing to conclusions and an innocent man is in danger of being convicted."

"What leads you to believe so?" asked Holmes.

"Mossgarden is holding Edgar Mason in a cell at Scotland Yard on suspicion of murdering his father. Mason is also the prospective son-in-law of the well-known barrister, Charles Anderson, whom I have had contact with in the past. He personally asked me to take a second look into this case when he could get no satisfaction from questioning Mossgarden."

"Why you and not the Chief Inspector?" I asked.

Lestrade shifted in his seat, "Anderson and the Chief Inspector do not get along. There have been too many times when they have wrangled in court and it has not gone well for the latter. He thought that by discreetly coming to me he would have a better chance of success.

"But if Mossgarden finds that I'm investigating his case, he will report me to the Chief Inspector who, as you know, disapproves of inspectors becoming involved in each other's cases. It would bring about a confrontation with Mossgarden that I would prefer to avoid until I have my proofs."

I could not believe my ears and spoke up at this confession. "Surely, Inspector, you are not afraid of such an individual? I've seen you in action on many occasions and you are one of the bravest men I've met. I've never known you to kowtow to anyone. Even in those instances when Holmes disproves your methods or theories, you accept them with grudging respect, without apology."

Lestrade looked me in the eye and answered, "It's kind of you to say so, Doctor, and normally I believe I can stand up to almost any man alive. But this fellow ..." he shook his head in exasperation, "This fellow has the most irritating character that I've ever come across. He's a conceited, arrogant, bully who won't listen to reason if it contradicts his own thoughts. I wouldn't be a bit surprised if he was a descendant of Captain Bligh himself![1]

"However, if I can tell the Chief Inspector that you gentlemen have taken an interest in the case, and that I joined you due to the fact that we have worked on many cases in the past, it might be more acceptable."

Holmes stood and announced, "Then we shall gladly accompany you, old friend, for we cannot risk a miscarriage of justice due to some overly ambitious inspector's ego."

We wrapped up warm against the weather and the three of us caught a train for East Finchley. From there, we hired a trap and set off for Fortis Keep. The weather was cooperating, for there had been no snow for twenty-four hours, but the temperature was still freezing.

Thus, it was that less than two hours from Lestrade's knock on our door, we arrived at the scene of the crime. Fortis Keep, part of an ancient long-demolished castle which once guarded the northern approach to London, still had a single tower with high walls surrounding the living quarters, courtyard, and stables. At some point in its past, a man-made moat some twenty feet wide was dug surrounding the structure.

"This seems like an odd place for a judge to retire," I commented. "You would think that some old manor or a townhouse in the city would be more appropriate."

"It's his inheritance," answered Lestrade. "The Judge's family dates back centuries in this place."

We crossed the moat via a bridge and a surly looking groom took charge of our trap and led the horse to the stables while we advanced upon the main door. Lestrade announced us to

---

[1] Lieutenant William Bligh, Captain of the HMS Bounty, whose despotic rule so enraged his crew that they mutinied near Tahiti in 1789.

the butler, Carson by name, and requested that we be allowed to examine the scene of the crime.

After allowing us in from the cold, Carson turned to us, hesitating as to his next action. He was an elderly gentleman, tall with a full head of wavy grey hair. A pair of silver-rimmed spectacles protruded from his breast pocket. Finally, he spoke.

"Your colleague, Inspector Mossgarden, has already been here and performed just such an examination, sir. He left earlier today with Mr. Edgar in custody, and said that he had all the proofs he needed and that we could put things back as normal."

Chapter Two

"Of all the incompetent fools!" cried Lestrade.

Holmes spoke up, "As long as we are here, Inspector, I believe that we should still examine the scene of the crime for ourselves."

"Quite right, Holmes," agreed Lestrade. "Carson, would you please take us to the room where this murder took place."

The inside of the keep had been upgraded to modern lighting and plumbing, yet still retained the ancient tapestries and trappings of a medieval castle. We passed a dining hall with a large stone fireplace engraved with the motto: *Veritatem et Iustitiam in Omnes*[1], and an armoury where suits of armour and armaments still lined the walls. I also noted a glass-covered case that held smaller weapons: knives, flintlock pistols, and moulds for projectiles and early lead bullets. The butler led us up long flights of stairs to the tower room, where Sir Jameson had set up a study for himself.

Before entering, Holmes questioned Carson.

"Who has keys to this room?"

"Sir Jameson, of course, and he habitually locked himself in so as not to be disturbed while he was writing his memoirs. There is also a set of master keys which I keep in my pantry. Only Sir Jameson and I have … or rather, had the pantry key."

---

[1] Truth and Justice for All.

Holmes nodded, "From the newspaper account I understand that you were summoned by Sir Jameson's son when he failed to get a response from his father?"

"Yes, Mr. Holmes. Mr. Edgar had gone to call his father for breakfast, which was a common occurrence. Sir Jameson often lost track of time when he was writing. When there was no answer and no sound from within, he came to me and we both returned here so that I could unlock the door."

Holmes bent to examine the lock with his lens. Satisfied, he bid Carson to go ahead and open the door. Once we could see the interior, the detective held up his hand to indicate that we should not yet enter.

Turning again to the butler he asked, "What did you observe when you first opened the door?"

Carson thought back, visualising the scene in his mind. "Sir Jameson was lying on the floor over there." He pointed towards a spot away from the desk, near the window. "He was face down, and the carpet at his feet was dishevelled."

The window referred to, was actually an archer's arrow slit, only about a foot wide and four feet high. There were three of them allowing light into the room from various angles.

There was also a fireplace, a suit of armour, and a floor-length tapestry of the family coat of arms. Holmes bent to examine the carpet which was an oval shape with a maroon and gold pattern.

"The area has been trampled over by too many feet to yield any clues. What happened when you opened the door? Please be precise."

Carson cleared his throat and pointed towards the spot that he had indicated before, "Sir Jameson was lying there and his son immediately cried out and ran to him. He turned him over and said, 'My God, he's been shot! Carson, send for a doctor!'

"I ran downstairs and out to the courtyard where I called for one of the stable boys to go and fetch a doctor. I then returned to the tower room with towels, bandages, and water. When I arrived, young Edgar was slumped on the floor against the desk. His father still lay where we found him, his chest covered with blood. There was also a pool of blood on the floor where he had fallen forward."

The memory seemed to affect him deeply. He grew pale and quickly sat in one of the chairs by the fireplace, lowering his head into his hands.

I knelt at his side and encouraged him to keep his head down and breathe deeply to avoid fainting. Lestrade strode over to the window and looked out while Holmes examined the spot where the body lay.

The Inspector looked from the window to where Holmes knelt on the floor and made an observation.

"See here, Holmes," he said, as he pointed outside. "There's a tree opposite this window that would make a fine perch for an assassin."

Holmes nodded, hesitated a moment, and then joined our comrade at the archer's slit. There, about fifty yards away, was a good-sized tree, bare of leaves but tall and sturdy.

"Such a shot would require considerable marksmanship," observed the detective. Turning back to the butler, who had somewhat recovered, he asked, "Did anyone hear a shot?"

Carson summoned the strength to stand again and replied, "No, Mr. Holmes, it was a quiet night. There was a light snowfall and a full moon occasionally broke through the clouds. I could observe it from my quarters where I was reading a novel."

Holmes digested that remark, called Carson over to the window, and asked, "Is that tree visible from your quarters?"

"Not from where I was sitting, sir. I would have to be standing by the window to observe that particular tree."

Holmes nodded, then he suddenly went to the floor, lay down, and asked, "Is this approximately where the body was when you first saw it?"

Carson suggested a slight adjustment and Holmes complied, then enquired further, "Could you see the wound when his son turned him over?"

Carson answered immediately, "Inspector Mossgarden asked me the same thing, sir. I could not originally see it. Mr. Edgar was kneeling between Sir Jameson and where I stood frozen at the door. I did not see the actual wound until I returned."

Holmes contemplated that and stood. "Now, about the carpet, can you show us how it was disturbed?"

The butler knelt and curled the edge of the rug back towards where the body's feet would have been.

Holmes took in the scene and closed his eyes. I strode over to where Lestrade had remained by the window and looked out at the aforementioned tree. Holmes was correct. It would have taken someone with the skill of Colonel Sebastian Moran[1] to make such a shot. As he was safely locked away in Newgate, I could not imagine who else could achieve the task from that distance at the upward angle required.

"Have you attempted to clean this bloodstain, Carson?"

"No, sir. I felt it unfair to subject any of the servants to that task. I was going to have the rug sent out."

"Look here, Lestrade. Does the colour of bloodstain not seem lighter than should be expected?"

The Inspector knelt and peered at the rug, "You're right, Holmes. I would have expected a much darker red. What does it suggest?"

"I wouldn't like to speculate at this point, but it is a fact worth noting."

Holmes put his hands on his hips and asked one more question, this time directed at Carson, "What was the state of the fireplace when you opened the door?"

Carson hesitated at the incongruousness of the question, then answered, "It was down to just a couple of smouldering embers, sir. The room was much colder than Sir Jameson usually kept it."

"Yet there was plenty of wood in the rack, was there not?"

"Yes, sir, it was half full. The stable boy refills it every day."

Holmes strode over to the desk and observed the papers, books, and writing apparatus lying there. At last, he

---

[1] Colonel Sebastian Moran, famous big game hunter, attempted to assassinate Holmes with an air rifle in Arthur Conan Doyle's *The Adventure of the Empty House*.

announced, "I believe I have gleaned all I can from inside this room, Lestrade. I should like to examine that tree now."

We made our way out across the bridge and approached the tree Lestrade had noted. Holmes carefully eyed the snowy ground surrounding its base. He then walked around the tree, studying its bark. Suddenly he reached up and pulled himself up into its branches. He seemed to be observing the limbs until he reached a high perch. From there he looked towards the keep through a fork in a branch. He examined it with his magnifying lens and then made his way quickly back to the ground beside us.

"What did you find, Holmes?" enquired Lestrade.

The great detective brushed the snow from himself and replied, "It is a pear tree, not a prime choice for a climber. As you can see the branches thin out quickly and one cannot ascend to great heights. However, the fork where I stopped does enjoy an excellent sightline to the window where Sir Jameson was standing."

Lestrade clapped his gloved hands together, "So, it could be the killer's perch!"

Holmes cocked his head to one side as he looked back up at the branch in question and replied, "Our perpetrator very likely climbed this tree. There are scuff marks on various limbs and several broken twigs. However, there are no marks at all on the fork, which would have been the ideal place to steady a rifle. Surely, the weight of the gun and the recoil of the shot would have left some scraping along the bark. There is also the fact that no shot was heard. I do not believe a silent air gun could have the range necessary to perform a fatal wound at this distance. For now, I suggest that we return to Scotland Yard and question Edgar Mason and Inspector Mossgarden."

"Wait, Holmes" I stated. "Aren't you going to question the servants? Search the grounds? Look for alternative suspects?"

"All in good time, Watson," he replied. "At this point, I have insufficient data to contradict Mossgarden's actions. Once we meet with him and Mason, I shall be able to determine our next steps."

London. He would be happy to act as your agent in giving your career the type of boost it most certainly deserves."

Following Holmes's lead, I pulled out a pencil and notebook and nodded at the giant before me. Although I had never *actually* written such reports for the press, technically Holmes hadn't lied, only saying that my reports were 'worthy enough'. The effect on the Inspector was quite phenomenal. His balled fists loosened, his puffed-up chest relaxed and the fierce expression on his face turned into a calculating smile.

"Hmm, maybe I'll give you a try. But my name must appear prominently in every report," he demanded, as he picked his chair off the floor with one hand and sat back down behind his desk.

Holmes smiled, "I promise you, Inspector, that your name will figure distinctively in the accounting of this case."

The Inspector handed Lestrade a copy of his report. As our friend perused it Holmes asked Mossgarden, "How did you conclude that Edgar Mason killed his father?"

The big man huffed, "It was obvious. The room was locked from the inside. No secret passages. The windows were too small for anyone to enter, yet there was no bloody weapon in the room. When I questioned the manservant, I knew there was only one solution. The old judge had tripped on the rug and while he lay unconscious, the son saw an opportunity to do him in. With his body blocking the view from the butler, the latter could not tell if he were alive or dead. When the butler went for help, the son stabbed his father in the chest and tried to dispose of the murder weapon by throwing it into the moat. That was the clincher. The moat was frozen over. The knife, which has been verified as belonging to the younger Mason, buried itself into the thin layer of snow on top of the ice. It was easily found when I searched the grounds below the window."

"Have you ascertained a motive?" I asked as I made notes.

Mossgarden leaned back in his chair, which squeaked in protest, hooked his thumbs in his belt, and proclaimed, "Take your pick. Come New Year's Eve, he was about to get married to a woman of whom his father did not approve. Fortis Keep, while nowhere near the value of Alexandra Palace up the road, is located on prime land which certain developers are clamouring after. But the old Judge wasn't willing to sell. As the only heir, Edgar can now make a killing. Ha, ha!"

His laughter at his own pun was disturbing, but before I could protest, Holmes spoke up.

"I should like to see the murder weapon. I am making a study of knives, swords, and other cutting weapons for a monograph on the subject of murder by blade."

"It's with the body and the police surgeon. Just a formality of course, but he needs to match it up with the wound for his report."

"Very good," said Holmes. "Dr. Watson and I are going down to the cells to interview Mason and see if we cannot punch some holes in his story to back up your case. Should anything new arise we shall inform you."

Edgar Mason was in his late twenties, clean-shaven with wavy brown hair. His appearance was a little dishevelled, as we learned that he had been taken into custody early that morning while he was dressing. He stood upon our entrance. I gauged him to be about five foot six inches tall with a stout body, leaning toward flabbiness that came with too much sedentary work.

Holmes took the lead in the conversation and made introductions. I sat on the bed to rest my aching war wound, which is always exacerbated by cold weather. Holmes indicated that Mason should be seated at the other end of the bed while he stood over him. Lestrade leaned against the cell door.

The interview was brief. We learned that the younger Mason, like his father before him, had entered into the practice of law. His studies and work as a clerk in a well-known legal firm had left him little time for social activities, but recently he had met the daughter of one of the firm's partners and become engaged.

His father, exhibiting his prejudices against that particular law firm without ever having met the young lady, was opposed to the marriage on the face of it. They argued over that issue but it had never become violent.

"Did your father ever threaten to disinherit you?" asked Holmes.

The young man seemed startled by the question. "The subject never came up, Mr. Holmes. I am his only heir. I can't imagine he would do such a thing."

"How do you explain your knife being found in the snow?"

"I only carry my knife when I leave the house. It's a small multiplex pocket knife, hardly suitable as a murder weapon. I thought I'd lost it when I was out riding the other day."

Holmes mulled that over and in the brief silence I spoke up and asked a question that had been bothering me. "Forgive me, but since it appears that your father was stabbed, why did you exclaim to the butler that he had been shot?"

He shook his head, "I can only assume my mind jumped to that conclusion based upon the circumstances. He was near the window and the room had been locked. There was no knife. There was just ..." he hesitated and caught his breath, "a hole in his shirt with a large blood stain."

He put his head in his hands.

Holmes knelt, "Just one last question. Are there any current enemies in your father's life? Anyone he was having a dispute with?"

The young man took a handkerchief from his pocket and wiped his eyes, then looked at Holmes's face.

"My father made many enemies as a judge. Any man who has finished his sentence or is out on parole could hate him enough to do this. The only current dispute I am aware of is the land developer who wants to buy Fortis Keep, John Bridger. He is highly determined and has been to the house several times with revised offers."

Holmes asked one last question, "Are there any of the servants, or a frequent visiting relative, or neighbour whom you suspect?"

Young Mason seemed taken aback by the question but finally answered, "I was his only living relative. The neighbours are few and far between and none drop in on any regular basis, except for the gentleman next door, William Gutman. He's a land developer and has consulted with my father several times regarding property laws, especially regarding ancient grants. I believe Bridger is trying to acquire his place as well.

"As far as the servants are concerned, the newest additions would be the cook, Widow Parker, her son, Billy, who is one of the stable boys, and the gamekeeper, Jack Knox. They've all entered service within the last two years. All the others were retained from my grandfather's days.

"I've no reason to suspect the widow. Her son is a bit of a wild one though, and has had some scrapes and brawls. Seems to have a sour attitude since losing his father. Always seems to be in want of money, but I don't know that he would murder for it or how killing my father would benefit him.

"Knox is a bit of a puzzle. As a boy he was in trouble with the police I believe, but ever since he has been here he does his work well enough. He is a quiet lad and can seem distracted at times. There have been a few occasions when it took him a while to respond when called. Again, though, I don't see how my father's death would benefit him."

Holmes thanked the young man, stood and turned to Lestrade and suggested, "That is sufficient for now. Let us be off and visit the police surgeon and see what we can learn from him."

Chapter Four

During the journey Lestrade questioned Holmes, "On the whole there seems to be few other suspects. Mossgarden may be right. Though this John Bridger fellow, if he was desperate enough might have done it to get the property."

Holmes tilted his head and replied, "Or he may have paid someone who was familiar with the ways of the house. Or there may be an ex-convict out there, who was exacting revenge upon the judge."

Upon arrival, we were led to the laboratory of the police surgeon, Dr. Sylvester Fox. He welcomed us with open arms and a slight Scottish accent when I introduced myself.

"I've heard good things regarding your medical work for the police, Dr. Watson. I should be happy to assist you in any way I can." Turning to my companion he said, "It's good to see you again, Holmes."

Holmes nodded and gave a quick smile to the eminent doctor and pathologist who had replaced Holmes's original mentor, Dr. Donald Drake when he had retired. "Thank you, Doctor. What have you for us regarding Sir Jameson?"

While he showed us the body, Holmes and Lestrade busied themselves with an examination of the clothes and the knife. The ex-judge's shirt was marred by a large pool of blood, the shade of red varying from light to dark as the stain ran downward from the hole. The knife was as Edgar Mason had described, a multiplex knife with the largest blade being less than four inches in length.

On discussing the body with Fox, I discovered that he had determined a very significant fact. "As you can see, Doctor," he prompted, as he handed me a lens to examine the wound, "the blade which made this wound was double-edged. The knife sent down with the body is not the murder weapon."

I explored the wound and agreed. Then I noted something else.

"This wound is remarkably thin and straight," I pondered. "Yet, there is also a bulge in the centre."

Holmes's head snapped up at that and he crossed the room to the examination table in a flash. Snatching the lens from my hand, he bent down and observed the laceration minutely.

"Did you find anything inside the wound?" he demanded.

Fox replied, "I was just about to probe the wound when you gentleman arrived."

Holmes handed the lens back to me, "If my surmise is correct, Dr. Fox, there will be nothing to find. Had you looked earlier there may have been trace elements of the weapon."

The Doctor stiffened at this admonishment. "Look around, gentlemen. I've two other cases demanding my time as well. Mossgarden's report stated that he was about to make an arrest. That put his case as the lowest on my list of priorities."

"That is unfortunate, Doctor. I do sympathise. However, Mossgarden has the wrong suspect and it would be a shame to have an innocent man spend Christmas in jail and to miss his New Year's Eve wedding."

Holmes went on to ask if Fox had certain chemicals and the pathologist pointed to a cabinet. Holmes then took up the bloody knife and went to a table where he performed some delicate tests.

In the meantime, Fox probed the wound in Sir Jameson's chest. As Holmes suspected, he found nothing. My friend though, made an interesting discovery.

"The stains on the knife are definitely blood," he stated. "However, it is likely that from a bird, and not human. Note the minute traces of feathers in the hinge of the blade."

Lestrade spoke up, "Then Edgar Mason is not the killer."

Holmes waved his statement away. "I knew that the minute Mossgarden proposed his theory of the crime. The evidence we have gathered now, however, tells us the weapon that was used and in so doing narrows our suspect list considerably."

"What weapon could leave a wound like that?" I asked.

"A most diabolical one, I assure you, Watson."

On the way back to Fortis Keep, Lestrade insisted that Holmes reveal why he was sure that Edgar Mason wasn't the killer.

"Inspector, it is simplicity itself," exhorted Holmes. "If the son stabbed his father in the chest after he turned the body over, the blood would only be on the father's shirt, and possibly on that of the son's too. In actuality, there was also blood on the carpet corresponding to where the body lay face down *before* it was turned over.

"Furthermore, young Edgar is not athletic enough to have climbed that tree. However, I am convinced that our perpetrator did climb the pear tree to see if he could make a shot from there. He determined that such an act would likely have roused the house and he would have had to flee for his life. Instead, it was while in the tree that he realised another method that he could apply. One which would be silent, and which he could use to manipulate evidence against the son. Thus, ruining both the ex-judge and his heir at the same time."

"So, who is it, Holmes?" I asked. "And how did he do it?"

Holmes pondered a moment, "That is yet to be determined precisely," he finally replied. "However, I am certain that it is a member of the staff and that the weapon is still in the armoury. What I do not yet know is whether they were hired by Bridger, or possibly Gutman who may be in league with Bridger on some land development scheme."

Chapter Five

Arriving back at East Finchley, Holmes made some enquiries at the nearest bank. He discovered that Bridger had a loan pending for a land development deal that would require that he obtain both Mason's and Gutman's properties in order to be successful.

He turned to Lestrade, "Two more suspects for your murderer, Inspector. I believe that we have enough now for reasonable doubt. But I think that another visit to Fortis Keep should give us the final clues, if I'm not mistaken."

At Fortis Keep, Holmes had Carson show us the way to the flat roof of the tower, where archers would have shot down between the stone castellations.

First, he explored the snow-covered surface while Lestrade and I watched. Then he examined the area directly above the arrow slit where Sir Jameson has been standing when he was killed. Finally, he called out.

"See here," he said, pointing to some fresh marks on the wall. We joined him and saw some small strands of hemp caught in the cracks as well as areas where the snow had been compressed or brushed away. "This is where the murderer tied a rope and lowered himself down to the window where he made the fatal shot."

Lestrade protested, "I thought that we'd established that he'd been stabbed."

"That takes us back to the armoury, gentlemen. If you please."

We went back downstairs and Holmes requested that Carson assemble all the servants in the armoury. While the butler went to attend to that, Holmes opened the glass case and began examining the various items. Picking out one at last he held it out for the Inspector and me to see.

"This is the mould used by our murderer, gentlemen. Normally filled with molten lead."

Lestrade accepted it from my hands and enquired, "Isn't this for a crossbow bolt?"

"Indeed, Inspector," answered Holmes. "If you will just step over here."

We both joined Holmes at the wall where several weapons were on display.

"Note the level of dust upon these items. Yet this one," he said, picking a crossbow off its pegs, "is perfectly clean and freshly strung. Here is your murder weapon."

He handed the medieval contraption to the Inspector who began examining it. Holmes, while our attention was on the weapon, surreptitiously made his way over to stand by the armoury door. Several servants started to enter and we turned at the sound. Suddenly one of them, seeing us with the murder weapon in hand, turned on his heels and bolted for the door. Holmes blocked his path and put him down with a sharp jab to the *solar plexus*. As the man lay gasping on the floor, we joined our friend who explained.

"Our killer, gentlemen. Sir Jameson's gamekeeper."

Having finally regained his breath, the man spoke out in protest as he raised himself up on his elbows.

"I didn't kill no one!" he shouted.

"Then why did you run when you saw that we had the murder weapon?" sneered Lestrade.

"I weren't runnin'," he replied in his working-class accent. "I just remembered I left somethin' on the stove back at me cottage and thought it best to take it off when I saw how big this meeting was goin' to be."

Holmes chided him, "The game is up, my man. Your boots left tracks in the snow around the pear tree and on the roof. The snowfall hasn't been heavy enough to obliterate them as you hoped."

Holmes reached down and lifted the man's right foot off the floor, causing him to fall off his elbows and lay prone again.

"This boot has a distinct wear pattern to its heel, just like the tracks we found. It would have been easy for you to snatch Edgar Mason's knife and plant blood on it from one of the birds that you shoot as the gamekeeper. Only you could have wandered the grounds outside the building without arousing suspicion, since it was an element of your duties. You picked the locks and gained access to this room to steal this weapon and used the privacy of your cottage to create the bolts that you needed for it.

"Once all was ready you gained entry to the keep and climbed the stairs of the tower to the roof carrying your rope and crossbow, then you lowered yourself from the battlement, attracted Sir Jameson's attention by some pretext to get him to come to the open window where you were hiding just to the side. Once he was there you swung into place and shot him through the heart. You tossed his son's knife towards the ground below the window to implicate him, but your aim was off and it landed on the frozen moat. You then climbed back up, returned the crossbow and mould to the armoury, and went about your usual business. My only question for you is did you do this on your own, or were you hired by the land developer?"

Holmes dropped the man's foot to the floor. Being in such a vulnerable position, surrounded by accusing on-lookers, and faced with such a detailed account of his actions, he couldn't hope to deny his guilt. He slowly got to his feet and faced us.

"All right, you've got me. But I'm not sorry for it. Not one bit. The old fool deserved what he got and more. I'll tell you my story and you see if I weren't justified in what I done."

Holmes had Carson dismiss the rest of the servants and sat the gamekeeper down while Lestrade handcuffed him. He then began his tale.

"My real name is Peter Silcox and twenty-two years ago I was an orphan on the streets of London. My father was a sailor whose ship sunk when I was just seven. My mother died of consumption when I was twelve and I was turned over to the workhouse. It was a filthy place and I run away the first chance I got.

"I lived by me wits and odd jobs here and there. Got handy at pickin' a pocket to get by from time to time. I even got the knack for pickin' simple locks too. That's how I got in the keep once the butler had locked up for the night.

"Anyways one day I got me a rich haul. Found a gentleman's wallet in an alley outside the rooms of a certain lady who was known for her favours. Well, it had over twenty pounds in it and I thought I'd died and gone to heaven. But then this gent comes back 'cause he'd gone orf to play cards and realised he didn't have his wallet, and catches me with it. We struggles over it for a bit when a copper comes along and grabs me by the collar. Naturally, he takes the gent's side when he says I picked his pocket.

"So orf to court I go. I'm only sixteen at the time so I figure worse case, I'll get eighteen months for a first offence. But this Judge Mason, who was only a magistrate then, won't listen to me story about finding the wallet. Says because I stole an amount of such 'grand proportions' as he put it, sends me down for the maximum he can.

"I was lucky to survive the beatings and the abuse, and I vowed if I ever got out of that place alive, I'd make that Mason pay as dear a price as I could.

"When I was finally released, I got me a job on an estate as a gamekeeper's apprentice. I'd changed my name to Jack Fox so me criminal record wouldn't follow me. I learned my new trade, but I never forgot Mason. It nagged me for years until I decided to get even so I did some pokin' about. I found out that he'd become a High Court judge but that he'd retired and was livin' in this place so I came here two years ago with good references. He didn't recognise me, and why should he after all this time?

"I waited for my chance. I learned the habits of the household and when he took to writin' his memoirs late into the night, I began makin' my plans. It's true, those footprints by the pear tree were mine. I had thought it would make a fair perch for a shot at one of the windows of the tower room. But there were too many problems to deal with. I'd have to wait for the leaves to come back out in the spring to avoid being seen before I took the shot and who knew if he would still be writin' up there then? The noise of the shot would draw people out here since nobody normally hunts at night, and I'd risk gettin' caught. Then there was the problem of getting him to come to that particular window. Besides all that, it was a difficult shot to make. Fifty yards straight up at night into a target only a foot wide? I've gotten to be a pretty good shot, but those odds weren't in my favour.

"But while I was up in that tree, I saw an owl take off from the roof of the tower. That gave me the idea of lowering myself down to the window. I got to thinkin' that maybe I could pull this job off and not get caught. I'd have the satisfaction of gettin' my revenge and still keepin' my new life.

"At first, I thought I could kill him quietly by stabbing him with a sword, or spear. That would make for a silent killing and give me lots of time to get back to me cottage. But I realised it would be awkward and I might only wound him if he had time to jump back out of reach before I could position myself for a fatal thrust. That's when I decided on the crossbow."

I interrupted at this point, for there was a glaring error in this scenario.

"But we found no crossbow bolt in the wound. It looks more like a stabbing."

"Ah that was the genius of it," he smirked. "Earlier this winter I saw the icicles form along the roof lines and realised what a formidable weapon they could make if delivered properly. So I stole the mould and made up some ice bolts during the cold nights when they'd freeze up good and firm. I kept them intact by puttin' them in a cold metal tray on the window sill of me cottage. Then I returned the mould so nobody would notice it gone. I knew that the judge's body heat would melt the ice and figured the heat from the fire would evaporate the water on the floor before it burned down to embers.

"When the time was right on that really cold night, I got to the top of the tower and lowered myself down next to the window around midnight. Then I started hootin' like an owl to attract him. I knew he wouldn't be able to concentrate and he'd come to the window to shoo the owl away. Soon as I heard him open the window I swung around with the crossbow and fired. He stumbled back and tripped on the rug. But I saw his face before he fell and I'll cherish that look for the rest of my days."

Lestrade had the next question. "But why frame the son? He'd done nothing to you."

Silcox slammed his manacled fists down on the table. "He had the life I should have had! He was the free son of a rich man and about to marry a beautiful woman and live happily ever after. That should've been me! So I decided to take my revenge on both father and son!"

Holmes spoke up again, "I think we've heard enough, Lestrade. It's time to visit Inspector Mossgarden and conduct an exchange."

Chapter Six

It was nearly dusk when we arrived back at Scotland Yard. Mossgarden was not happy to see us. He had obviously heard from the police surgeon. He stared menacingly at Lestrade.

"So, you've come to Shanghai my case after all," he accused. "And who's this fellow?"

Inspector Lestrade shoved Silcox forward. "This is the real murderer of Sir Jameson. He's confessed it all. Now it's time for you to free Edgar Mason."

Mossgarden reluctantly led us back to the cells and locked up our prisoner. When we went to free the son, we found that he had visitors.

Mossgarden unlocked the door, but it was Lestrade who announced, "You are free to go young man. We've caught your father's killer."

He had been sitting on the bed with an elderly gentleman and a young lady at his side. Upon hearing the news, they all stood immediately and the man, whose name it later transpired was Anderson, spoke.

"Charlotte, this is Inspector Lestrade of Scotland Yard, and Sherlock Holmes and Dr. Watson. They're the men I told you about."

Anderson, a portly fellow with an expensive suit and balding head, was a partner at the law firm where Mason worked. He stepped forward and immediately shook hands with Lestrade, Holmes and myself.

"Thank you, Inspector. I'm glad to see that *one* member of the official police force knows what he's doing," he said, glaring at Mossgarden as he did so. "My daughter and I are sincerely grateful for your help."

Charlotte Anderson was an attractive woman in a cherubic-like sense. Her plump face beamed with a smile that could melt a man's heart. She walked over to us and shook hands with Lestrade and me, then suddenly, overcome by emotion, she threw her arms around Holmes and began sobbing her thanks.

"You have saved our wedding and our Christmas, Mr. Holmes! Oh, thank you, thank you, thank you!"

Peeling himself away, Holmes replied, "You are quite welcome, Miss Anderson, I assure you."

Edgar Mason came up and put his arm around his fiancée, who turned her full attention back to him.

"I cannot thank you gentlemen enough. Who was that fellow who killed my father?"

Holmes gave a summary of Silcox's actions and motive and we soon left the Yard with Mason a free man. He invited us all back to Fortis Keep for dinner, but Holmes declined, stating that we needed to get back to Baker Street. Anderson brought up the subject of Holmes's fee, but my friend merely nodded toward the happy couple climbing into a cab and said, "Let this one be a Christmas present for their sake."

Lestrade returned with us to Baker Street, where Mrs. Hudson had a warm fire going and prepared hot toddies for all of us. As we sat by the fire and drank, I asked Holmes to explain his reasoning for the steps he took.

"It was obvious from the start, Watson that the killer had to be someone familiar with the Sir Jameson's habits and who could access that room in some fashion. That narrowed the suspects to family members or servants, although it was possible that an outsider might have been hired for the job. I determined that the lock had not been picked and thus, even though it was improbable, the arrow slit seemed the only method of delivering the fatal blow.

"After examining the pear tree which our perpetrator had climbed, I deduced that it was impossible to make the shot from there, except by using a high-powered rifle which would have been heard. It also offered no cover for the shooter and no guarantee that the judge would come to the window. Why would he, during a cold night when his desk was by the fire?

"The state of the fire was also critical to discrediting Mossgarden's theory of the crime. Remember Carson said that it had burned down to its embers. That meant that Sir Jameson had been dead for some time, unable to maintain the fire, and not killed by his son upon entering that morning."

Lestrade spoke up, "That still doesn't mean that the son couldn't have done it during the night."

Holmes lit his pipe and blew out a puff of smoke before he answered, "It's true that the timing does not exonerate young Mason, Inspector. Remember, however, that I noted the athleticism required to climb the pear tree and to later descend from the rooftop, acts that are quite beyond the young man's capabilities. Add to that the size of the footprints around the tree and later on the roof."

"How did you determine the weapon that was used?" I asked.

He smirked, "Simple deduction, Doctor. The only weapon which could have silently delivered a projectile made of ice with sufficient force had to be a crossbow, which I observed the first time we walked through the armoury."

"How did you know that it would be a bolt made of ice?" asked Lestrade.

"Our killer had decided to frame the son by leaving the knife in a compromising position, which would look like Mason had tried to get rid of it. Thus, he needed the real instrument to be one that would disappear. There have been theories about ice bullets, which melt away and leave no trace. But such items are impossible due to the explosive nature required to deliver them. Firing an ice bolt with a crossbow, however, would work over a short distance. When I examined Sir Jameson's shirt, the bloodstains were lighter in colour close to the wound, this is where the melting ice diluted the blood. You also recall the lighter shade of red on the carpet. That confirmed my theory and I knew that the police surgeon would find nothing in the body and that there would be a clean cut, with no distortion caused by the inevitable twisting removal of a knife or sword."

Lestrade, now sipping his his second toddy, spoke up, "When did you decide that it was the gamekeeper?"

"I don't *decide* these things, Lestrade. That was Mossgarden's mistake. A man seeking an easy solution will find it, even if he has to make it up. I *deduced* that our suspect was a servant and had narrowed it down to either the gamekeeper, or someone who worked in the stables such as Billy Parker, since they would need privacy and the proper tools. I admit I was leaning toward Silcox after Mason told us about him not always responding to be called right away. I reasoned that this might be because he was using a false name. But that was only a hypothesis. That is why I had Carson summon the whole staff to the armoury. I hoped that the sight of us with the murder weapon in hand would create a reaction, which is precisely what happened when Silcox attempted to flee."

The Inspector rose to his feet as did we, but he was a trifle unsteady now as he was about to finish his third toddy. He raised his glass to the detective and declared in a slightly slurred voice, "You are a brilliant man, Sherlock Holmes. Thank you for joining me on this case."

Knowing such unbridled praise was probably a result of intoxication, Holmes and I took his remark in our stride. We clinked glasses with him and the detective returned Lestrade's compliment.

"Thank you for another little mystery to solve, Inspector. It is as fine a Christmas gift as I could ask for."

And together we drank to a happy Christmas for all.

Pride

The Etherege Escapade

Chapter One

On a Saturday afternoon in the summer of 1887, I was enjoying a pipe and reading the latest issue of *The Lancet* in the sitting room I shared with the private consulting detective, Sherlock Holmes. He was occupied at his chemistry table, performing some experiments with small amounts of gunpowder mixed with various other substances. An occasional popping sound would emanate from that corner of the room, as certain mixtures proved more explosive than others.

I had rather tuned out this intermittent cacophony, to the point that I did not hear the ascending steps of Mrs. Hudson and a guest until a knock came to our door. I rose from my chair to open it, finding our good landlady in the company of Scotland Yard Inspector, Morgan Smith.

The stocky fellow with the porcine face burst through the door past Mrs. Hudson and quickly located Holmes as he scanned the room. "Holmes. There you are. I need your help, man!"

At that moment the loudest explosion of the day sent up a white cloud of smoke at Holmes's chemistry table. Smith threw an arm up to cover his face as he ducked. Mrs. Hudson retreated and closed the door behind her. Holmes merely pulled off his goggles and made a note on the tablet next to him.

"Good God, Holmes!" cried the Scotland Yard officer when he straightened up again. "I hope that you haven't turned to bomb-making now?"

My friend stood to walk over towards our sitting area, "Calm yourself, Inspector, merely a chemical experiment. Have a seat by Watson there and tell us what brings you to our door in such a state of rude agitation."

Smith sat on the sofa next to me, removed his bowler, and wiped his wide brow with a large handkerchief. Holmes filled his churchwarden with tobacco from the stuffed Persian slipper hanging on the mantel and took the seat opposite us. Smith started speaking, even before Holmes had lit his pipe.

"It's this missing solicitor business," he began. "It's fairly plain what's happened, but the widow wants a definitive answer and her father, old Justice Shipley, is putting pressure on the Yard to solve the case."

"You are referring to the disappearance of Mr. Etherege?" I asked, having read the news story earlier that week.

"The very same," replied Smith.

"*The Times* gave few details, Inspector," noted Holmes. "Yet it seemed straightforward enough that I found it to be of little interest. Please give us the precise facts."

I took that as a cue to bring forth pencil and paper and to begin jotting down the story that Smith was about to relay to us. He cleared his throat and began.

"A week ago yesterday morning, Mr. Andrew Etherege left for his office at eight o'clock. He was dressed in a black suit with a grey checker waistcoat, black overcoat, black, square-toed shoes with grey spats, and wearing a black and burgundy four-in-hand tie. He carried a black leather briefcase which he used to transport papers to his office and various appointments.

"He is fairly young to be so successful, as he is but twenty-eight. However, he began working for his father in his chambers when he was twenty-one. He inherited the business two years ago, upon his father's death from a stroke. He is five feet seven inches tall and weighs about eleven stone. He has short, wavy brown hair and a neatly trimmed moustache. I have a photograph for you here."

He pulled a sepia portrait of the young man, standing next to a seated woman, from his inner breast pocket, and handed it to Holmes. Both wore serious expressions, as was common for formal portraits. He was on the left side of the chair with his left hand behind him and his right on top of the chair back. The young lady, whom Smith noted was Millicent Etherege, his wife of six years, sat up straight with both hands atop the handle of a parasol. A garland of white flowers perched on her hair, which piled up behind the adornment and rolled down the sides of her round face with large curls.

"That was taken shortly after their wedding," continued Smith. "Etherege's office is a small space in a building on Cannon Street. There is a sitting area for clients and two enclosed offices for private consultations. Behind those is a back room containing supplies, files, and a fairly substantial safe. Etherege has not hired anyone since his father's death and runs the office by himself. Of course, he spends considerable time at the stock exchange, as most of his clients are large companies whom he advises on things such as acquisitions and mergers. Mostly contract law, you see. He is generally in the office for several hours after the exchange closes. As a result, he often returns home between seven and eight o'clock for dinner.

"On that Friday, he had yet to return by ten o'clock. Mrs. Etherege had not been overly concerned, as he occasionally goes out with fellow businessmen after work, or to his club. Usually, however, he informs her ahead of time and is always home by ten. She contacted her father and he in turn contacted the Yard. Of course, due to his position, priorities were rearranged and I was assigned to the case. Examination of his office showed signs of a struggle, some blood, and an empty safe. The next morning Etherege's coat, with significant amounts of blood on the collar, was found at low tide in the mud at the base of the most northerly of the five supporting arches of Blackfriars Bridge. Dragging the Thames has proved fruitless thus far. We've concluded that he was robbed, injured in a struggle, and then kidnapped for ransom. Perhaps his injuries proved fatal, or maybe he attempted an escape which led to his death. In any case, he has not returned home, nor has any man of his description appeared in any of the local hospitals. Two days later his briefcase turned up in a pawnbrokers in the East End."

"How did you identify the coat and briefcase as being his?" asked Holmes.

"The coat was his size and the label was that of his tailor, Henry Poole & Co., Savile Row. The briefcase had his initials, A. T. E., embossed upon it."

"You seem to have the case in hand, Inspector. What would you have me do?"

"Justice Shipley is insisting that we enlist your aid, Mr. Holmes. He has heard of your reputation. Even though we reminded him that you are an amateur, he is adamant that we leave no stone unturned."

If the word 'amateur' rankled Holmes, he hid it well. Removing the pipe from his lips, he pointed the long stem at the Inspector and replied, "Then I suggest that we start at the scene of the crime. While we do so, would you please let Mrs. Etherege know that we should like to come around to speak with her this evening at six o'clock? I presume that you wish to come along also, Doctor?"

I put the pencil and paper into my pocket and replied, "Certainly, Holmes, if I may be of assistance."

"There's a good fellow. Well, Smith," he said, rising from his chair." Let us be off to Cannon Street."

Chapter Two

It did not take us long to traverse the three miles to Etherege's office. It was in a building full of small business establishments. Smith led us up two flights of stairs and down a hall to the last office in the row. He opened the door and stood aside to let Holmes enter.

Holmes stood in the doorway, taking in the layout of the space. Over his shoulder, he asked the Inspector, "How many of your men have been in here since the constable discovered the scene?"

Smith looked down at his hands as if counting the number on his fingers, "The constable, his sergeant, the doctor who tested the stains we found, and myself. That's all I'm aware of."

"Yes, your shoeprints are readily apparent," replied Holmes, "as are the prints of the two policemen with their standard footwear. If you'll wait here, gentlemen, I should like to examine the carpet more closely."

My friend entered, walking sideways along the edge of the partition that led through the reception and divided the two offices. Carefully he eyed the marks in the carpet, which were all but invisible to the untrained eye. He stopped just short of the two office doors which faced each other perpendicular to the hall created by their presence. He took particular notice of the floor outside the office to the right. Smith called out, rather condescendingly, I thought, "Etherege's office is the one on the left, Mr. Holmes."

Holmes ignored him, opening the door to the right-hand office. Still peering down at the carpet, he crouched, oscillating his head back and forth. He then rose, his gaze gathering in the room's contents, like a hen gathering her chicks, nodding his head slightly as some observation became registered in his brain. He did an about-face and stepped across to the already open door of Etherege's office. He repeated the process from the doorway, then stepped inside, gesturing for the stocky Scotland Yard official and me to come and wait by the door. From where we stood, I could see that Etherege's umbrella and overcoat still hung on the coat rack. That was a foreboding sign to my mind.

We watched as the detective circled the perimeter of the room, attempting to replay activities indicated by the footprints he could see. "It was foresighted of you, Smith, not to allow the cleaners in here. Their carpet sweeping apparatus would have destroyed valuable evidence."

The bulky Inspector smiled at the compliment, "I never thought I'd have to call you in, Holmes. But I did wish to leave the scene intact for as long as possible, especially with the judge's son-in-law involved."

"I see that a woman has been here recently," remarked the detective. "May I presume that Mrs. Etherege was allowed to come in the office?"

Smith tugged at his collar and cleared his throat, "Ahem! Yes, we allowed her the courtesy to visit the scene. We watched her carefully though. She was not allowed to remove any evidence, save for her husband's cheque book in order to pay some bills. The cheque book was in the safe, in the room at the end of the hall."

Holmes walked to the window, which looked out onto flat rooftops below. Even from where we stood, I could see that it was capable of being used as a fire escape. Smith spoke up, "No one came in that way. The frame is swollen and impossible to open without noise. You can see that the latch has not been tampered with."

"Yes," replied Holmes in that distracted voice I've heard often. Then he asked, "What was Mrs. Etherege's countenance when she came upon the scene of the crime a mere two days after its occurrence?"

Smith seemed a little taken aback, "How did you know it was two days later?

Holmes merely turned back towards us and gave him a look, as one does when asked a foolish question.

"Er, yes, of course," replied the Inspector. "She remained calm and business-like, though she did give a slight gasp at the sight of the blood stain on the floor by the safe."

Holmes said, "Yes, I can imagine."

He sat in the chair with the window behind him and examined the layout of items on the desk, as well as the contents of the drawers. One drawer, the second one down on the left-hand side, drew his attention. It was completely empty. He pulled it all the way out laying it across the desktop, examining it with his lens. Then, running his fingers over the bottom, he smelled his fingertips, nodded thoughtfully and called over the Inspector.

"Did your men find a gun in this drawer?"

"No, Mr. Holmes, it was empty just like that."

Holmes pointed to the stain, "This is gun oil. If he had access to a gun then why did he not use it to defend himself?"

"Perhaps he was overpowered before he could shoot," offered Smith.

"Maybe they already had him at gunpoint and forced him to hand over his weapon," I suggested.

Holmes stared at the drawer thoughtfully, then replaced it. Then he stood and said, "Let us go and examine the room in which the safe is kept, Inspector."

Smith led us to the end of the hall and opened the door. There was no carpet in this small room, just solid oak flooring. It contained cabinets and shelves for the storage of files and stationery. The safe was a large Chubb model with a combination dial. It stood about four feet high by three feet wide. The door was open revealing several empty shelves.

Off to the right, beyond the safe, was an irregularly shaped red stain on the floor. Holmes knelt by it, using his magnifying lens to examine it closely. He even used his penknife to scrape up some of the discoloured wood slivers. Then he waved me over.

"Take a look, Watson," he murmured. "Note particularly the colour, smell and shape."

"What's that, Holmes?" called out Smith.

My companion stood and replied, "I am just asking Dr. Watson to take some notes for a more precise medical opinion. I presume that you realised that the location of the stain would indicate that the assailant was likely to be left-handed."

"How can you know that?" asked the Inspector, with some scepticism, folding his arms across his wide frame.

"Observe," replied the detective. "Etheredge stands here, opening the safe under the threat of harm, no doubt. Once it's opened, his knowledge is no longer needed so he's knocked unconscious and falls to the floor. As he fell to the right, he was most likely struck on his left-hand side. A left-handed man would swing his arm that way quite naturally, rather than a right-handed one, hitting him with a backhanded blow. However, I do not discount the converse entirely.

"Has anyone gone over the contents of the safe to determine what is missing?"

"Tis impossible to say, Holmes," replied the man from Scotland Yard. "He had no partner, nor did his wife know anything of his business affairs."

"May I have your permission to examine what is left in the safe?"

"Yes, indeed, sir. After all you have been given that authority by the judge himself."

"Very well," replied Holmes. "I should like to return later and perform that task this evening, after our visit to Mrs. Etherege, if you will inform your officer on guard to let me in."

We began walking back out, but Holmes turned abruptly into the office that he had first observed. Smith and I followed him in but stayed close to the door. The Inspector huffed, "There's nothing here, Holmes. This was young Etherege's office before his father died, and prior to him moving across the hall. It hasn't been used since, except as a storage space for books and files."

Holmes answered back over his shoulder as he opened the double doors of a cabinet perpendicular to the desk that faced the doorway, "Yes, I can see you came in here for a short time, Smith ... but there are other footprints here, from our victim, no doubt, which indicate that he had put this office to some use recently."

We could not see into the opened cabinet as one of the doors blocked our view. However, we immediately went to Holmes's side when he declared, "Well then, what have we here?"

What he had revealed was a counter with a sink bowl and water jug on top of a lower cabinet. There was a mirror above the sink with candle sconces on either side. What was unusual was that, on the inside surface of the two doors, were mounted two full-length mirrors.

"Merely a vanity closet," remarked Smith. "Nothing related to our case."

Holmes opened the top drawer of the cabinet beneath the sink and found shaving utensils, a toothbrush and powder, moustache wax, towels, and the like. He ran his fingers around the sink and checked the water level of the jug. He examined the towels and countertop with his lens, sweeping some small fragments into one of his ever-present envelopes for later examination. Leaving the cabinet doors open, he sat in the chair behind the desk, turning his face towards the mirrors. Examining the desk drawers, he found little of interest, though he did spend some moments noting indentations in the carpet to the left of the chair and made a quick measurement of them.

At last, we stepped back into the space between the two offices and faced the doorway. Holmes asked, "What is your working theory, Inspector?"

The stout official gripped both his lapels in his hands while making his statement:

"Late on that Friday, likely just after the normal closing of business hours when the rest of the building was nearly empty, two unknown persons came in to see Etherege. It may have been by appointment, or they may just have burst in unannounced. They confronted the victim in his office, forcing him to go back and open the safe. He was struck down when the task was complete. They took what cash and any redeemable certificates that they could, stuffing them into Etherege's own briefcase. Perhaps they realised that they needed his signature on certain papers, or perhaps kidnapping was a part of their original plan. They dragged the victim to the door. You can see the drag marks of his heels there on the carpet. They carried the unconscious man down to a waiting conveyance. Perhaps prepared to explain to anyone they ran into that Etherege was ill and that they were taking him to a hospital. We believe that he was initially taken for ransom. At some point, he may have attempted to escape and slipped out of his coat. He was probably killed in the attempt or succumbed to his original head wound. They disposed of his body and coat in the Thames, but his coat washed up on shore. Without being able to offer proof of life, they abandoned their ransom scheme. Neither they nor Etherege have been heard of since. The pawnbroker could only tell us that the person who brought in the briefcase was tall, thin, and wore a moustache."

Holmes nodded, "You seem to have created a plausible theory based upon the facts you have in hand, Inspector. After we make our call upon Mrs. Etherege and once I have examined the papers in the safe this evening, perhaps I could offer some suggestions."

"I would be grateful, Mr. Holmes," replied the harried man. "I have other cases vying for my attention. This seems like a waste of valuable time."

"Until tomorrow then, Inspector," answered Holmes.

Chapter Three

While returning to Baker Street, Holmes stared out the window of our cab in silent contemplation. I knew better than to interrupt his train of thought. Instead, I merely went over the notes I had taken, ensuring that I had everything in order. Upon arrival back at home, we stepped out onto the pavement. Holmes stared up at our sitting room window.

Shaking his head, he murmured, "It will not do, Watson."

"What's that, Holmes?" I asked.

"Can you imagine you and I carrying a third person between us down the seventeen steps from our room to the entrance hall? These supposed kidnappers had to carry Etherege twice that far, in a public building, then out to a waiting vehicle."

"It was likely after dark by the time they did so," I suggested. "On a Friday evening, most of the other offices would certainly be closed. I admit, three men abreast, two carrying the other, on that stairwell is unlikely, but what other explanation is there?"

"What indeed, Watson?" he said, as he opened the door to 221B and we returned to the comfort of our sitting room. He immediately went to his chemistry table, retrieved the envelopes from his pocket, and began running experiments. I poured myself a brandy, took a seat on the settee, looked at my notes, and contemplated what I had seen and heard.

Some forty minutes later, Holmes looked up from his microscope. "What was your opinion on the blood stain, Doctor?"

"Yes, I have a note on that," I replied, flipping through my pages. "Ah, here we are. The colour and consistency were unusual. It was far too red for what should have been dried blood. It was rather thick and smooth. I would have expected it to be a crusty texture and reddish brown in hue. I can think of no medical condition that would cause blood to congeal in such a fashion. Also, there was only the puddle where he fell. There was no splatter from the initial blow."

"Excellent, Watson!" cried Holmes. "My chemical analysis confirms your findings. We are entering deep waters, my friend. A cunning mind is behind this case. We can take nothing at face value, which is the error Smith has made."

I nodded in agreement, then asked, "Why did you not request to see the scene where Etherege's coat was found?"

"After a week's worth of tides coming and going, there would be no evidence left to be found. If it indeed washed up on the embankment, there was no way to know where it entered the water. I have no reason to believe that it is the actual scene of any crime."

"Why would you conclude that?" I asked.

"Let me recall your attention to the unique contents of the coat rack in Etherege's office."

"His umbrella and overcoat were still there."

"Indeed, those were the unique contents," Holmes smiled enigmatically. "I should like to step out for a while, Watson. I shan't be long, then we can proceed to interview our victim's wife."

Holmes returned in plenty of time to retrieve me. Then on we went to the Etherege home in Clerkenwell. We arrived just before six o'clock at a well-appointed house with a colourful flower garden in front of its red brick Georgian façade. We strode up the steps and Holmes rang the bell. A matronly woman opened the door. "Would you be Mr. Sherlock Holmes, sir?"

Upon our affirmation, she invited us into a modest entrance hall, took our hats and overcoats, and placed them by the door. "This way, gentlemen," she said. We followed the lady to a sitting room where Mrs. Etherege sat by the fire. It was a well-furnished room, with several pieces in the French provincial style. She was reading a book but looked up when we were announced. Placing the bookmark where she had left off, she set the volume aside, stood slowly then held out her hand. She was about five foot four in height and a little heavier than in the picture we had been given. Her voice was high-pitched and rather strident, I thought. Holmes and I each bowed over her hand in turn. She waved us to the sofa to be seated.

"Now then, Mr. Holmes, I understand from my father that you are some sort of a detective with a fair reputation for solving unusual mysteries. Did you find anything in my husband's office that may give us hope of finding him alive?"

Frankly, I found her attitude to be a bit cavalier. Were someone I loved to be missing for a week I would be frantic. Yet this woman seemed as if she were merely inconvenienced. Holmes replied to her enquiry with one of his own.

"I have found several interesting clues, Mrs. Etherege, but I need time to follow them to their conclusion. I should like to ask you whether your husband has any enemies or unhappy clients of late?"

"We do not discuss his business at home, Mr. Holmes. As long as his income maintains our lifestyle, I care nothing for his work."

I could not resist a question of my own, "How long have you and your husband known each other, Mrs. Etherege?"

"What an odd question, Dr. Watson. We've known each other since childhood. Our families were always very close. It was just naturally expected that Andrew and I would marry."

Holmes asked, "Did Mr. Etherege always wish to follow in his father's footsteps?"

"Of course! He studied for it at Cambridge," she answered, matter-of-factly.

"Did he have an office here at home, or maybe a desk where he worked? I should like to go over it for any further clues."

"Yes, he used one of the rooms upstairs as a study. I'll have Marian show you." She rang a bell on the table next to her. The same lady who had shown us in appeared. "Yes, madam?"

"Marian, please show these gentlemen to Mr. Andrew's study."

We followed the servant upstairs and into what appeared to be a converted bedroom. This was decidedly more utilitarian with solid oak furnishings. There were paintings on the walls by Millais, and others depicting scenes from Shakespeare. There was a single bed against one wall, but the rest of the room was taken up by a cabinet, a heavy chair with burgundy upholstered seat and arms, as well as a roll-top desk. Holmes, however, first stepped over to the wardrobe making a mental inventory of the clothes therein. He also took note of various hats on the top shelf as well as shoes and a full set of luggage on the wardrobe floor.

While he was doing that, I was tasked with examining the cabinet. My findings were insignificant as it contained mostly older files which were likely kept for only historical reference.

Satisfied with the wardrobe, Holmes stepped over to the desk. The top was down and locked, but using his lock picks, he had it open in mere seconds. He went through each of the cubby holes and drawers, examining various papers and notebooks. One file in particular caught his interest. After he scanned its contents, he handed it over to me. I opened it to find programmes from various theatres and numerous plays. The file itself was labelled, 'theatrical'. I did not see why Holmes felt it significant.

"Theatrical companies always need investors, Holmes. It's not as lucrative as the stock market, but certain parties do like to support the arts. He probably kept these as a portfolio of sorts to determine which companies were most successful for investment by his clients."

"Oh, I quite agree, Watson," he replied. "That is why I would like to retain that particular file."

"You think an investor whose money went into an unsuccessful play is responsible for Etherege's disappearance?"

"What I think, is that there is more to this little drama than meets the eye."

He took two more files and handed them over to me. Then he closed and locked the desk. Before leaving, he also made a cursory examination of the bed, pulling back the covers, checking the bedding, and even sitting on the mattress. Standing again, he threw the covers back over the pillows. Marian immediately straightened them and tucked them smartly back in.

"I believe that is all we need glean at this juncture, Doctor. Let us bid our hostess farewell."

This time the lady remained seated and merely let the book drop to her lap as she asked with a sigh, "Did you learn anything, gentlemen?"

"Possibly some helpful data. With your permission I should like to take these files to compare them with papers I will be examining at your husband's office tonight. I will see that you are kept informed as to any progress."

"Very, well, permission granted. Good night, gentlemen."

She went back to her novel and the maid saw us out. As we stood on the pavement waiting for a cab to hail, I remarked, "I cannot understand her attitude, Holmes. She seems almost disinterested in her husband's case."

"What does that tell you, Doctor?" my companion asked.

"Well," I hesitated over the thoughts that occurred to me. "Either she has completely accepted her husband's fate, or she is somehow involved in his disappearance."

A hansom pulled up, Holmes held the door for me as he said, "Excellent, Watson! I have no doubt that Mrs. Etherege has played a significant role in this act."

Chapter Four

He refused to expound any further. We rode in silence to Etherege's office. The constable on duty snapped to attention at our appearance, though Holmes merely waved him to sit back down at his post in the waiting room.

"First of all, Watson," he stated as he crouched in the doorway, "take a close look at these drag marks made by the heels of our solicitor's boots."

I lowered myself gently to the floor where I could get the best angle on the indentations in the carpet. "What am I looking for, Holmes?"

"Note how the depth is not consistent. Every eighteen inches or so, there is a slight hump in the track. This tells me that no body was dragged to the door. Rather, the marks were made by a man dragging a pair of boots along as he moved backwards on his knees. At the end of each pass, he got up to re-position himself and start again. Note that every so often you can still see the indentations made by his knees."

Holmes helped me to my feet, realising that my war wound was not conducive to this activity. "Now, let us examine that blood stain again."

We walked back to the room with the safe and, this time, he did not require me to kneel. "You saw for yourself, Doctor, this fluid resembles fresh blood. However, after a week it should not."

He produced a vial from his coat pocket and poured a small amount of liquid from it on to the carpet about a foot from the original stain. In appearance and consistency, it matched perfectly. I sounded him out, "Something tells me that's not human blood with a strange medical condition. What is it, Holmes?"

"Indulge me, Watson, there's more," he replied. "Wait here one moment."

He went into Etherege's office. Seconds later he stuck his head back out, "Doctor, I wish you to pretend that you are Etherege. Come into this office and do what you think he would do if he were just arriving from being outside."

I walked in as if I were a businessman coming to work for the day. I took off my overcoat and hat and hung them on the coat stand, which Holmes had emptied, along with my walking stick. I then moved to the desk, pulled out the chair, and sat down. "Did you wish me to go through the motions of working on papers?"

"That won't be necessary, just open the second drawer down on the left."

I did so, noting that the drawer had a stain on the bottom. "Is this stain significant, Holmes?"

"It adds intrigue to the scene, Watson. That stain is from gun oil."

"So there was a firearm here in the drawer?"

"Very likely," said my companion.

I could see he was warming to the task and so enquired, "You have a theory, Holmes. Out with it."

He rubbed his palms slowly together, just below his chin while he sat in one of the guest chairs, an upholstered affair with green velvet on a mahogany frame that matched the desk and other furnishings.

"Consider the layout of the items on the desk and the location of the gun. Etherege was obviously left-handed. This begs the question, why did he not use the gun so close at hand? It also explains why the blood stain landed where it did. Etherege acted out the whole thing in his mind but did not take into account that an assailant would likely be right-handed. Now, note the coat rack. What do you see?"

"My hat, overcoat and stick."

"And what was left behind after our victim's disappearance?"

"His overcoat and umbrella ... no hat!" I realised.

"Very good. Now, suppose that you were going to carry a man out of here. Would you bother to put on his hat?"

"Not likely," I replied.

He nodded and said, "Now, come next door."

We walked into what used to be the younger Etherege's office and Holmes opened the doors to the vanity cabinet again. The mirrors reflected our images multiple times. Holmes opened the drawer, then turned to me.

"While the water has evaporated, I did find some dried shaving soap and several hairs on this towel. There was enough to convince me that our missing man had shaved off his moustache.

"Note also the wear pattern in the rug on this side of the room."

I looked down noticing that it was far more worn than the rest of the room. I said, "He obviously always came and went from this side of his desk, Holmes. That would make sense since this is the side where the vanity cabinet is located. Being left-handed coming around this side of the desk would seem natural."

"An excellent surmise, Doctor, though not quite complete. Now, step over here."

He led me behind the desk, pointing out the marks on the rug that he had noted on our earlier visit, "What do these suggest to you, Watson?"

I leaned over my cane, which I had retrieved from the coat rack, and peered at the circular indentations. There were four marks in a rectangular pattern, roughly eighteen inches by six inches. Too large for a briefcase. Then it struck me.

"A carpetbag?"

"Precisely."

"So, you're saying Etherege staged this disappearance, right down to the fake blood, the abandoned coat, and the pawned briefcase? To what end, and where is he?"

"The method he chose is interesting. As to motive, and his current location, that will require more investigation. I suggest that tomorrow we pay a visit to Justice Shipley. I also need to send out some telegrams tonight. For now, I intend to go through the files that he left behind and compare information with that we've brought with us."

We returned to Etherege's office and started removing files from the cabinets. Holmes gave me some indication of what to look for. We spent the better part of two hours in a hunt for pertinent data. I was fortunate to find some relevant papers, as did my companion. Together, we managed to compile quite a little scenario, circumstantial, I admit, but suspicious nonetheless.

It was quite late when we returned to Baker Street. Mrs. Hudson, bless her soul, had left us a note indicating that a cold supper was to be found in the kitchen. I prepared a plate for myself, but Holmes, as usual when on a case, chose to forego food, going straight to his indexes and newspapers. He also wrote the telegrams that he wanted to send in the morning, and was still working when I decided to retire.

As I lay in my bed, contemplating the day's activities, my mind drifted into various possibilities. Not for the first time, I marvelled at how Holmes's mind worked to make sense of such disparate facts.

Chapter Five

The next morning, Sunday, I awoke to find Holmes gone to who knew where. He had left me a note though, stating that he had requested a meeting at Justice Shipley's home at one o'clock and hoped that I would be available.

I breakfasted courtesy of Mrs. Hudson and enjoyed a splendid meal. I was grateful for the repast, as we would likely not be offered lunch at the judge's house. Being the Sabbath, I had no patients scheduled. So I settled at my desk and organised the notes that I had taken thus far. I was interrupted twice by telegrams addressed to my fellow boarder. I set them on the table next to his favourite chair by the fireplace.

It was about eleven o'clock when Holmes finally returned. Once he had removed his hat and coat, he greeted me heartily and fell into his chair picking up the flimsies I had set there. The first confirmed that the judge had accepted our meeting. The second was a little longer. He read it carefully. At last, he sat back and crossed his long legs. Staring off into the distance, he tapped the piece of paper against his chin. I was tempted, but I refused to interrupt his thoughts. I waited until he at last folded the paper and placed it into his waistcoat pocket. When he still did not speak, I broached the subject.

"What have you learned, Holmes? You seem to have a look of satisfaction about you."

"Pieces are falling into place, Watson" he replied. "A plot is developing, but like any good writer, we must gather our inspiration from facts as they come to light. I believe that the judge may provide another spotlight or two."

At one o'clock we arrived at a substantial residence not far from that shared by Etherege and his wife. This one was more masculine in its furnishings and décor. Oak panelling prevailed in the interior. A bearskin rug lay before the hearth. Mounted heads of deer and boar adorned the walls of the judge's snuggery, which also featured the Shipley coat of arms with its sable lozenge upon an argent escutcheon. A gun case stood off to one side of the judge's desk, filled with shotguns, rifles, and a pair of pistols.

Justice Shipley sat behind his desk, commanding the scene as if it were his courtroom. He did not stand upon our entrance. Instead, he bade us to sit down. We settled into black, leather-bound wingback chairs with brass studs.

"Mr. Holmes, Dr. Watson," he intoned with his stentorian voice. "How are you progressing in finding my son-in-law's killer?"

Holmes folded his hands in his lap as he crossed his legs, defying the formality of the situation. "I have been tracing several leads, your Lordship. I need not remind you that no body has been found, so there is still hope that he is alive."

Shipley sniffed, "Come now, Holmes. Even though circumstantial, surely the bloodstain, the coat found by the river, and the pawned briefcase must point to Andrew's demise."

My companion tilted his head in acknowledgment and replied, "Strong indicators, certainly, but not proof by any means. I presume no ransom demand has been forthcoming?"

"None at all. What are these leads that you have been following?"

I was curious as to how Holmes would answer Shipley's question. He chose to be vaguely promising, "I am looking into disgruntled clients and other possible enemies. Not all of his investments or legal advice on behalf of his clients have been successful. I have also gone as far as contacting Cambridge to ensure that no old college grudges may be surfacing."

"Cambridge!" cried the judge, "Hah! You're wasting your time there, Holmes. He was a highly popular student and an excellent halfback. He even performed in the student amateur dramatics club[1]. No, you should stick to your disgruntled client theory, or look for a criminal gang."

"Do you know which members of his club he was close to?"

"The Garrick? I don't recall him being particularly close to anyone. I believe he has mentioned a fellow named Thomas, but I don't know if that was a first or last name."

I made a note of that while Holmes asked his next question.

"What about his finances, your Lordship?" asked the detective. "Could he have made a poor investment or borrowed from the wrong people?"

"Impossible! He inherited a fortune as well as a successful business, which he has grown even more so. Marrying my daughter also brought him a very substantial dowry. No, I cannot imagine that he has any money trouble. I would have heard something, especially from Millicent. She can be very, shall we say, *boisterous* in letting her feelings being known."

"I take it that she has never been in want for anything?" said Holmes.

The judge acted offended as he replied, "Certainly not! I've never denied her any desire that could be afforded. That's what money and success are for, after all."

"And their marriage is quite happy, I presume?"

"Well, of course. He is a successful young man and keeps her in the lifestyle to which she has always been accustomed."

"Forgive me for being so bold, Your Lordship. What will become of her, if Andrew is indeed deceased?"

The justice hesitated slightly at the thought as if he were truly contemplating the full meaning of it for his daughter for the first time. Then he replied, "She will be a wealthy young widow. I will certainly see to her care, but I'm sure there will be no shortage of suitors after a decent period of mourning."

He sat up straighter. If he had his gavel, I'm sure that he would have pounded it on the desk as he said, "You need to

---

[1] This would have been the University Amateur Dramatic Club founded in 1855, with its membership drawn largely from Trinity College.

find his body or his killer before that can happen, Holmes. So, I suggest you get to it!"

We took that as an order of dismissal and left him with assurances that all our efforts would be concentrated on his case.

As we stood on the pavement outside attempting to hail a cab, I asked my companion, "I'm sure you have good reason for not voicing your theory that Etherege is still alive, Holmes. May I ask why?"

"For the same reason that the police theory is based upon circumstantial evidence," he replied. "My theory has yet to be proved, though I believe it more viable than Smith's. Still, without absolute proof, I prefer not to raise anyone's hopes. The coat by the water may have been a plant by Etherege, but it may also have been the result of a falling out with a co-conspirator. The only thing I am sure of is that Etheredge left that office alive and deliberately."

A four-wheeler came in to view. Holmes bid the driver to take us to The Garrick Club. We were delivered to Garrick Street where we disembarked in front of the large two-storey structure with its facade noted by its long row of arched windows on the first floor and a large oak double front door. Since its founding in 1831, it has remained one of the most distinguished clubs in all London. Membership is limited to actors, and literary personalities. As we entered, Holmes stopped to note its wall-mounted motto stating 'All the World's a Stage'.

I spotted his look and commented, "Recalling your days in the theatre, old man?"

He shook his head with a slight smile, replying, "Just ruminating on the truth of that statement, Watson."

A porter came up to us and asked about our business. Holmes questioned if Thomas Kent was about. The gentleman asked us to wait while he enquired. It was only a minute or two later that he returned with a tall string-bean of a fellow. Holmes introduced me to Mr. Kent of *The Daily Telegraph*. The gentleman took us off to a side room where we could talk in private. Once settled in some chairs around a card table off in a quiet corner where we would not be overheard, he asked in a high, reedy voice, "Have you a story for me, Holmes, or are you seeking information today?"

"Information for now," replied my friend. "And confidentiality is paramount. I do promise you though, that you will receive an exclusive from me at some future date."

"Ah, how intriguing," replied the journalist as he took out his cigarette case and offered it to each of us. Holmes accepted, so I did as well.

Once we had shared a match, Kent continued, with an easy smile, "Well, you've always been as good as your word. What can I tell you, that the great Sherlock Holmes does not already know?"

Holmes smiled and replied, "You are aware of the missing solicitor, Andrew Etherege, of course. My investigation has led me here to seek out a friend of his named 'Thomas'. I believe that man is you and I have some questions."

Kent paused, taking the cigarette from between his lips. He rubbed the thumb of his other hand across his moustache, then curled his fist, with the knuckle of the index finger under his nose and his thumb rubbing under his chin as his elbow rested on the chair's arm. He stalled for time by taking another puff of his cigarette, then flicked ashes into the receptacle on the table.

Finally, he spoke, "I admit, I do know of Etherege, but only as a fellow club member. After all, he is a solicitor and I'm a journalist of some distinction, who only dabbles in a news story when someone like you brings one my way. What could I possibly tell you?"

Holmes leaned across the table and looked him directly in the eye. "I believe quite a lot, sir. Let me start with a piece of information I have discovered. *Cambridge, Amateur Dramatics Club.*"

Kent looked to the ceiling, took a deep breath, then, stubbed out his cigarette. "I'm sorry, Holmes. Just as I would not break a confidence with you, I'll not break one with him."

He started to rise, but the detective waved him back to his seat, "Two minutes, Kent. Let me tell you what I have already deduced. At that point, you can decide whether to let me help your friend, or leave me to expose the truth on my own, which shall surely lead to scandal and possibly incarceration."

Kent sat back down. Holmes poured out a tale that I now understood. I berated myself for not having assembled all the clues my companion had pointed out along the way.

When finished, he extinguished his cigarette and held an open palm out to the journalist, "Well, what shall it be?"

Chapter Six

This time Kent stood and looked down upon us. "I will not break his confidence, Holmes. I will convey to him what you know, as well as what you propose, and then leave it up to him. I want your word as a gentleman not to follow me, or report this conversation to the police. I will meet you at Baker Street tomorrow morning at nine o'clock with his answer."

Holmes stood and shook the journalist's hand in agreement. Kent showed us to the door and we obtained a cab for home.

The next morning, as we sat expectantly before the morning fire at precisely nine o'clock, Mrs. Hudson announced that we had visitors. While I wondered at the plural, Holmes gave that quick smile of his, that you can miss if you blink, and nodded for her to show them up.

We stood by the door as our landlady led the gentlemen to our threshold. She asked if we would care for coffee or tea. Holmes looked to Kent's companion who bowed to her responding, "Tea would be lovely, madam. Thank you."

I looked upon the gentleman. He was the right size and weight for Andrew Etherege, but the resemblance stopped there. He was clean-shaven with long, straight black hair with sideboards. He wore tinted, silver-framed eyeglasses and a grey suit, which, most certainly, did not come from Saville Row. He also carried a large manila envelope.

Holmes extended his hand to each man. Without hesitation, he called Etherege by name. I also shook their hands in welcome. My friend waved towards the sofa by the fire as we took up the chairs opposite them.

Etherege got right down to business. "Thomas tells me you know everything, Mr. Holmes. Before I share my story, I should like to know how you discovered my secret."

Holmes folded his hands together, elbows on the armchair, index fingers steepled just below his chin as he gazed upon the solicitor. "Very well, sir," He finally answered letting his hands fall into his lap and crossed a leg over his knee.

"To start with the fact that there were not enough footprints upon the carpet to indicate anyone other than the police, the doctor, you, and your wife had been in your office since its last cleaning. Then there was the blood. You used stage blood to make sure that you had enough to indicate a serious injury. Since I was called in a week after your disappearance it should not have retained the bright red colour and smooth texture. Your gun was missing from its accustomed place in your desk drawer, yet there were no indications that you used it to defend yourself. You faked the drag marks of your boot heels on the carpet, but having to stop periodically they were not of a consistent depth. I also found evidence that you had shaved your moustache. Finally, you left your overcoat and umbrella but took your hat. An unlikely action of a kidnapper."

Etherege spoke up, "My hat was supposed to be found with my coat."

"It was not. Being lighter it was most likely to have been blown away by river breezes," replied the detective.

Mrs. Hudson arrived with her tea tray at that moment. I poured for all of us. With cups in hand, Holmes continued his summary.

"Now convinced that your abduction was a prevarication, I began to look for a motive. Examination of papers left in your office and home led me to believe that the vast majority of your cases were in a state of completion, or close enough that they could easily be taken up by another solicitor. I commend you on your loyalty to your clients."

Etherege saluted with his cup, "My clients did not deserve to suffer for my situation. I made it as easy as possible for them to carry on without me."

Holmes nodded, "In your old office there was a wear pattern to the carpet along the side of the room where the vanity cabinet was located and also in front of the unit itself. The larger mirrors told me another story. You are not a vain man, but you felt a need to observe your appearance. The most likely reason is that you were contemplating a change in career to one that required you to project a specific presence. However, the pacing up and down on that side of the room and the change in your appearance told me a different story. When I went to your home and discovered the file on theatrical productions and the Shakespearean paintings on the wall of your study, I felt I was on the right track. I contacted your *alma mater* in Cambridge. Thus, I discovered your participation in the amateur dramatics club. This confirmed to me that your pacing was the result of your process of memorising lines."

"If you've been to my home, I assume you met Millicent?" he asked.

"Yes, I also noted the condition of the bed in your study. It is far too worn to be merely a daybed or a sickbed."

"Couples often sleep in different rooms, Mr. Holmes," replied Etherege. "Especially if one of them is a prodigious snorer."

I noted that he did not indicate which one. Though recalling Mrs. Etherege's strident voice, I could easily conclude to whom he was referring.

"I also noted that after six years of marriage, you have no children."

Etherege stiffened, "I prefer not to discuss intimate matters with you, Mr. Holmes. Infer what you will, I'll not speak of such things except to her alone."

"As you wish, sir," said Holmes, retreating diplomatically. "Regardless, I determined that you wished to leave your present situation behind to embark on a career in theatre.

Justice Shipley recalled that you had a friend at The Garrick named 'Thomas'. I have known Mr. Kent for several years. If he was not the Thomas I sought, he would likely know who was. I questioned him accordingly and here we are."

Etherege finished his tea with a gulp, setting it down on the table. "Thank you, Mr. Holmes. At least I know I did enough to fool the police. I had not counted on Shipley calling you in too.

"My intention was to let Millicent twist in the wind until she could legally have me declared dead. It was fitting for what she had put me through. It would also have saved any other poor fool from falling into her clutches until, perhaps, she mellowed with age. You have made that impossible, thus I am forced to take another tact."

He pulled some papers from the manila envelope and flipped to the last page. "This is my declaration which will lead to divorce, gentlemen. I intend to sign it, and to have you both act as witnesses. Then you may deliver it to her so that she can enact it through the divorce courts. She is entitled to none of my savings or income and is wealthy in her own right, thanks to her father spoiling her all these years.

"I am sailing for New York later today to pursue my new career. I would appreciate your delaying delivery until it is too late for her to ask the His Lordship to stop me."

Holmes leaned on his elbow to one side and placed an index finger to his lips as he considered Etherege's proposal. I, on the other hand, asked a question, "What of your marriage vows, sir?"

The gentleman, having placed the papers on the table before him in preparation for signing, leaned forward with his elbows on his knees as he replied, "In all your experience, Dr. Watson, have you not run across a situation where a woman was forced into an arranged marriage with a man who was completely wrong for her? Did you not feel sorry for her, being required to endure this lifetime of unhappiness?"

"Well, yes, but ..."

"It's the same thing here, Doctor. Only in this case, *I* am the one who is stuck in a loveless marriage and forced to carry on in my father's footsteps. The advantage I have is that I intend

76

to put an end to it. With this document, her father should be able to use his influence and get a private act of divorce through parliament. She will be free to pursue someone who can make her happy if such a person exists. I will finally be able to take a pride in myself and my work and be free to follow my own dreams and ambitions. Perhaps even find true love. In any case, it puts an end to a bad situation. Is that not reasonable and best for all, sir?"

I looked at him and could see the sincerity in his eyes. I glanced at Holmes, who merely nodded, then I stood and retrieved pen and ink from the desk across the room.

After the departure of Etherege and Kent, I asked Holmes, "How long should we wait?"

"It matters not, Watson," he replied. "First, we must report this to Inspector Smith so he can be relieved of his search. Then, there will be plenty of time to inform Mrs. Etherege."

The trip to the Yard and finding the Inspector took the better part of an hour as he was in a meeting on another matter. He was relieved to discover that Holmes had found Etherege alive. An unsolved murder would not reflect well on his record. He was sorely disappointed that we did not have the name of the ship Etherege would be sailing on. He felt duty-bound to curtail a matter of family abandonment. Holmes merely pointed out there would not likely be many ships sailing for New York that day. If he hurried, perhaps he could still catch the rascal.

As we left the Yard and headed for Mrs. Etherege's home I said to my friend, "I noted that you neglected to mention Etherege's change in name and appearance. I presume that was a purposeful omission?"

"It is of no consequence, Watson," he replied. "Even with a description, Smith's first effort will be to send a telegram to check the passenger manifest and stop Etherege from boarding. He will not find Etherege's name. Assuming that Etherege is sailing at all, it will be under his new identity, which only he and Thomas Kent know. There is only one ship sailing for New York today. Smith will be too late to stop it. Kent knew that when he set the time for our meeting. He could barely reach it in time."

"You said *assuming that he is sailing?*"

My companion smiled, "Etherege has been very clever throughout, although some of his execution has been less than perfect. It would not surprise me if his statement was meant merely to throw us off, in case we should not keep our promise. With his new look, name, and profession, he could go anywhere in England. He could even remain here in London, with no one the wiser, save his friend Kent."

We arrived at the Etherege home at half past eleven. We were told by Marian, the housekeeper, that Mrs. Etherege had gone out to a luncheon and would not be returning until three o'clock.

As we stood there, I asked Holmes if we should deliver the papers to the Justice Shipley.

He replied that these were a private communique for Mrs. Etherege and only she should decide who should see it. "Besides, Watson, Shipley is likely to be on his bench all day. You know how busy the courts are on Mondays."

Thus we left the papers with Marian and returned to Baker Street. The next day, very early, we were set upon in our sitting room at breakfast by Inspector Smith and Justice Shipley together. The latter was furious, demanding Smith arrest us for aiding Etherege's escape.

Holmes, still in his dressing gown, asked me to ring for Mrs. Hudson. She soon joined us. He then went into his defence. "First of all, Your Lordship, we were engaged merely to find proof of what happened to your son-in-law. At this we were successful. I have every right to invoice you for my services, though I have decided to forego my charges in this instance. I am not the official police, therefore I had no powers to arrest Mr. Etherege. I remind you that he still had his firearm as well as a rather large bodyguard who was with him, isn't that right, Mrs. Hudson?"

As he said this, he raised his palm several inches above his head, indicating to her that he meant Kent's height, not his bulk. She took the hint and readily assured our accuser, "Oh it's true, sir. He barely fitted through the door. I'd certainly not want to confront such a man myself."

78

"Thank you, Mrs. Hudson, you may go," said Holmes.

He now turned back to our visitors, "As you can see, sir, we signed as witnesses under a threat that hung in the air like a choking cloud. I also remind you, that as soon as they left us, we immediately made our way to Scotland Yard to inform Inspector Smith. Afterward, we set out and delivered the papers to your daughter. We have acted in good faith throughout. Should you persist in this false arrest I will see to it that every newspaper in town is informed of your daughter's situation. I have no wish to expose her scandal, but neither do I desire to sit in jail, even temporarily, for doing what I was tasked to do."

Fuming, the judge sputtered as he tried to form a reply. Finally, he merely said to his companion, "Come along, Smith. We'll arrange to have him arrested when he lands in New York. Then we'll see, Mr. Sherlock Holmes, just how true your testimony is."

He stomped out with the Inspector at his heels. Holmes walked over to the landing watching them descend the stairs and storm out of the front door. Then, he called to Mrs. Hudson for a fresh pot of tea.

As he returned to the breakfast table, I commented, "A very clever use of words, Holmes. All true enough, but not accurately portraying the situation. I was wondering about your use of the word 'threat', however."

"Ah, Watson, recall that I did not say Etherege threatened us. It was the threat of our exposing him to which I referred. Dear, Mrs. Hudson," he cried as she brought forth a steaming pot of tea. "You were quite the heroine this morning. Thank you."

"You're welcome, I'm sure, Mr. Holmes," she replied with a wink and left us to finish our breakfast.

Two months later, Holmes and I had heard nothing more from Smith nor Shipley. We were taking in a performance of

Hamlet when Holmes nudged me with his elbow, leaned over, and whispered, "Observe Polonius, Doctor."

I took up my opera glasses and trained them upon the evil counsellor. Even with his stage makeup on, I recognised the fellow and looked back at my friend who merely replied quietly, "All the world's a stage, Watson, and our friend has found his part in it."

Wrath

The Game at Chequers

Chapter One

It was the spring of 1920 when I happened to be visiting my friend, the retired detective, Sherlock Holmes, at his beekeeper's cottage in Sussex. We had been lunching when a telegram arrived:

> SHERLOCK STOP YOUR PRESENCE REQUIRED STOP
> SEE MOST SOONEST STOP M STOP

The housekeeper had laid it on the table by his plate. A quick perusal by him resulted in a grunt and a toss of the paper over to me. Cryptic as it seemed, I had known Holmes long enough that I recognised the significance immediately.

"It appears your brother, Mycroft, has something beyond his ability to solve from his desk in Whitehall or his chair at the Diogenes."

Sir Mycroft Holmes[1], according to my companion, was the smarter of the two brothers and held an unusual government post of key importance. His one flaw was his lack of ambition in proving the solutions that he had deduced. His physical bulk

---

[1] Mycroft Holmes was knighted after the Great War, ostensibly for his decades of loyal service. Sherlock Holmes suspected it was rather to placate him for the government ignoring his advice regarding post-war treatment of Germany. Mycroft had predicted that the harsh terms imposed by the Allies would build nothing but resentment and determination for the German nation to rise again (see *The Five Gold Rings* in *Sherlock Holmes: Further Adventures for the Twelve Days of Christmas* by Roger Riccard).

made him notoriously inactive. When proof was required through on-the-spot investigation, he often called upon his younger sibling to 'do all the tramping about to uncover the physical evidence necessary'. This would usually occur when there were legal or political ramifications necessitating absolute proof, as opposed to Mycroft's stated theories.

"An astute deduction, Watson," he replied, though I could not tell if there was sarcasm behind that remark or not. "Would you care to accompany me up to London this afternoon to see if we can put Mycroft's mind at ease?"

"I wouldn't mind a dinner at the Diogenes," I replied, nonchalantly, giving him back a little of his own. Not being a member of the Diogenes myself, I was only able to sample the exquisite cuisine on those rare occasions when I was an invited guest.

"I shall see to it, Doctor, though it may have to be after the case is solved since Mycroft appears to be in a hurry."

Having agreed to terms, we finished our lunch, packed our bags, and were at Eastbourne station in time for the three o'clock train. We brought a third companion with us whom Holmes seemed to feel might be helpful on whatever task Mycroft would lay before us. Upon reaching Victoria, we took a cab to my practice where we dropped our friend off. We then proceeded on to the Diogenes, assuming that Mycroft would keep to his normal custom of going straight there after his office hours.

The Diogenes Club was founded by Mycroft Holmes, among others, for the purpose of having the benefits of a club where members could have privacy away from work or home in absolute peace and quiet. Thus it welcomed the 'unclubable' gentlemen of London. Those who were socially distant or supreme introverts. There was no talking allowed, save in the Strangers's Room where Holmes and I always met with his brother. Even the dining room was silent. One was given a card with the choices of the day, completed it, and was served accordingly. There were also refreshments available in the Strangers's Room, such as tea and biscuits, wine, sherry, or brandy.

As so happened, our arrival coincided with that of the elder Holmes. We greeted him as we disembarked from our cab, whilst he was just beginning to ascend the stairs. He was in his seventies now, being seven years his brother's senior. He had lost some of his bulk with age, though he was still overweight. His hair had receded halfway back upon his scalp and, along with his mutton chop whiskers, had gone completely white. His cane now was a necessity rather than an affectation. Hence he held the hand rail tightly as we made our way to the front door.

We walked inside and to the Strangers's Room where Mycroft ordered brandies all around as we sat in a triangle of overstuffed chairs. The room itself was panelled in walnut with several tapestries of historical moments in British history. In addition to decoration, these tapestries also provided a measure of sound deadening. Therefore, any conversations would not filter through the walls into the silent areas of the building. There were heavy green drapes drawn across the windows now that dusk was falling. The chairs and settees were a combination of solid and patterned upholstery in green, tan, mauve, and burgundy.

Mycroft began the conversation with a statement, "You are aware that the Chequers estate has been turned over to the government for the private, exclusive use of the Prime Minister."

Surprised by this opening remark, I recalled that in October 1917, it became public knowledge that the historical estate had been bequeathed as a gift to the government of Great Britain. It was to be used as a country home for the Prime Minister, in perpetuity, whenever the pressures of No. 10 Downing Street required a respite from London and Parliament.

Chequers was an ancient edifice. It gained its name from the office of Exchequer, or Treasurer, held by many of its inhabitants. The final private owners, Sir Arthur Hamilton Lee (now Lord Lee), Minister of Agriculture and Fisheries and First Lord of the Admiralty, under Prime Minister David Lloyd George, and his wife, referred to as Lady Ruth Lee, had undertaken major renovations to the manor in 1909-1910, while they were still leasing the property. In 1912 they bought it outright. Chequers had also served as a military hospital during the war.

Mycroft continued, "Its use as a hospital has been concluded and the few remaining patients have been transferred to other facilities. Preparations are under way for the Prime Minister's occupancy, we must be certain that the manor is secure. Lord and Lady Lee are not in residence at the moment. They're taking a holiday in Rome. While they are gone, you are to go up to Chequers and examine the estate for any security weaknesses. Your government is requesting your observation skills in this matter, Sherlock. Report your findings to me and suitable corrections will be made."

"Then it is well that I brought Lestrade along," said Sherlock Holmes. "He should be quite adept at sniffing out irregularities on a country estate."

I stifled a chuckle at this statement as Mycroft nodded at his brother's foresight. The *Lestrade* we were discussing was the Basset hound which Holmes had been given as a gift from a grateful client.[1] Holmes named him after our friend, Inspector Lestrade, who had passed away during the Spanish Flu epidemic after the Great War. He was an excellent scent hound and just as determined as the old Scotland Yard official.

---

[1] See *The Five Gold Rings* in *Sherlock Holmes: Further Adventures for the Twelve Days of Christmas* by Roger Riccard.

Chapter Two

The next morning, we left Marylebone station for the forty-mile journey northwest to Great Kimble near Chequers. Once beyond London's city limits, we passed through some of the greenest meadows and woods in all of England. While I enjoyed the view of spring's arrival, my companion was focused deeply on papers provided by Mycroft regarding the history and layout of the estate. Lestrade was curled up sleeping quietly on the seat beside me.

About two minutes before pulling into the station, Holmes suddenly folded up the documents and put them into his bag.

"Finished already, Holmes?" I asked.

"Hardly, Watson," he replied. "The history of Chequers dates back to the 12th century. However, we are about to reach our stop."

I looked out of the window. My seat faced forward while Holmes's view was to the rear. All I could see were green fields. "How could you know that, Holmes?" I asked, just as the locomotive sounded its whistle. "You've never checked your watch and the station is not yet in sight."

"I knew how long the journey was scheduled to take, dear fellow. I also know how fast I read, depending on the type of material I am perusing. It was a simple calculation to know how many pages I could review in the time allowed."

I shook my head as the train slowed to a stop. Even after four decades, there were still depths of Holmes's character I had yet to learn.

Mycroft had arranged rooms for us at the Crowe's Nest Inn. A moderate cab ride deposited us at the establishment, which was less than a mile from the manor house. It was located in the hamlet of Butler's Cross, directly across the street from The Russell Arms, an attractive building steeped in history. Originally it was an 18th-century coaching house, its name being deriving from the family that once owned Chequers. Many of the staff from Chequers now lived there to the extent that it no longer offered accommodation to the public.

The landlord of Crowe's Nest, Harvey Boyle, was a tall, lean fellow with receding brown hair and a prominent nose. He wore a white shirt with black braces and a bow tie. He greeted us with enthusiasm, "Welcome gentlemen, it's an honour to have Sherlock Holmes and Dr. Watson at my humble establishment. I've arranged a ground floor room as per your request, Mr. Holmes. It's near the back door for the convenience of your hound."

"I made no such request, Mr. Boyle," stated my companion.

The fellow handed Holmes a telegram from his pocket, "I received this two days ago."

Holmes glanced at it and handed me the form, saying one word, "Mycroft."

I read it aloud, including the signature, 'M Holmes, Foreign Office'.

Addressing Boyle I asked, "How did you get 'Sherlock' from the letter 'M'?"

He replied, "I thought at first that it was a typing error and was supposed to read either 'S' or was an abbreviation of mister. Frankly, I thought you were retired, Mr. Holmes."

"My brother seems to have anticipated me," Holmes mumbled. "Again."

To Boyle, he replied, "It seems that one never retires from his duties as a British citizen, Mr. Boyle. This is Lestrade."

"Yes sir," replied the manager as he knelt and gently petted Lestrade who welcomed the attention as he sniffed the man's hand. "Ah, he smells my Galahad. We should introduce them, just to get acquainted and avoid any unpleasantness later on."

Holmes agreed and a quick whistle from Boyle brought forth a heavy Clumber Spaniel. With his thick white coat and brown ears, he approached us cautiously. Being a short-legged breed, he went easily nose to nose with Holmes's Basset. They sniffed each other, as dogs do, and seemed satisfied with each other's company.

Boyle showed us to our rooms. As promised, they were in the back, away from the noise of the reception area. There were two bedrooms and a common room. I noted that there was also a padded basket for Lestrade. Holmes thanked Boyle and we set about to unpack.

The landlord handed Holmes two keys for the room and a third oddly shaped key. "Your automobile is in the carriage house out the back and filled with petrol. Dinner is served at six-thirty. Let me know if you need anything else, gentlemen."

"You could satisfy my curiosity, Mr. Boyle," I said. "Why the name Crowe's Nest for an establishment so far inland?"

The man smiled ruefully, "A concession to my father, Doctor. He was a seafaring man and always wanted to retire and own a pub. It's the name he would have called it, had he lived to realise his dream."

"Ah, I see. Thank you."

In our younger days, the journey to Chequers would have been a pleasant walk on a spring day. Now, however, we were given the use of a Crossley to drive back and forth.

Completing our unpacking, Holmes and I went out to the carriage house. The automobile was parked in an area pointing towards the door. Other carriages and wagons were in place around it and a small stable of horses was adjacent. There was also an area fenced off for numerous crates and barrels of supplies for both the Russell Arms and the Crowe's Nest. While there we ran into a burly fellow by the name of Brockmeyer. He identified himself as being from the Russell Arms and was gathering a few supplies for the day. I thought it a convenient arrangement for the two establishments to share a common storage space. Barrels of beer, foods, extra bedding, tablecloths, and various and sundry equipment were all stockpiled in an orderly fashion.

As to the car; Holmes, being in better physical shape than I, operated the crank while I inserted the key and adjusted the timing and throttle stalks. I admit I was somewhat perturbed at Mycroft for his choice of vehicles. There were certainly easier ones to start and operate and this had no side windows to protect against weather. However, I accepted the situation and followed Lestrade's example. The hound sat patiently in the back seat and gave a sharp bark when the engine started.

Holmes insisted that I drive slowly, as he wished to examine the road leading to the manor. It was a pleasant day with scattered clouds and a bright sun. We headed due south on Missenden Road. It was a narrow affair exhibiting fresh spring growth along the embankments on either side. Lestrade sat up straight and woofed on several occasions at movement in the hedgerows. Rabbits and squirrels seemed to abound. We passed only one structure, about halfway along our journey. It was a good-sized building made of multi-coloured brick with a scalloped roofline of descending arches. A pair of black Labrador retrievers roamed the front garden, confined by a wrought iron fence.

As I was occupied with driving, Holmes was forced to make his own notes. His frequent scribbling and grumbling told me that he already was unhappy with the security offered by the road which led to the prime minister's country home.

The trees on our right thinned out about three hundred yards before the turning to Chequers, giving us a view of the high roof and chimney stacks of the structure itself. We turned down a long drive, bordered by thick hedges. There was no gate, merely a small sign posted stating 'Private – No Admittance'.

"Well," I said, sarcastically, "that should certainly keep intruders out!"

Holmes merely grunted and replied, "Our task appears daunting, old friend. Let us hope the house itself affords better protection."

At least there was a wrought iron gate at the entrance to the east circular drive, which was open wide and there were no guards posted. Arriving at the main house, we found a magnificent manor with manicured grounds. The multi-storey structure of red and tan brick almost seemed out of place in its bucolic surroundings. Its many large, multi-paned windows spoke to the appreciation of its builders for the surrounding view of the lush countryside.

A well-dressed gentleman was waiting for us in front of the high-arched eastern entrance. I took him to be about forty with dark brown hair cut short and clean-shaven. He raised his hand and pointed to a spot where I should park the vehicle. He walked smartly over to us and reached for the door, but Holmes beat him to it, stuffing his notepad and pencil into his inner breast pocket before extending his hand.

"Good afternoon, Major," said the detective as he took the gentleman's hand. "I trust that your lookouts informed you of our approach by telephone, and that our speed did not leave you standing here too long, but I insisted that the Doctor here drive slowly so that I could make my initial observations."

As good a soldier as he was, the officer could not hide his surprise at Holmes's statement. By this time, I had also exited the automobile and come around to join the two of them. He shook my hand almost absent-mindedly as he pondered a response. Finally, he spoke.

"A pleasure, Dr. Watson. My name is Nathan Hunter, gentlemen. I'd prefer that you did not use my rank, as my true purpose here is unknown to the staff and workmen. They believe me to be the major-domo, acting on Lloyd George's behalf. Did Sir Mycroft tell you about me, Mr. Holmes?"

"Only your name, Mr. Hunter," answered my companion. "Your rank was a mere deduction. As to your scouts, I observed them and their binoculars trained upon our vehicle and the singular phone line which runs straight from there to this property, in addition to the regular telephone service."

"I am aware of your reputation, sir," replied the Major. "I confess that I did not believe such things were possible until I was assigned to Sir Mycroft and observed him do the same thing. How did you deduce my rank?"

Holmes conceded to answer, "My brother has a penchant for using brave and bright military personnel for certain assignments. A military presence for security could certainly be assumed for the estate of the prime minister. Such responsibility would be entrusted to no less than a captain, but not likely to be thrust upon a colonel. Your military bearing gives you away as a soldier. As we drove up you were, out of habit, standing at parade rest. Your attire is crisp and clean with trouser creases sharp as a sword and shoes shined to a mirror finish. You have shaved off your moustache, so common to military men, but there is a slight difference in the skin tone, indicating that it has been done recently and not had a chance to obtain the same tanning as the rest of your face. When you raised your hand upon our arrival, it moved towards your forehead, as if in salute, until you caught yourself and waved us to this parking spot. Finally, your age indicates that you are likely to have risen above the rank of captain to that of major. For someone who is still a captain at your stage of life has not likely distinguished himself in a manner which would gain him such an important assignment as this."

Major Hunter nodded, "Very good, Mr. Holmes. You noted our outpost and the extra telephone line. You should also be aware that we have a wireless radio set up there with a receiver in a special attic room here."

Holmes nodded, "Excellent, Mr. Hunter. Might I suggest that the telephone line from the outpost to here be run through an underground conduit? That would make it less likely to be spotted and pulled down by an attacking force."

"I'll make a note of that," replied our host. "Do you wish to step inside or walk around the grounds first, gentlemen? I have an office set aside on the ground floor for your work."

He nodded towards me and my walking stick, as if he had made this concession to our ages and my game leg. I returned his nod with one of my own as Holmes replied, "I think that we could use a perusal of the grounds, Mr. Hunter. Between the train and the car, it would be pleasant to stretch our legs while we have a warm spring day to do so. What say you, Watson?"

"It is a nice day for a walk and I'm sure Lestrade could use the exercise," I replied.

"Lestrade?" queried Hunter.

"Our companion," I answered as I opened the car door and coaxed the hound out of the back seat to join us.

Chapter Three

With most people, Lestrade has a natural tendency to draw one down to a kneeling position to pet him, for he has a winsome appearance and friendly countenance. Major Hunter, being a disciplined soldier, did not deign to do so.

"You've brought your dog with you?" he asked, curiously.

Holmes, in an uncharacteristically doting fashion, crouched and stroked the animal's back, "Lestrade is an invaluable assistant to my work. Like the Scotland Yard Inspector he was named after, he is brave and determined. If I put him on a scent, he will run it to ground. He is also adept at warning of danger and is a fair judge of character."

Standing again and taking the hound's leash from me, he asked Hunter a question, "Before we begin, I should like to know if there will be a military force assigned to these grounds and whether or not they are to be on display or clandestine?"

The Major, still looking askance at Lestrade, answered, "There will be a military presence here, Mr. Holmes. As to how many and in what capacity, that is still under debate. I only know that it will be increased whenever the Prime Minister is in residence.

"Personally, I prefer a strong show of force to discourage anyone who has any thoughts of attacking this property or doing the Prime Minister harm. However, I have heard the argument made that this estate should present a peaceful image to the British people and, except for ceremonial guards, any

Troops attached would be assigned to quarters which are either underground or hidden from public view by high hedges."

"Very well," said the detective. "We'll delay that discussion for now. If you'll lead the way, Mr. Hunter, I should like to observe the exterior of the house and any approaches from the surrounding woods."

We started off towards the south side of the estate where there lay several hedge parterres surrounding multiple rose gardens. Each square was designated for a particular type or colour of rose. The spring blossoms created a heady fragrance as we strolled through. To my mind, the roses provided a thorny barrier to any advancing foot soldiers while the hedges were too low for effective concealment. South of that area the land was flat and green for a goodly distance with only a single line of trees running perpendicular to the manor house some one hundred and fifty yards away.

Swinging around to the west, we found multiple tennis courts surrounded by a grove of trees some fifty feet thick. Beyond the western border of that grove, the land was again flat for well over two hundred yards before reaching a border of boxwood beyond which was a small wood of about a quarter of an acre. Coming around to the northwest corner, there was a scattering of trees some two hundred feet from the north side of the manor. About two hundred and fifty yards due north, there were the woods which had been on our right as we had driven down Missenden Road. After a hundred yards of trees, it flattened out again to a wide level field, directly across from the house that we had passed.

Other than the occasional woodland creature drawing his attention, Lestrade seemed quite content with his walk and showed no sign of alarm. Holmes had had me make a few notes regarding the aforementioned measurements and the types of trees. He then requested Hunter to conduct us on a quick tour of the house so that we could see what we were up against from a security perspective.

Room after room of magnificence and splendour greeted us. Marvellous works of art and historical memorabilia were everywhere and I shall not attempt to list them here. Suffice to say that they were worthy of a museum. Holmes questioned Hunter on the provenance of several pieces and how long they had been in the house. He was particularly concerned with anything that may have been added after the plans were announced to turn Chequers into the Prime Minister's country home.

One such piece was a bust of Oliver Cromwell, which sat on a shelf immediately behind the desk in what would be the Prime Minister's working office. Lestrade had sniffed at it rather anxiously, even sitting up on his haunches and waving his paws like some circus animal. A rare feat I hadn't seen in him before and one of which I was not aware he was capable.

This caused Holmes to examine the bust carefully, then he lifted it off the shelf and held it down for the Bassett to get a good sent. Lestrade immediately barked and Holmes told us all to clear the room as he set the piece on the desk where he could scrutinise it more closely.

Hunter started to question this command, but I took his elbow, along with the dog's leash, and hurried them both out into the hallway. We waited there for an anxious two minutes before Holmes called out to the Major.

"Mr. Hunter, I'm taking this bust out through the window and getting it away from the house. Please meet me outside and lead me discreetly to the garage."

"Mr. Holmes," cried the man. "That was a gift from the Duke of Holdernesse. Certainly, it cannot be dangerous."

"I've no time to explain, sir. Please do as I say," ordered the detective in his most commanding tone.

"Watson, tie Lestrade up somewhere safe and come and meet me by the window. I need your assistance to hold the bust while I climb out of the window."

I did as instructed and, once at the window, was able to feel the weight of the bust. Somehow it did not seem appropriate to the size. After Holmes came out, he took up the work of art and carried it to the garage where he carefully set it down on a workbench.

Hunter and I had followed him and the Major declared, "Are you telling me that the Duke of Holdernesse sent a bomb intended for David Lloyd George, Mr. Holmes? That's preposterous!"

"I quite agree, but we'll get into that later. Do you have any ordinance experts nearby who can disarm such a device?"

"Not presently, Mr. Holmes. What do you propose we do?"

Holmes reached into his pocket and pulled out his multiplex knife. Carefully he began scraping away at the back of the base of the bust. Soon a small pile of wax shavings was lying on the bench and Holmes used the tweezer feature of his knife to grasp what appeared to be a piece of string and pulled it gently out about an inch.

"What we have here Major is a fuse to a bomb."

Hunter's composure remained calm, but his next question was filled with concern. "What do we do with it?"

Holmes thought briefly, then said, "I am loathe to destroy it as that would let the would be assassin know that we are on to him."

He picked it up gingerly and looked at the bottom, "It is likely filled with black powder since that would have been less likely to have exploded if it were dropped in transit. I believe I can extract the powder by drilling a hole in the bottom of the bust, rendering it harmless."

Hunter asked, "How could they have possibly hoped to set it off?"

Holmes replied,"

"It was a black powder device," See how this fuse at the back of the base of the neck, was nearly impossible to detect when covered with wax? They must have assumed that someday they would be able to infiltrate the staff and some servant could enter the room with refreshments or what not for the Prime Minister, then scrape away the wax with his thumbnail, pull out the fuse and light it, while the Prime Minister was distracted, giving him several seconds to leave the room.

Hunter's demeanour changed immediately, "Surely Holdernesse could not be involved in this!"

"Very likely not," replied Holmes. "Do you still have the card which came with it?"

"Yes, it is in my files awaiting an opportunity for the Prime Minister to send out thank you notes."

"Do you know who put the bust in that position?" asked the detective.

"We've had multiple workmen of varying specialties working on this project," replied the chagrined officer. "I'll have to check the files and see if we can reconstruct who did what."

"Very well. Let's remove the powder, re-cover the fuse with wax, and return Cromwell to his original position before anyone notices him missing. Then we shall go to your office and learn what we may about the arrival of this device."

Having re-secured the bust, Holmes, Lestrade, and I were soon in Hunter's office as the Major began scouring various ledgers for information. It was a dark-panelled space, unadorned by the artwork and décor that permeated the rest of the mansion. There was no window due to its location, thus it was dependent on ceiling lights and a banker's lamp on the desk for illumination. Shelves of ledgers and several dark wooden filing cabinets took up the majority of the room. Altogether a utilitarian space meant for work, not comfort. Holmes and I were seated in hard wooden chairs in front of the desk with the dog laying at the detective's feet.

At last, Hunter seemed to find the information that we sought. First, he handed Holmes the card that had come with the Cromwell bust. "You can see for yourself, Mr. Holmes, the Duke of Holdernesse signed the letter."

I looked over at the document in Holmes's hand. It appeared to be quality stationery, worthy of a peer's station. It was a single typed paragraph with Holdernesse's bold signature affixed at the bottom. An envelope was attached by a paper clip and my companion gave it a cursory glance before handing it back to Hunter.

"This is a forgery," declared Holmes. "We once provided services for the Duke and were rewarded with a sizable cheque.[1] One does not forget the signature on such a significant document. It is similar, but even accounting for His Grace's advancing years, there are certain characteristics inconsistent with his penmanship.

"Also, the stationery does not bear Holdernesse's custom watermark, nor does the envelope include his seal. It was a clever ruse to get the bomb inside the manor. Have you found who is responsible for placing it in the Prime Minister's office?"

The major-domo consulted a ledger that he had opened on his desk. Running his index finger across an entry he shook his head as he read, "That particular task was the responsibility of Mrs. Katherine Casey. She is a noted historian and was recommended by the Cashman Museum in Oxford, where she is an assistant curator."

"Where is she now?" asked Holmes.

"She completed her work three weeks ago. Just in time, I should say," recalled Hunter. "She was heavy with child and has probably given birth by now."

Holmes tilted his head, "I presume she was vetted by your people?"

"We verified her identity, of course," replied Hunter. "We were assured by the museum that she came to them upon her graduation with honours from Somerville College as Katherine Doyle in 1914. She married Sean Casey, a prominent solicitor in Cowley with a good reputation, in 1917. He was exempted from war service due to an injury he suffered during his army training which severed his left foot."

As I sat listening to this, it seemed that such detail was rather thorough and I wondered how the young woman could be involved in this apparent plot. Holmes steepled his fingers at his lips momentarily, then asked, "If she was that far along in her pregnancy, I presume that she had someone to assist her with the placing of the heavier articles in that room. Do you have any idea who that might be?"

Hunter shook his head, "It could have been any of the servants or workmen. All such items are received into the cellar

---

[1] See *The Adventure of the Priory School* by Sir Arthur Conan Doyle.

where they are catalogued and assigned. There are still many items down there awaiting to be sorted. They will be stored and rotated for display on various occasions or to fit the tastes of the particular Prime Minister in residence at the time."

"We will need to examine that area, of course," declared Holmes. "Is the telephone in the Prime Minister's office a private line? I need to call London."

Chapter Four

Hunter unlocked the door to the office, for Holmes had locked it before he passed the bust out of the window to me. We gave him his privacy on the phone and I enquired of the Major if there were somewhere convenient where I might obtain water for the hound panting at my feet. He took me to the kennel that we had walked past on our excursion earlier. "There are no dogs in residence at present," he remarked. "Your Basset is free to wander this area as it pleases. There is a water pump over there and containers of dog food in that shed."

I took Lestrade off his leash and let him wander about as I filled a metal bowl with water from the pump. I found more bowls and food in the shed and set out a fair-sized meal for the hungry hound. I knelt and spoke gently to the animal as I scratched behind his ears, assuring him that I would be back. He seemed to accept that, going immediately to his food bowl.

The Major and I returned to the house and met Holmes exiting the office, having finished his telephone call. Hunter spoke first, "What next, Mr. Holmes?"

My friend glanced at the floor and replied, "I presume Lestrade is enjoying a meal out in the kennel. We will require him later. For now, let us continue the tour of the house."

The rest of the afternoon was spent going floor by floor and room by room. Holmes had me take so many notes I nearly filled my notebook. This was only a cursory tour and a more detailed examination would take place over the next few days. We found many other items regarding the Lord Protector. Hunter informed us that John Russell, a grandson of Cromwell, had married Joanna Thurbarne who had inherited Chequers in 1707.

We finished with a cursory examination of the attic, before descending to the basement where we examined the kitchen and pantry. Holmes paid particular attention to the dumbwaiter and he even took some measurements.

Finally, he turned to Hunter and said, "I believe that we should retrieve Lestrade and examine the cellar."

Our canine companion was napping in a shady spot when we returned to the kennel but perked up immediately at the sound of the opening gate. He trotted over to Holmes in that swaying fashion unique to stout, short-legged dogs, sat down, and stared up at his master. Holmes gave him a biscuit from his pocket and attached the leash.

"I should like to take a closer look at the outside entrance to the cellar, Major. Please lead the way."

Hunter did so and, upon arrival, took keys from his pocket to unlock the doors, prompting Holmes to question, "Who else has keys to this area?"

"Only the kitchen steward, groundskeeper and I can enter through here. From the inside the door to the kitchen has a lock, but it is a vestige from when servants were less trusted. Nowadays it is never locked."

Once inside, Hunter turned on the electric lights and I noted a quiet hum. When I questioned the noise, the major-domo replied, "That is a dehumidifier, Dr. Watson. You'll notice that this room does not exhibit the damp feel or smell typical of most cellars. It prevents the growth of mildew and the spoilage of food."

Holmes knelt by the Basset and pulled the envelope of black powder from his pocket to give the hound a scent. He then ordered, 'seek' and walked around the room with the hound sniffing all about the place. Everything seemed to pass muster until they reached the coal bin. The bin itself was nearly empty. However, there were several crates of charcoal next to it and

Lestrade crouched and barked until Holmes put him at ease. Using a crowbar that hung there for the purpose of opening such crates, Holmes pried the top off of one and dumped the contents onto to floor. One would expect coal dust to have settled to the bottom of the crate so it was no surprise when the briquettes tumbled out amidst piles of black powder. What was concerning was the amount. The crate was probably two thirds full of black powder with just two or three layers of actual charcoal on top.

Holmes called the Major and me over, pointed at the pile on the floor, and said, "More gunpowder. We are in deep waters, gentlemen. Major, do you have men who can come and haul away these crates tonight under the cover of darkness?"

"Yes, Mr. Holmes, I can arrange that," replied Hunter.

"Good. You will also need to replace the crates. None of the servants may know that we've discovered this deadly cache."

Holmes looked about the cellar once more, "Are all the supplies and artifacts delivered to this room directly from the supplier, or is there another storeroom from which you draw items that have been bought in bulk?"

"There are two such places that we use for overstock," replied the army officer. "I can get the names and addresses for you from my office if you would like."

"That would be prudent," answered Holmes. "I presume they are nearby?"

Hunter's answer sent an alarm off in Holmes's mind and he demanded, "I must use the telephone again, quickly Major!"

Late that afternoon, we left in time to be back at the Crowe's Nest before dark. This time, Holmes drove and I sat with Lestrade on my lap, poking his nose out the side of the car. When we reached Wendover Road and were almost there, Holmes turned left instead of right. When I enquired where we were going, he stated, "I'm expecting a telegram to be waiting for me at the station."

"Why did you not have it delivered to the Crowe's Nest?" I said.

"I prefer to pick this one up as discreetly as possible," was his only reply.

After forty years of friendship, I knew better than to question Holmes's reasons and merely sat back and enjoyed the ride. The temperature was beginning to drop, but our overcoats were sufficient for now. I waited in the car with the hound while Holmes went into the station. He was out in about five minutes, stuffing the message into his inner breast pocket.

"Forgive my tardiness, Watson," he apologised. "It required another inquiry on my part."

"Are you writing to Mycroft?" I asked.

"Among others," he said.

"Could you possibly request another vehicle? This old bucket is deucedly cold, uncomfortable, and nearly impossible to crank up. I should hate to have an emergency come along and need to start it without your assistance."

He smiled, "Already done, my friend."

Upon return to our lodgings, Holmes backed our automobile into the carriage house and parked it where it had been. When we got out, though, instead of immediately going into the inn, Holmes chose to examine the supplies in storage. This went on for nearly ten minutes before he was satisfied. He would not answer my query as to what he was looking for, merely stating 'something that is not here'.

We took to our rooms and cleaned up for dinner. The menu at the Crowe's Nest was in keeping with its sea-faring name. On offer was a variety of seafood in addition to the more common dishes of the English countryside. The dun-coloured walls were decorated with fishing nets, harpoons, and mounted fish. There was a large painting of an old ship on one wall, and an anchor leaned heavily in a corner. The list of available drinks was extensive and included various beers, Guinness, a selection of spirits including Jameson whiskey and wines to suit every taste.

Such an atmosphere inspired me to have a halibut steak with assorted vegetables. Holmes chose to eat lightly as he so often does on a case when he eats at all. His plate arrived with various cheeses, a platter of bread, and a glass of wine. Our table was off in a corner, as Holmes preferred not to be overheard.

"You have suffered your usual patience with this investigation, old friend. As always, I appreciate your silence so that I may concentrate my thoughts. Now, however, I would require you to speak your mind upon any conclusions that you may have drawn."

I took a sip of white wine to wash down my last bite of fish. I dabbed my lips with my napkin and sat back. Looking at my companion I sniffed, "I could hardly have seen any more than you, Holmes. I daresay likely not a tenth as much."

Holmes shook his head, "I need an intelligent layman's perspective, Doctor. Your education and military background are ideal, for you are the type these assassins are attempting to bypass."

"Very well then," I paused, hooked my thumbs into my lapels, and looked to the ceiling to gather my thoughts. Finally, I leaned forward, arms folded upon the table to keep my voice low, and spoke.

"There could be any number of enemies who would want to harm the prime minister. This could be the work of German agents in retribution against the treaty terms they were forced to sign. It could be radicals of the opposition party. At some future point there may be a ransom note forthcoming from some criminal element and failure to pay would have required a demonstration of their power."

"You are convinced then, that it is a group plot and not an individual?"

I shook my head, "Too many elements for one person, or even two. Had it just been the bust in the office, we may be able to lay the blame at the feet of this Katherine Casey person. But even then, she would require the aid of a servant to set off the bomb at some future date. The stockpile of black powder in the cellar indicates a much larger group."

Holmes hummed in apparent agreement, then asked, "Why an explosive? A servant could just as easily slip poison into the prime minister's food or drink."

"Poison is too quiet," I responded. "Whoever is behind this wants a public demonstration. Death by poisoning could be covered up as merely a heart condition or other such ailment.

The public may never know the truth and these people want to make a statement."

Holmes pulled his pipe from his pocket and sat back to light it, "You are a reflection of luminescence my friend, as always. Thank you."

Chapter Five

The next morning there was a knock upon our door at seven-thirty. Lestrade sat up in his basket as I went to answer. Holmes emerged from his room just as I opened the door to reveal Lieutenant Harry Wiggins. He was not in uniform, as he was during our adventure just the previous Christmas[1], so I merely said, "Wiggins, it's good to see you again."

The young man shook my hand, "Doctor, always a pleasure, sir."

Turning to my companion he held up a key as he said, "Ah, Mr. Holmes, I believe that you requested a new car? I've been sent to take that relic off your hands."

Holmes exchanged keys and thanked the young man. I could never get over the resemblance of the Lieutenant to his father, Joe Wiggins, former head of the Baker Street Irregulars and now the owner of Jabez Wilson's old pawn shop. He then held out a briefcase to Holmes saying, "From Sir Mycroft."

Holmes took the case, removed a folder, and began a quick perusal of the papers within. "As I thought," he said, without expounding. Looking back at the young man he asked, "Will you be joining us, Wiggins?"

"I'm afraid not, sir. Though I will be gathering information that you may find useful while I'm on assignment to Oxford. I will send any findings to the railway station, per your request.

---

[1] *Five Gold Rings* from *Sherlock Holmes: Adventures for the Twelve Days of Christmas* by Roger Riccard.

A telegram to the Oxford constabulary will reach me if you need anything."

"One question, if I may," I said. "Why on earth did Mycroft inflict that old heap on us to begin with?"

Wiggins shrugged his shoulders, but Holmes answered, "It was merely an identifier, Watson. The lookouts were told to watch for such a vehicle on the day we arrived. It merely established our *bona fides*."

I shook my head, looked at Wiggins, and said, "Tell Mycroft that he should try something out himself first before inflicting it upon others. Thank you for bringing us something better." I paused, "It is better, isn't it?"

The young man smiled, "Yes, Dr. Watson. No more cranking to start, and it has side windows against the weather."

"Thank goodness," I replied. "You be careful on your assignment young man."

"Yes, sir," he said, starting to salute, but caught himself and shook my hand instead.

After Wiggins left us, Holmes sat at our common room table, beginning a more thorough examination of the papers, saying to me, "You go and have breakfast, Watson. I need to digest this information rather than any food. Meet me at the car in forty-five minutes."

I took his advice to heart and ate a hearty breakfast, not knowing whether Holmes's plans for the day would allow any time for lunch. I returned to the room and found him and Lestrade both gone, and so I exited the back door and was greeted by the sight of a beautiful automobile. It was a four-door model with a royal blue body and a black roof, and it featured windows to enclose both the driver's and passenger's compartments from the elements.

I was greeted with a bark from the Basset who was seated at the back with the window partially open and the car already running. I slid into the passenger seat and Holmes drove us smoothly out onto Missenden Road and at a moderate pace to arrive at Chequers in less than five minutes. We pulled into the same spot as the day before, and Hunter greeted us.

"All is as you requested, Mr. Holmes, the crates with the black powder were replaced last night and taken away by horse-drawn carriages, so as not to draw attention. I and my men are the only ones currently spending the night here. The nearest neighbour is only a half mile away and I felt that motor vehicles in the middle of the night may arouse suspicion. My men down the road have been examining the crates and found that the ones containing the explosives had a unique identification mark. We also found one packed with dynamite along with a concealed fuse, much like the one in the bust. We have left the fuse intact, but replaced the dynamite with empty tubes, just in case someone checks."

"Excellent work, Mr. Hunter. Has everyone shown up for work today?" asked the detective.

"All accounted for, Mr. Holmes."

Holmes held up the briefcase, "Mycroft's agents have been digging deeper into certain backgrounds. We may uncover this conspiracy very soon." In the meantime, I should like to lock this up somewhere and then go about a more thorough inspection of the house."

We went on to examine the known secret passages and rooms and to ensure that they were either locked or sealed and that nothing harmful was stored in any of them. There were more than I expected. But then, this estate had been through many a war and persecution. Priest holes and even a 'prison room' were a part of its history.

Holmes also inspected the gas pipes and electrical circuits, making note of vulnerable areas where more precautions should be taken. Every ground floor entrance, whether by door or window, was checked for locks or bolts. These proceedings took up most of the morning and even Lestrade was exhibiting signs of wanting to rest.

At last, Holmes stated, "I believe that is sufficient for this morning. Mr. Hunter, if you could prevail upon the chef to provide us with a light lunch it would be most appreciated. Watson, would you see to Lestrade? I'll be in the office."

After provisioning our four-legged friend with food and water, I stopped by the kitchen where a trolly with trays of food and beverages had been prepared. I offered to wheel the cart myself, but the kitchen steward insisted on serving us. Thus, he followed me to the office where Holmes was going over Mycroft's papers in greater detail.

Holmes glanced up briefly at our entrance and nodded to the gentleman, "Thank you … Walsh, isn't it?"

"Yes, Mr. Holmes," the steward replied. "Will there be anything else, sir?"

Holmes took a quick look at the top tray and answered, "This should be quite sufficient."

Walsh turned on his heels and left us. I set a plate with a sandwich and some fruit next to Holmes and took one for myself. I also picked up a bottle of brandy, but before opening it, Holmes asked to inspect it. I handed it over and he carefully examined the foil and cork and even checked the bottom of the bottle. Handing it back to me he merely said, "Thank you, Watson. You may pour."

"Really, Holmes," I said as I poured us each a measure of the amber liquid. "Do you think someone would dare to poison us while we are here?"

"It would be foolish to poison both of us, Doctor," he replied. "It would bring down suspicion rather hard and make their further plans even more difficult to move forth. However, we have dealt with fools before."

I looked at the bottom of the bottle after I had poured our drinks and enquired, "I assume you were looking for needle marks in the foil or through the cork. But why the bottom of the bottle?"

Holmes took a sip of his brandy and replied, "A diamond drill could be used to make a hole for inserting poison. Someone could then re-seal the hole with wax."

I sighed, "Sometimes I pity the way your mind must work, Holmes. Always having to be on guard like that. It must be a terrible strain."

"On the contrary, Watson," he replied. "It has become second nature to me and I rarely notice the extra precautions I take, unless they prove to be life-saving."

Major Hunter stuck his head round the door just then and enquired if we needed anything else before he went to eat lunch with his men in the radio room. Holmes handed him a slip of paper with two names written upon it and asked for the personal records and references of each of them. "After you've eaten will be sufficient, Mr. Hunter. At that point, I may need to use the private telephone in the P.M.'s office again."

The information Hunter returned with an hour later did, indeed, prompt a telephone call by Holmes. Afterwards, he informed Hunter that we would be leaving for the day and returning later that evening. He asked if we could leave Lestrade to the Major's care and he agreed.

When we got into the automobile, I asked Holmes where we were going. He replied, "The sparks that have been going off in my mind are starting to burn more brightly, Watson. I just spoke with Wiggins. He gave me a piece of kindling and is now investigating another possible match. We are headed towards Oxford, but first, we must make a quick stop at the Crowe's Nest."

Arriving at the inn, Holmes pulled straight into the carriage house. As the previous evening, he strode among the supply area for the two establishments. This time, however, I saw him making notes as I stayed out of his way, standing by the entrance. I was smoking a cigarette and also serving as a lookout. I let out a loud 'Halloa' when I saw Boyle coming from the inn. Holmes quickly opened up the engine compartment of the automobile before the manager came into his line of sight. Boyle asked if anything was wrong.

"I saw you pull in a few minutes ago, Mr. Holmes. When you didn't come in straight away, I thought I'd see if I could help you with something."

"Thank you, Mr. Boyle. The engine seemed to be running a little warm," answered the detective. "I was just letting it cool down so that I could check the water level. It appears adequate. I should like to borrow a container if I may, in case it acts up on our next drive."

"You're going out again today?"

"Just a quick trip over to Oxford. One of my old tutors has asked us to tea with him this afternoon."

"I'll fetch something for you right away, Mr. Holmes."

"We do appreciate your assistance, sir. The Doctor and I will just step inside for an ale, then be on our way." Holmes closed and latched the engine cowling and the three of us walked back to the pub where Doyle pulled Holmes and me two pints of local beer.

As we drank, Boyle disappeared for a minute, then returned with a full, two-quart-sized canteen. We thanked the man, stopped by the toilet, and then returned to our car for the trip westwards to Oxford.

As we turned right on Ellesborough Road, I turned to my friend, "I assume that was a ruse about tea with an old professor?"

Holmes kept his eyes on the road and replied, "Certainly, Watson. All of my professors at any of the schools I attended are long retired to warmer climes or have passed on. We are meeting Wiggins to pick up more information and then calling upon a young lady."

He would say no more but, after retrieving a report from the Sergeant on duty at Blue Boar Street, our next stop was the hospital whereupon Holmes asked for a piece of equipment from my ever-present medical bag. We made our way towards the maternity ward and he asked me to keep a watch outside the room of Mrs. Katherine Casey.

As it was mid-afternoon, Mr. Casey was likely to still be at work. This allowed for my friend to be alone with the new mother, who was still recovering from giving birth to a son, whose name, Wiggins had learned, was Patrick.

"Good afternoon, Mrs. Casey," Holmes's smooth mellifluous voice filtered out into the hallway where I stood. "I am Dr. Scott. How are you feeling today?"

"I'm much stronger, Doctor. Frankly, I feel that I could do better if I could take Patrick home and start eating decent food again."

Despite the words, the complaint was couched in a humorous tone which I found to be a pleasant sound. Holmes replied in like manner. "I understand. Hospital food is not exactly *haute cuisine*. Well, let's see what your heart tells us."

Holmes, using my stethoscope quite expertly, listened to her heart and lungs. I should have known that, after all the years of observing me, he would be able to mimic a cursory examination.

"Your heart and lungs are fine," he stated. "Any pelvic pain?"

"It has quite subsided, Doctor. Only hunger pains now," she joked.

"Very good," replied Holmes with a chuckle as he took her wrist to check her pulse. "I see on your notes that you are married to Sean Casey. Would that be the solicitor of Casey, Stengel, and York?"

"Yes, that is his firm," she replied with no little pride. 'You know of it?"

"I've written an opinion for them on a medical case years ago but was never called to testify. I understand that they are quite successful."

"Yes, my husband has many prominent clients. Just recently he was entrusted to deliver a gift for the Duke of Holdernesse to the Prime Minister for his new estate at Chequers. I was doing some work there as an historian and was able to assist in the delivery. It was a bust of Cromwell and the Duke was quite insistent that it be placed overlooking the Prime Minister's desk as a source of inspiration."

"How interesting," replied Holmes. "You were most fortunate to obtain such a prestigious post. Were you solicited or did you apply for it?"

"My husband heard of the position and used his connections to make a recommendation. I was thrilled to obtain it. I only wish that I could have finished, but Patrick had other plans."

Out in the hall, I was finding this lady quite charming, even though I could not see her.

"Did you get to meet the Duke yourself when he handed over the bust to your husband?" asked Holmes

115

"No, Sean was given it while meeting at the Duke's estate. His Grace preferred to have him deliver it rather than entrust it to some delivery service, for it was rather fragile."

"I presume Mr. Casey drove you there? He did not let you carry anything too heavy?" said Holmes, feigning concern.

"Oh, no, Doctor. He insisted on driving me and setting the bust up in the office himself because of the weight.

"Very good," replied the detective. Then added, "Your blood pressure is slightly elevated, but not alarmingly so. Have you done your walking exercises today?"

"Yes, Doctor. I'm feeling quite well. No pain, no dizziness."

"You seem fine to me and I shall add my voice to a recommendation for your release. Congratulations on your new son. Good day!"

As Holmes and I were walking away from the room a nurse came by with a tea trolly. Holmes, the stethoscope still around his neck, asked the young lady if it was for Mrs. Casey. "Yes, Doctor, it's her afternoon tea."

"I believe that from now on that she can have something more substantial."

"Very good, Doctor," said the nurse. We continued to our vehicle and I questioned my companion.

"She seemed quite sincere, Holmes. It appears that she had no knowledge of the explosive device."

"Her charm can be quite disarming, Watson," he replied. "She is also attractive. A two-edged sword in the weaponry of deceit. However, I believe that you are correct."

"What tipped the scales towards her innocence in your eyes?" I enquired.

"I was taking her pulse the whole time I questioned her. There was no significant change as there would have been if she were lying or hiding something. Just a slight elevation due to her pride in her husband and her son. No, she is innocent in all this. More's the pity, for her words have all but condemned her husband."

Chapter Six

"**W**ill you have Sean Casey arrested then?" I asked as we stepped into the automobile.

"Not yet, Watson. We need more proof and this admission does not explain the dynamite in the cellar. There is more data to gather and more players in this little game at Chequers."

We drove back to Oxford police station and met with Wiggins and a police sergeant. Holmes instructed them on actions they needed to take regarding the solicitor and left them so that they could fulfil their duty. The return to Chequers went smoothly. Walsh answered our knock on the door and informed us that Hunter was awaiting us in his office. The Major greeted us enthusiastically when we appeared and bade us to close the door and sit down.

"I've found a discrepancy, Mr. Holmes. We get regular coal deliveries by way of a company that brings in a truck once a month and fills the cellar bunker via the coalhole chute. Charcoal is used in small quantities, primarily by the estate forge, and it also serves as a reserve in the event of coal not being available due to a strike or other delay in our regular deliveries. The crates we found were ordered just recently at a time when there was already sufficient charcoal for several months use and so it was sent initially to the storehouse of the Russell Arms."

"Ordered by Walsh, no doubt," declared Holmes.

Major Hunter's countenance fell as his thunder was knocked out from under him. Recovering, he asked, "Why, yes, Mr. Holmes. How did you guess that?"

Holmes shook his head impatiently, "I never guess, sir. As head kitchen steward, Walsh was the only one in authority to make such an order, save for Lord Lee himself, until you arrived. It also fits the pattern I have detected."

"What pattern, Mr. Holmes?"

"I believe a group of militants are planning this attack to disrupt the government for their own ends."

"We should take him into custody!" demanded Hunter.

Holmes shook his head, "There are more players in this game than he. We need absolute proof before we make our move to round them all up."

"You mean Brockmeyer at the Russell Arms? Likely a German agent if you ask me."

Holmes shook his head and responded, "People are being used, in this plot, Major. I'm awaiting one further piece of evidence before we close in on the true culprits. In the meantime, we remain diligent and do not let any potential target visit until we've sprung our trap.

It took two more days and Holmes continued a vigilant inspection of the grounds and buildings. At last, we brought in an army stenographer to transcribe all the notes he and I had taken into some semblance of a report of recommendations for Mycroft to act upon. When a telegram from Wiggins arrived at Little Kimble station, Holmes emerged waving the flimsy in the air as he returned to the automobile. Handing it to me he cried, "We have them, Watson! Walsh and Boyle were both involved with the Easter Uprising of 1916 albeit under different names. Now we can act."

The following Saturday afternoon, a tea was planned for the staff and other special guests who were so instrumental in the preparations of Chequers for the Prime Minister's occupancy. A contingent of soldiers was brought in for ceremonial purposes and the servants were relieved of their normal duties so that they could be waited upon by an outside agency that had been specially commissioned for the event.

All the servants and workmen were invited, including Mrs. Casey and her husband. Brockmeyer, Boyle, and other suppliers were brought in as well. All were gathered in the long gallery until Hunter, in his role as major-domo, stood before them.

"I welcome you all to this special occasion where Lord and Lady Lee wish me on their behalf to express their gratitude for your diligent work in the preparations for this grand estate to be turned over to the government for the use of all future prime ministers. They have returned from Italy, but are currently detained in London. Hopefully, they will arrive in time for dinner. In the meantime, you are all to proceed to the dining room where tables have been arranged for your comfort and refreshments will be served."

The dining room held seating for twenty-five around a long table with additional seats around the outer edges of the room. There was a large fireplace to one side and windows to the other.

Holmes had stayed out of sight, not wishing to be recognised by Mrs. Casey, but I knew that he was in disguise as one of the waiters who had been brought in for the occasion. Hunter stayed close to Walsh and Casey as we entered.

When Walsh saw crates of charcoal stacked by the fireplace he visibly froze. Turning to Hunter he asked, "What is that charcoal doing here? Where's the firewood?"

Hunter explained, "The recent rains have curtailed our supply of dry wood for the present due to a hole being discovered in the woodshed roof only yesterday. In addition, the coal bunker is all but empty, but fortunately we have ample charcoal which will provide more than adequate heat for this little gathering until supplies of wood and coal can return to normal."

When Holmes, in his servant guise, placed a whole box of charcoal on top of a pile of kindling in the fireplace and then set a match to it Walsh grabbed Casey's arm and whispered "We must get away from here, now!"

Expecting this reaction, Hunter and three of the soldiers grabbed Walsh and Casey as they turned to flee, while Mrs.

Casey cried out in confusion at being left behind. Several feet away, Boyle had also tried make for the door but was detained by two more guardsmen. Walsh looked back at the fireplace in horror as the flames began to grow. In panic at last he screamed, "It's going to explode! You must get away now!"

He struggled against his captors to no avail as Holmes, while removing his false beard, called out to those assembled, "No need to panic ladies and gentlemen! The explosives he refers to have been removed and everything is quite safe. I am Sherlock Holmes and there are some arrests to be made, but the rest of you please feel free to relax, have some refreshments, and enjoy yourselves."

The guests returned to their conversations, much more animated than before. Casey, Walsh, and Boyle were handcuffed and taken away. As they were led out, Boyle shouted *"Tiocfaidh ár lá!"*[1]. Hunter pushed him up against a wall and muttered in his ear, "Not today, you Irish blaggard!"

Mrs. Casey went up to Holmes and demanded, "How dare you pass yourself off as a doctor! What is the meaning of all this? Why have you arrested my husband?"

Holmes bowed his head to the lady, "I am sorry for your situation, Mrs. Casey. I have no doubt you are an innocent pawn in your husband's game."

She started to protest, but Holmes held up his hand and pointed to me, as I was standing close by. "This is Dr. Watson, he will introduce you to the Duke of Holdernesse, who is a guest here this afternoon. He will confirm that he never gave your husband the Cromwell bust. It was a bomb meant to be set off by your husband's uncle, Mr. Walsh, to kill the Prime Minister. I'm afraid that they are both members of an Irish rebel group, as is Mr. Boyle of the Crowe's Nest."

"No," she cried, on the verge of tears. "It cannot be." Her voice faltered and she began to swoon. I caught her and eased her into a chair. Holmes caught Holdernesse's attention and he came over to speak with the unfortunate lady.

---

[1] Translates to 'our day will come'.

Later, after the soldiers had taken away their prisoners, Holmes and I met with Hunter in his office, away from curious guests.

Hunter began the discussion, "How did you make the Irish connection, Holmes? I thought surely that Germans would be behind this."

Holmes nodded as he lit a cigarette, "With the late war so fresh in our minds, gentlemen, it was natural to lean toward German agents perpetrating this scheme. But a different spark was struck in my mind at the mention of Katherine Casey's name. When I heard her maiden name as *Doyle*, then her husband's *Sean Casey*, I left that ember to smoulder in the background. Then, when you informed me that the supplies were stored at the Russell Arms that was another link. I knew at that moment that Boyle, another Irishman as evidenced not only by his name but also by the drinks that he serves, was involved. His establishment being used for the storage of charcoal gave him the perfect opportunity to sabotage it. That ember in my mind began to burn like kindling. Finally, there was *Walsh*, the steward. Certainly, you realise that we had the makings of an Irish bonfire here?"

"My agent's name is *Doyle* and he's a Scotsman," I interjected.

"One of the many names developed from the Gaelic language roots they share. Just as is *Walsh*, which is also a Welsh name," answered my friend patiently, and went on, "When I had Mycroft and Wiggins dig deeper into the family backgrounds of these people my suspicions were confirmed. Walsh and Boyle were both involved in the Easter Uprising four years ago, though under different identities. Casey blames the British government for the loss of his foot and was a natural recruit for his uncle. The Irish see the weakened state of England after the War as an ideal time to strike for total independence. The wrath of centuries of Irish hatred for the English is at its highest peak since Cromwell invaded Ireland in 1649. Which made it all the more fitting that they chose his bust to be the bomb. The assassination of the Prime Minister would have put the government in upheaval and provided the

Irish a position of strength with which to negotiate their independence."

Hunter nodded, "You are sure that the wife is not involved?"

"Mrs. Casey, despite her Irish roots on her grandfather's side, loves Great Britain and is passionate about our history. It is what makes her a successful curator for the museum. It was shameful of her husband to use her so. I only hope that this bitter experience will not dampen her enthusiasm and turn her against England."

I spoke up at that, "If she recognises the lack of trust her husband had in her, and that his love for her was not as deep as hers for him, then I am sure that will go a long, though painful, way towards her resolve to go on and provide a good life for her son."

"I leave the thoughts of women to your expertise, Doctor," he replied, waving his cigarette in my direction. "All the same, I do believe a recommendation to Mycroft to keep an eye on her, and her son as he grows up, would not be out of order. The Irish independence question is not likely to go away for at least a generation to come."

"Likewise Holmes, perhaps in a century's time the Prime Minister of this great nation will still be occupying this splendid property, who knows?"

Greed

The Case of the
Merchant Mogul

Chapter One

It was an early August evening in 1882 when Holmes and I returned to our Baker Street rooms from a night at the opera. We had thoroughly enjoyed Gioachino Rossini's *Guillaume Tell* based on the Swiss legend of William Tell. Holmes, being a violin aficionado, was in a particularly good mood after the performance. As was frequently the case, he was eager to get home, pull out his Stradivarius, and attempt some of the movements that he had heard that evening.

However, when we arrived, Mrs. Hudson greeted us with the news that a young man had been awaiting our return for over an hour. Knowing that we would be late, she tried to persuade the fellow to come back in the morning. However, he had insisted on waiting, and she had kept him in her parlour, not feeling comfortable at the prospect of leaving a stranger alone in our sitting room.

The fellow must have heard her greet us, for he appeared in her doorway and cried out, "Mr. Holmes, at last! I am sorry for the lateness of the hour, sir. But I simply must see you regarding the murder of my father-in-law."

I noted the gentleman's appearance. He was in his early twenties and of average size and build with neat reddish-brown hair and moustache. He wore a dark grey linen suit of high quality. Holmes merely sighed. Rossini would have to wait. "Very well. Come upstairs and give us your story."

We marched up the steps and entered our sitting room. From behind I now noticed that the gentleman also wore a black cloth yarmulke. Holmes asked the fellow to sit in the usual chair he preferred for clients where the gaslight catches their face and reveals every twitch, blink, or other nuance. He then asked me to pour some brandies to help dispel the chill of the evening.

Our client, however, declined alcohol, preferring to get right to his business. I set Holmes's snifter on the table as he lit his briarwood pipe. Then he asked, "Well, let us start with the facts. What is your name, and who do you say has been murdered?"

"I am Jethro Feldman. My father-in-law is … was Abraham Loew."

I responded, "The department store mogul?"

"Yes, Dr. Watson," he replied. Then he spoke in a softer, conspiratorial voice, "We kept it from the newspapers and were warned not to call in the police, but Abraham was kidnapped five days ago. We delivered the ransom yesterday morning as instructed … £2,000. At the exchange point, we were given instructions to where we would find him. But when we arrived, he was dead.

We informed the local police inspector at that point, but he was stymied, and all he seemed to be able to do was berate us for not having contacted the authorities earlier. I had read a newspaper article about a case where you had provided the solution to the police and that is when I decided that you may be just the man we need. Can you come out to Harrow and investigate, Mr. Holmes? Money is no object. I assure you that our family is quite wealthy."

I could well imagine that statement to be true. Loew's department stores had grown into a chain with three locations in London, Ealing and Richmond. They sold everything from clothing to appliances, furniture, office supplies, and other sundries. Their slogan was 'Come to Loews for low prices all in one place'.

"What was the manner of death?" asked the detective.

"There were no wounds on the body, Mr. Holmes. It has gone to the police surgeon for an examination to see if it may have been poison."

As a medical man, I recognised that a man of Loew's age may have also succumbed to fear. "Did he have a heart condition? He may have perished out of anxiety by having a heart attack."

"No, Dr. Watson," he replied. "He was as healthy as an ox. He ate well, drank and smoked only in moderation, and exercised every day by walking his dog for at least a mile, weather permitting."

Holmes changed the subject. "We'll see what the police surgeon has to say officially before we speculate. In the meantime, Mr. Feldman, I take it that in addition to being married to Loew's daughter, that you also work for them. Tell me about the family."

Feldman seemed a little taken aback at Holmes's deduction and asked, "How did you know that I worked for them?"

Holmes pointed the stem of his pipe at the man's coat and replied, "Though you did not work today, there are still the creases of a bulge in your coat pocket where you habitually keep your sales book. Your attire is professional and the fairness of your skin, despite your ancestry, indicates that you spend little time outdoors. Thus, you occupy your working hours inside. Being of Jewish faith your position as son-in-law makes it highly likely that you would work for your wife's family unless you were a successful businessman in your own right, but your age suggests that you have not attained that status yet."

Feldman sighed, nodded, and replied to Holmes's query, "All true, Mr. Holmes. Well then, I am married to his only daughter, Sarah. I work at the Richmond branch of the store. Mr. Loew's wife is Meriam, to whom he was married for thirty-six years. He has two sons, Caleb, who is the hardware manager at the Oxford Street store, and Daniel, who is a solicitor."

Holmes interrupted, "Is Caleb married, or does he live at home?"

"He is engaged, Mr. Holmes, but for now he does still live under his father's roof."

Holmes nodded, "And how about Daniel?"

"Daniel is the eldest and is married. He handles the family legal matters, but he also has many other clients as well."

Holmes nodded, "Pray continue."

"He has two brothers, Herschel and Kenan. Neither of them is involved in the business. Herschel is a rabbi, and Kenan has a farm in Harefield."

"Harefield is not far from Harrow. Where is the rabbi's synagogue?"

"It is also in Harrow. It's where the family worships."

"So, is it safe to say that the family is close and gathers together frequently?"

Feldman frowned, then replied, "All except Daniel. He's ... well, not exactly the black sheep, but there was tension between him and his father. Abraham expected Daniel to follow him into the family business as the first-born son, but Daniel's temperament wasn't meant for working his way up as a store assistant and then into management. He always had a passion for the law. Abraham's opinion of solicitors was more along the lines that of William Shakespeare when he wrote, 'the first thing we do, let's kill all the lawyers'[1]. The only time they saw each other was during the holy day celebrations of Passover, Rosh Hashanah, Yom Kippur, and Hanukkah. Daniel would make the effort to come home at those times for his mother's sake. Otherwise, he and his wife live in Kensington, where his practice is located. He does not keep with all our traditions."

"Very well," said Holmes. "I always desire to have an impression of all the players in the game. Now let's talk about the crime itself."

---

[1] *Henry VI: Part 2*, Act IV, Scene 2.

Chapter Two

"It was on Monday last, Mr. Holmes," continued our client. "The last time anyone saw Abraham alive was when he bade goodnight to the staff at the store in Oxford Street and went outside to walk towards his club, The Sons of Isaac. He usually went there to have a drink and chat with some of his fellow businessmen before coming home for dinner on the train. But if you recall, it was raining that day and he never made it to his club that afternoon."

"What time did he leave the store?" asked Holmes.

"He left at four o'clock as usual. That gave him enough time to spend at the club and still be home at six-thirty for the seven o'clock meal."

"Did he have any enemies? Perhaps among his competitors?"

Feldman looked shocked. "Certainly, none that would go so far as to kill him, Mr. Holmes!"

Holmes wagged his finger at the young man. "We don't know that it is murder just yet. Dr. Watson is correct in not ruling out a heart attack. I will check with the police surgeon in the morning. Still, it would be helpful to know if he has had any disagreement with anyone of late."

"He had not mentioned any problems with competitors lately. There are always ongoing issues with suppliers but certainly none that should resort to such a drastic action as kidnapping."

"How did the kidnappers contact you?"

"We received a note by post on the Tuesday."

"Do you have that with you?"

"No, Mr. Holmes. Mrs. Loew has it at the house."

Holmes shook his head. "I shall need to examine it. Meanwhile I presume that none of you recognised the handwriting?"

"It was printed in pencil in block capitals. Almost as if a school child had written it."

The detective nodded. "A typical practice among kidnappers. It also means that it could be someone you know who was afraid of their handwriting being recognised. Mr. Feldman, I must ask, who benefits from his death? Is there a particular family member who has the most to gain?"

"Mr. Holmes!" cried our client. "Are you suggesting that one of us had something to do with this?"

"If I am to determine the truth, I must explore every possibility and eliminate those that I can, however unpleasant those explorations may be."

Feldman fidgeted, obviously uncomfortable at this line of questioning. Finally, he replied, "I do not know the terms of his will, Mr. Holmes. I can only assume everything gets left to his wife with some provisions for his sons and daughter."

"What were the instructions from the kidnappers? Try to be precise as to the wording."

Feldman closed his eyes and tried to picture the note. At last, he said, "We have your husband. For his safe return, we demand £2,000. You have until nine o'clock Friday morning to gather the money. Do not involve the police or dire consequences shall result. Instructions for the exchange shall follow."

"And what were those instructions, and when did you receive them?"

"They came by Thursday's post. Same printed lettering. They said, 'Bring a satchel with cash to St. Mary's church in Harrow at 10 a.m. Go to the last pew on left'."

"We did so. Kenan and I made the delivery, for we were afraid to send anyone alone. Instead of finding Abraham, we found a coil of rope along with another note that said, 'Bring

130

this rope up the bell tower steps and climb out onto the roof. You will find a basket. Follow the instructions inside'.

"The climb to the top of the bell tower starts with a narrow, spiral staircase to reach the room from where the bells are rung. From there two steep ladders go into the belfry and then up inside the spire itself. But there is also a low door that leads out onto the roof. Kenan and I stepped out onto the slightly pitched affair and immediately saw the basket near a battlement at the far end.

"In it, we found another note that read, 'Place the satchel with the money in the basket and lower it to the ground. Wait thirty seconds then haul the rope back up. In the basket you will find instructions on where to find Mr. Loew'.

"Well, we did so, Mr. Holmes. We looked over the side to see if we could identify the person who picked up the satchel but they were covered in a large black cloak and wide-brimmed hat so we could not see their face or even determine their size. When we brought the basket back up there was another printed note directing us to the cemetery at Kensal Green along with a key that would allow access to where Abraham was supposedly being kept. To our shock, the location was a mausoleum.

"We rushed down the winding staircase but found that the door was closed tightly and a wedge was jammed under it to keep us from pushing it open. It took several minutes of pounding and yelling before one of the clerics came to our rescue."

"A clever ploy," said Holmes. "The kidnapper delayed you long enough to obtain a significant head start. I suppose the clergyman saw no one?"

"He did not, Mr. Holmes. The church is open during the day so anyone could have gained access."

"Once free we made haste for home, as it was on the way, and picked up Herschel and Daniel, who had just arrived at the house. We made our way to the cemetery and found the sexton who upon consulting a map told us where the mausoleum was located."

Feldman stopped, his emotions rising within him at the memory of what they found. I handed him a glass of water, which he gratefully swallowed up quickly. Then he concluded the tale of his adventure.

"We found the structure and opened it with the key provided. There were two coffins within, and room for more. Abraham was lying on one of the empty slabs reserved for some future member of a family named Esterhaus. He had two blankets and a pillow and there were boxes of food, a barrel of water, and some wine bottles, most of which were empty. There was also a large bucket off in one corner for his bathroom needs which only added to the stench of the stale air. While the mausoleum had ventilation which allowed some dim light in, any cries for help would have gone unheard through those thick walls in that desolated section of the burial grounds. He was cold to the touch with no pulse. We found no wounds. I went for a constable and the police took over the investigation from there."

Holmes asked, "What food was in front of him? Was it kosher?"

Feldman cocked his head to one side, confused by the question, then replied, "I don't recall. I'm fairly certain that I did not see anything that I did not recognise, but I really was not concerned to look closely at his food."

"Does anyone in your family know the Esterhaus family?"

"No one recalls that name, Mr. Holmes."

"Who is the Inspector in charge?"

"Korman. Henry, I believe, or Harry."

Holmes nodded, "Inspector Harry Korman. An older gentleman, a little on the stout side. Grey hair and muttonchop whiskers?"

"That's him, Mr. Holmes. Do you know him? Is he any good?"

The detective tilted his head. "He lacks imagination, and his observation skills leave much to be desired. But he is about as competent as any of the others at the Yard. I shall make it a point to visit him in the morning. What about your family? Do they know that you have come to see me?"

"My wife and I were with her mother late this afternoon when I declared that I was going to seek your opinion. I have not informed the police, but I would assume that Meriam told Caleb when he returned home from work. Shabbat rules would have prevented her from sending word to Daniel until after dusk tomorrow."

"I presume that there were no objections to your action?"

Feldman allowed himself a small smile. "Only that Meriam adjured me not to break the Shabbat and to wait until Sunday before seeking you out. But I understand how a trail can grow cold, Mr. Holmes. I believe Adonai would prefer justice over tradition."

"Yes," replied Holmes. "As necessary as religion is to maintain order in society, it can occasionally conflict with itself. Fortunately, the police surgeon is a Presbyterian and will be at work in the morning. Please write down the home and work addresses of your relatives. Advise them that I may be coming around to gather more information."

I handed the pad and pencil with which I had been making notes to Feldman and he began writing. He added, "I'm sure they will cooperate, Mr. Holmes. But none of them will receive you on this Shabbat while they are in mourning, except possibly Daniel. They are quite Orthodox in that respect."

Holmes frowned but acquiesced. "Very well. We shall begin our investigation with the police surgeon and Inspector Korman, then question employees at the store and see what they can tell us. Does Daniel work on Saturdays?"

"He generally avoids it, but that is more of a choice to be home with his wife and son rather than a religious obligation. When necessary, he does go into the office to work on cases where timing is critical."

Holmes nodded and then stood, indicating that he had finished asking questions for now. Feldman finished writing and stood as well. "I do hope that you can solve this, Mr. Holmes," he said as he donned his hat and coat. "Not just to retrieve the ransom, but to give the family satisfaction that justice has been done and that Abraham's death has been avenged."

"I will do all I can," replied the detective. "I suggest you and the family perform your rituals and include the resolution of this crime in your prayers. Good night, sir."

After he had left, I turned to Holmes, who had sat back down and was re-filling his pipe. "We've never discussed religion, Holmes. I am aware that you rarely attend church unless it is in conjunction with a case. But I've never known you to pray or ask for prayers."

He lit his pipe, blew out a puff of blue smoke, and answered, "I am familiar with the practices of Jewish, Catholic, and most Protestant denominations, Watson. I was raised Anglican as a child but lapsed in my attendance as I approached adulthood. I prefer to practice my beliefs in my work rather than merely attend a service once a week. As the epistle of James says, 'Faith without works is worthless'. As to prayer, I do not pray for supernatural interference. I merely use whatever talents with which I have been endowed. However, I find that it gives comfort to some of my clients, and so I will encourage them to indulge to the extent their faith allows. It helps to calm matters and makes it easier for me to work with them. If Adonai, Jehovah, God, Jesus, Mother Mary, or any of the Saints choose to respond with assistance, I certainly won't complain. But I will not count on it either, for God works in mysterious ways and often leaves us to our own devices."

Chapter Three

The next morning, despite the late-night visitor, Holmes was up and about quite early and had to rouse me from Morpheus's arms to accompany him to the mortuary and get the police surgeon's opinion as to the cause of Abraham Loew's death.

Dr. Donald Drake was examining some chemical test results when we arrived at his office. Holmes had known him from his days when he was resident in Montague Street, and the middle-aged doctor welcomed us both eagerly. "Ah, Sherlock, my boy! Good to see you. I expect you're here about Abraham Loew. Step over here and let me show you what I've found."

Holmes introduced me, and the preeminent doctor welcomed me with equal enthusiasm. "I'm glad to see Sherlock has another friend in the medical profession, Doctor. Perhaps between the two of us, we can keep him alive despite his atrociously unhealthy habits."

Holmes ignored the jibe and leaned over the table Drake had led us to. "I am aware of the post mortem restrictions that Orthodox Judaism places upon you, Doctor. Did you obtain any tangible results from the chemical tests that you were able to run?"

Drake pointed to the test tubes and beakers laid out before us. "His blood is clean. No trace of poison. However, it and the liquids that I extracted from his stomach, kidneys, pancreas, and liver indicate a high sugar and carbohydrate content. I believe that he went into a diabetic coma and died from heart failure."

"So, it was not murder?" I asked.

"Not likely deliberate, though it could have been avoided had he been fed properly," he replied. "You may have a good case for involuntary manslaughter. There is one other thing that may help you. Come take a look."

We followed Drake to another room painted a dull white with multiple wooden shelves and cubby holes with various boxes labelled with names of cases. Light filtered in through windows covered with dust from the outside making it necessary to have the lamps lit for proper visibility. This was where Loew's personal effects were kept for the time being. Drake pulled out a man's shirt collar and handed it to my friend. Holmes immediately held a section of it to his nose. Then, as he reached into his pocket for his magnifying lens, I noted a yellow stain on the bleached white collar.

Immediately I declared, "Chloroform?" To which my medical colleague replied, "Yes, Dr. Watson. That suggests the means by which Mr. Loew was incapacitated. Hopefully, it will assist in determining the method by which he was spirited away as well."

Our next stop was at the Scotland Yard office of Inspector Korman. The gentleman was just as Holmes had described him. His gravelly voice was tinged with suspicion when Holmes introduced us. "I've heard of you from Lestrade. You seem to have a nasty habit of butting into police business."

Holmes replied, "Is that *all* he said?" Then he folded his arms and stared back at the older man. The silence was just starting to grow uncomfortable when at last Korman relented. "Well, he did mention that you were actually helpful in some cases. So, why are you here?"

"We have been engaged by the family of Abraham Loew to find the kidnapper and bring him, or her, to justice. As I have no wish to duplicate your efforts or to impede your investigation, I've come to see what steps you've taken, what information you've gathered, and what your plans are."

Though he would be loathed to admit it, Korman appeared to be at sixes and sevens, but he did allow me to copy his interview notes with the employees at the store where Loew worked that day. He could give us little else. Loew did not appear to be anxious or fearful, and no one was aware of any threats that he had received. Further no witnesses to his actual disappearance could be found, and there had been no disturbance reported on the streets between the department store and his club.

"Yet, somewhere along the route to his club," observed Holmes, "he was chloroformed into unconsciousness and would have had to be conveyed away in some sort of vehicle."

"Indeed, Mr. Holmes," agreed the Inspector. "But at that time of day, Oxford Street and the surrounding areas are full of people. Someone should have noticed something amiss."

"It was raining, Inspector," said Holmes. "So, the number of pedestrians would have been significantly reduced. That leaves us with the most logical conclusion, that he entered the vehicle first due to the weather and was chloroformed once inside, out of view of any passersby. Have you been in contact with the Esterhaus family?"

Korman shook his head, "We know from the cemetery records that Walter and Matilda Esterhaus are the current occupants of the mausoleum. They were placed there four years ago when they both died in a fire. They have two sons, both of whom are elderly and no longer live in the area. We have sent word to their local constabularies to arrange for questioning, but I am not hopeful, Mr. Holmes. But we'll see if there is any connection to Loew."

"Very well, Inspector," said Holmes. "We shall leave that task to you for now while we explore other avenues."

Chapter Four

Knowing that the store would only be open until noon on a Saturday, we chose to make our first stop there. At the Oxford Street premises, we met with the general manager, Horace Stone. He made the necessary arrangements for Holmes and I to interview individual employees over the next two hours. All responded in like manner. Abraham Loew was a hard but fair taskmaster. He paid decent wages, complimented employees who went above and beyond to assist customers, and was an overall good employer. The only complaints we heard were of him resisting to allow his Jewish employees time off for any reason other than Shabbat or the major Jewish holidays. This gave roughly half of his workers no time for recreational or other activities. A few were witness to his leaving work on that last day and confirmed that he seemed in good spirits as he passed through the hardware department to bid good afternoon to his son, Caleb. Those who worked for Caleb felt him to be a bright and efficient lad, one they fully expected to be promoted to store manager someday. His interactions with his father were professional and cordial in front of the employees. He had seemed preoccupied the last few days, but they put that down to the fact that none of the employees were aware of the kidnapping.

When we left, Holmes hailed a cab and gave the Kensington address that had been provided by Feldman. I asked, "You don't suppose the solicitor to be the kidnapper?"

He shook his head, "Unlikely, but I should like to start with the one person that we know had a confrontational relationship with our victim," he stated. "Even if he is not the culprit, his insights into Loew senior could provide us with some valuable data."

Thus, we arrived at the house of the eldest son. Holmes had correctly presumed that he would be at home as a comfort to his wife and child over the family loss. Surprisingly, Daniel Loew himself answered the door to our ring of the bell. He appeared to be in his mid-thirties, slightly above average height at about five foot nine inches and somewhat on the lean side. He bore a handsome, clean-shaven face with straight black hair parted on the left. He wore a black armband, but there were no traditional Jewish signs of mourning upon his person. His sharp brown eyes gave us a quick examination before he spoke, "Gentlemen, this is a house of mourning. If you have business with me, I suggest that you come to my office on Monday."

Holmes quickly replied before he could shut the door in our faces. "Our condolences upon the death of your father, Mr. Loew. We have been hired by your brother-in-law, Mr. Feldman, to investigate. My name is Sherlock Holmes, and this is my colleague, Dr. John Watson. If we may have a few minutes of your time, it could save us the wait of a day and increase our chances of finding the criminal who brought this tragedy upon your family."

Loew hesitated, then replied, "The police are already looking into the matter."

Holmes responded, "We have just come from Inspector Korman and with his permission to assist Scotland Yard. I assure you, sir, we would rather not bother you during shiva, but time may be of the essence."

The solicitor looked down in thought, then finally opened the door wider and invited us inside. Pointing to a side room he stated, "I do not practice shiva, Mr. Holmes. My father and I were at odds over certain traditions which I felt were outdated. We can speak in there. I do not wish to upset my son while he mourns his grandfather."

We entered a typical drawing room with a brown sofa and some overstuffed beige chairs arranged around the space and small tables in between. It was on the east-facing side of the ground floor and had fortunately been warmed by the morning sun as the fireplace was not lit. I could tell that my friend was slightly annoyed when Loew led the way in and took the seat with his back to the window, making it harder for Holmes to read his expressions.

Loew, in a typically legal fashion, led with the first question. "Did my brother-in-law care to check with anyone else in the family before requesting your assistance, Mr. Holmes?"

"He informed your sister and mother, who in turn were to advise your brother, Caleb, when he got home from work yesterday. As to your uncles, I doubt there was time before the shabbat began. He came to see me late last night, as I was out for the evening."

"Jethro broke shabbat to come to you?" he asked with surprise in his voice.

Holmes replied, "As he put it, he believes that Adonai is more concerned with justice than tradition."

The solicitor pondered that statement for a moment and finally said, "A sentiment to which I concur. Very well, how can I help you?"

Holmes got right to the point. "He tells us that you and your father were at odds on certain matters. Could those issues you had with him somehow have been a source of contention with someone else, to the point where they would wish him harm or cause him grief through the loss of the ransom money?"

Loew folded his hands across his waist and stared at my friend. "I do hope that you are not insinuating that I was involved, Mr. Holmes. My father and I argued over many things, but I would never desire him harm."

Holmes shook his head. "As one who has studied law, you recognise, I am certain, that the public awareness of your disagreements with your father makes you a suspect."

Loew slapped the arms of his chair and started to rise, but Holmes waved him back to his seat with his next statement. "However, I have found in my line of work that the obvious suspect is seldom guilty merely from the fact that he is *too* obvious. The true criminal may use facts about that person to implicate him, but likely the one who commits the crime is someone with a hidden resentment or else a perfect stranger. We can eliminate the latter in this case because they knew your father's habits."

"How do you know that, Mr. Holmes?"

The detective went on to explain the police surgeon's findings and how they supported the premise that someone knew that Abraham Loew would be leaving at that time of day and was aware of his Jewish dietary restrictions.

"Do you think it was someone from his club?" asked Daniel.

"That is an avenue I will explore," replied Holmes. "If you have any thoughts as to his rivals or competitors, I would like to hear them."

"I have some successful Jewish businessmen as clients, but I do not know if any are members of his club since we only discuss business. As to competitors, there is Matthew Lehman, who is a large clothier and resents my father's clothing departments that undercut his prices. Marcus Strohman has a chain of appliance stores that has also probably lost customers to Loew's department stores. There are likely others, but I cannot imagine any of these people going to such drastic measures. Kidnapping father wouldn't put him out of business. Nor would killing him, for that matter. The stores will still go on with the management stepping in to run them for now, at least until the will is read."

"Are you aware of the contents of his will?" asked Holmes.

"I am not, Mr. Holmes. He uses the firm of Berkowitz and Falk for his personal affairs. I expect it will all go to mother with some provision for Caleb and Sarah."

"Nothing for yourself?"

"I would imagine anything coming to this branch of the family will go directly to my son, Peter. I had made it quite clear to my father that I expected nothing from him, and that he could not buy my obedience."

Daniel Loew could offer little else in the way of information or suspects, and we took our leave of him shortly afterwards. It was now that I asked Holmes why he had dismissed Daniel as a suspect when there were obviously strained relations between father and son.

"The obvious is often deceitful, Watson. It is a mistake the police frequently make, as it overpowers other factors which can lead to the truth. Yes, Daniel and his father were estranged, but they were not enemies. Did you notice the photographs on the wall by the window behind our host?"

"I noticed them but did not observe their content other than that they appeared to be groups of people."

Holmes pursed his lips, "What have I told you about observation, Watson? They were family images. Some from Daniel's childhood, others as recent as last Hanukkah. One appeared to be a photograph of Daniel with his bride standing with their parents on their wedding day. Abraham Loew was right next to his son. The pride was still there, even in the face of their religious and philosophical differences. This is not a man who would physically harm his father. Then there is the house itself. Daniel is well-to-do and does not need the ransom money. In short, he has no viable motive."

"I suppose we won't find someone with motive until we can see a copy of the will," I commented.

As the rest of Holmes's planned investigations involved the family and the club members who would not be available until after dusk, we returned to Baker Street where Holmes dived into his indexes to see what information he might have pertaining to Abraham Loew.

Just as Mrs. Hudson was serving us our afternoon tea, we received a surprise visit from Inspector Korman. Holmes bade the gentleman to sit down after he seemed to have overexerted himself climbing our stairs. I offered him a brandy but he declined. "I can't stay long, gentlemen, and I don't know if it is relevant to your case, but I thought that you should know that we found the body of a cab driver named Michael Jones whose area includes the West End where we believe Mr. Loew was kidnapped. There's no connection that we can ascertain, but I am telling you this, Mr. Holmes, in case he may have been an accomplice."

Chapter Five

"**W**here did you find his body?" asked Holmes.

"It was inside his cab on Glasshouse Street between Air Street and Sherwood Street."

I piped up, "That seems a rather public area for a killing."

Korman nodded. "We believe he was killed elsewhere, Doctor, and driven to that spot sometime late yesterday afternoon. So far, we've found no witnesses as to exactly when his cab stopped there. It was parked in front of an establishment where the windows are opaque so no one inside could have observed it. It was only discovered when a nearby shop manager attempted to find the driver to hail a ride. He opened the door to see if the cabbie was resting inside and found the body with a fatal stab wound to the heart."

Holmes obtained the cabbie's name, home address, and the yard from which he worked. It was one of the larger ones in Paddington and owned by a Mr. Geoffrey Conway. To Korman, Holmes commented, "Thank you, Inspector. It may have nothing to do with our case, but I loathe coincidence. We shall look into this, and I will let you know if the cases cross paths."

While we still had some daylight, we chose to go to Paddington and speak to Conway. We arrived just as he was about to hand things over to his night manager, and Holmes, to better ensure his cooperation, advised him that we were working with Scotland Yard on the murder of Michael Jones.

"Ah yeah, that's too bad 'bout Jonesy. He was a good cabbie. Always made sure we took good care of his carriage and horse. Worked long hours usually, as he wasn't married. Best foul weather driver I ever saw. Nobody could navigate London in such conditions like Jonesy."

Holmes waved the statement aside. "Did he have an unusually long day last Monday?"

"Let me check my log on that," answered the ostler. "Hmm, Monday, let's see," he murmured as he flipped the pages of a large ledger. "No, says here he returned at his usual time."

"Did he act in any unusual way?"

I turned to my companion and said, "Kensal Green is close enough to allow him to keep to his normal routine, Holmes."

"He seemed to be in a hurry when he left here. He usually has some coffee and talks with the stable lads for a while"

Holmes nodded, then said to Conway, "Did Jones have any enemies?"

Conway looked perplexed. "None that I know of who would kill him. Like all hacks, he occasionally had arguments over picking up passengers. They all vie for fares."

"Was Jones especially poor?" asked my companion.

"No more than most, I would guess. Certainly wouldn't turn down a big fare or a special request."

"May we see his cab?"

Conway took us to the back of the building, "We haven't had a chance to clean it yet. If no family comes forward, we'll put it up for sale."

"Its current condition is exactly what I need to observe, Mr. Conway. If you will give us a few minutes."

The proprietor shrugged and said, "As you wish, sir. I'll be in the office for another ten minutes if you need me."

Holmes climbed in. The bloodstains on the seat and floor were obvious. There was a significant amount and I offered, "This is a lot of blood, Holmes. It's likely that the killer got some on himself."

The detective merely grunted in agreement as he was now leaning over and examining the back of the seat with his magnifying lens. Suddenly he bent his head and sniffed the leather seatback. Straightening up, he backed out of the cab, handed me his lens, and said, "Please verify my findings, Doctor. Observe and smell the area I was just examining."

I climbed in and took a look at the spot. To assure myself I also ran a finger across it and smelt it. Looking back over my shoulder I confirmed to my friend, "Chloroform."

Holmes nodded and we made our way to the entrance, stopping by the office to advise the manager that we were finished.

Holmes nodded. "I believe that's all we need for now, Mr. Conway. Thank you."

As we turned to go, the gentleman asked, "Any ideas who done it, or why, Mr. Holmes?"

Holmes hesitated a beat, then replied, "I hope Inspector Korman or I will have an answer soon, Mr. Conway. Good evening."

We stepped out into the early evening, the summer sun turning orange as it was just about to settle into the western horizon. Holmes pointed his walking stick towards it and observed, "Nearly sunset, Doctor. I believe by the time we arrive in Harrow shabbat will be over and we may call upon the Loew family to offer our condolences and learn what we may."

"You don't wish to examine Jones's rooms?" I asked.

"That can wait until the morning," he replied. "I believe the most profitable path for clues lies within the Loew family."

We were fortunate to enter Baker Street station just ten minutes before the next Metropolitan line train to Harrow, and within the hour we had reached that fair village and were alighting a cab at the home of Meriam Loew.

The Loew home was a large, spreading brick structure with white framed windows surrounded by hedges and wrought iron fencing. The black-panelled front door was opened to us by a young gentleman in his mid-twenties. His appearance was reminiscent of Daniel, but on a smaller scale. He was dressed in a quality black suit that was slightly rumpled, his hair was a little shaggy and he was in need of a shave. Then I recalled that Jewish tradition is to refrain from laundry, haircuts, shaving, or the wearing of shoes during shiva. As I expected, the servants had been given the shabbat off to observe the holy day, I assumed this young man to be Caleb, the youngest son.

He looked upon us in the light of the porch lantern with some surprise and curiosity as to who would be calling upon his family at this hour on this day. "Oh! I'm sorry gentleman, I was expecting my fiancée. This is a house of mourning."

"Yes, we wish to express our condolences on the loss of Mr. Loew, sir. Jethro Feldman hired us to look into the matter. I am Sherlock Holmes, and this is my associate, Dr. John Watson."

"Oh, oh yes, mother did mention that Jethro was going to bring in a private detective. Please come in, gentlemen. I am Caleb Loew."

Just then another cab pulled up at the front gate, and a young lady stepped out. Caleb visibly brightened at the sight of her and held the door as we waited in the entrance hall until she could join us. She was attractive with a lean figure, and though her head was covered by a dark scarf, a red fringe cascaded onto her forehead. As they were in mixed company, Caleb greeted her merely with a bow and introduced her to us as his intended, Deborah Bass.

He explained to her, "These are the detectives that Jethro hired to assist the police in finding out who kidnapped father. They are Mr. Sherlock Holmes and Dr. John Watson."

She offered her hand rather tentatively, and we each shook it in turn. Holmes, as usual, could not help vocalising his observations. "I see you spend a great deal of time reading and writing, Miss Bass, and the slight indentations on either side of your nose indicate that you wear a *pince-nez* quite often. Would you be a teacher by chance?"

Taken aback by his pronouncement, she could merely reply, "Why yes, Mr. Holmes. I've been getting ready for the autumn term and doing a lot more reading lately. How could you deduce such a thing?"

"In my line of work, it is a practice to notice such things and to compare them to various categories of occupations. The slight ink smudges on your thumb and forefinger where you habitually turn pages indicates that much of your time is spent with books. In your case, I narrowed it down to a teacher or librarian and leaned towards the former as you have a good strong voice for lecturing.

"But that is not our concern for today," he continued. "Mr. Loew, I realise that it is a delicate situation for your mother, but time could be of the essence in tracking down these villains. Could you arrange for us to have a few minutes with her? I promise to be as brief as possible."

Caleb asked us to wait while he took Miss Bass with him to advise his mother of our arrival. He came back within a minute and asked us to follow him into her drawing room. The widow Loew was seated in a black leather, high-backed chair. On the sofa sat Miss Bass and another young lady who was introduced as her daughter Sarah Feldman. Meriam Loew was dressed all in black, including a black lace veil, which made it difficult to observe her expressions. Her voice, however, was quite strong and commanding.

"Gentlemen, I understand that Jethro has hired you to find my husband's kidnappers. I appreciate your waiting until shabbat has ended, though I did not expect you until tomorrow. Since you are here now, and as you say, time may be of the essence, I shall consent to answer your questions."

Holmes bowed, declined to take a seat, and replied, "I shall be brief madam, as I believe most of my questions can be answered by your sons or your brothers-in-law. However, as a wife may have knowledge known to no other, I must ask you, did your husband have any enemies or competitors who would stoop to stealing from him through this ransom?"

She tilted her head and replied, "Stealing, possibly, but murder? I hardly think so."

Holmes cautiously lowered his voice. "The police believe his death may have been accidental. Was your husband a diabetic?"

She cocked her head at the detective and replied, "His doctor did have him on a strict diet and advised against certain foods. Abraham never told me why. He just said not to worry and that so long as he ate properly everything was fine."

Caleb looked at his mother in surprise. "That's why he stopped eating some of his favourite foods lately? Doctor's orders?"

"Yes," she replied. Then she raised her voice and slapped a hand down on the arm of her chair as she addressed Holmes and me. "His kidnappers are responsible for his death, not his diet, and that's murder in my book, Mr. Holmes! You find them! Hunt them down, and kill them like the dogs they are!"

Caleb went to her side and placed a comforting arm around her shoulders. He gave Holmes a look, imploring that the interview be brought to a close. Holmes replied by stating that he would be looking into the gentlemen named by Daniel, and she agreed that they were the only two that she would have any concerns about.

Holmes asked her for the notes received from the kidnappers and she turned them over to him although she had not kept the envelopes, much to Holmes's displeasure. We then excused ourselves with assurances that we would be in contact should any new developments occur.

Once back in the entrance hall, Caleb questioned us, "Have you been to see Daniel?"

Holmes replied, "Yes, we found him at home earlier today."

"You are aware that he and Father were estranged?"

Holmes took a hard look at the man and replied, "Yes, Jethro mentioned that to me."

Caleb looked down at the floor, hesitating to voice his next question. Finally, he looked up and asked, "Do you believe Daniel was involved?"

Holmes replied calmly, "I have ruled no one out as yet. I am still discovering and prioritising possible suspects. When I have more definitive proof, I will let you know."

Chapter Six

We returned to Baker Street for a late supper that Mrs. Hudson had kept warm for us. After eating, we settled into our chairs smoking our pipes by a low fire. I was going over my notes for the day while Holmes was checking his indexes for any information that he had on Matthew Lehman and Marcus Strohman.

"Holmes," I asked, daring to interrupt his concentration, "In light of Caleb Loew's statement, have you reconsidered Daniel Loew to be a suspect in this case?"

The detective looked up from the page that he had been studying and stared across at me, the smoke from his pipe swirling about his head. "Watson, there is one factor of which you should be aware. More often than not, kidnap victims know their abductors. However, I still think Daniel is too obvious a suspect and not in need of the ransom money."

"Then could Abraham have been forced in at gunpoint by the occupant?" I countered.

Holmes answered, "Possibly since it was a rainy day and the streets were not crowded. However, the occupant would have had to stay back from the open door of the growler to avoid being seen with a gun.

That would allow Loew ample room to duck towards the back of the cab where there would be no clear shot. Think of it this way, Doctor. A man is pointing a gun at you. The fact he is doing so indicates that he is likely willing to kill you, if not immediately, then after you have served his purpose. Especially if you can identify him later. Would you step into that cab when you have a greater chance of survival by risking an escape move that would force him to hurry his shot and miss, or only wound you? Also, in that public setting, would it not be more likely that the culprit would not risk a shot where his cab could be either halted or easily identified by witnesses?

"No, I believe that he was joined in that cab by a friend or family member in disguise."

I nodded my understanding then said, "Perhaps a member of his club, since they would have been *en route* to the same destination?"

"Indeed, and we will call there in the morning to learn what we can from the members. But I'm still concerned about motive, my friend. Who did Abraham Loew know that was desperate enough to attempt this crime?"

"£2,000 is a great deal of money, Holmes. That would tempt many people."

"Yes, but it is a mere pittance compared to Loew's fortune. The kidnappers could have demanded much more. It's almost as if ..."

I waited for him to finish his thought, but after a year and a half of living with the detective, I also knew the look that came upon his face and realised that it would not be forthcoming. "You have an idea," I declared.

Holmes gave his head a shake, "Always, Doctor, but this one requires careful thought. I must smoke a few pipes and let it germinate. I beg you not to speak to me for ..." he looked at the tobacco remaining in his pipe and finished, "the next hour and ten minutes."

That told me this was going to be a multiple-pipe problem. I chose to pour myself a whisky and go to the writing desk to re-copy my notes into some sort of order so that I could more easily refer to them should I wish to at some future date. It took me less time than Holmes required for his thought process and so I settled in with the evening paper. There was nothing sensational that would interest my friend, but I did catch up on the latest racing results and sports scores. I also read a most interesting account of an eyewitness on the Audacious-class ironclad, *H.M.S. Invincible*. They detailed how the ship was saved from the guns of Fort Marabout during the Battle of Alexandria the previous month when they ran aground within range of the fort's guns. The gunboat *H.M.S. Condor,* seeing their plight, drew within 1,200 feet of the fort and began a ferocious shelling that effectively took the fort's guns out of action. The *Invincible* was saved until it could be set afloat again.

It was at this point that Holmes put away his pipe and poured himself a whisky as well. As he resumed his seat, I asked, "Well, have you come to a conclusion?"

He nodded, "The captain of the *Invincible* is going before a court martial to determine if he was careless or incompetent. Likely the former."

I shook my head, "How did you know what I was reading?"

"As a veteran yourself, you always get a certain look about you when reading of military matters. I noted that story earlier today and knew it would catch your attention."

"Fine," I acquiesced. "But I was talking about the Loew case."

Tactful and close-mouthed as ever, he merely said, "I've developed a theory which holds true based upon what we know at this point. The data I gather tomorrow should confirm or deny its plausibility."

"Do you care to share your theory?" I asked, already knowing the answer.

"Too soon, Watson, too soon." Hearing my harrumph of disappointment, he decided to throw me a bone. "Let me give you a thought to ponder. Miss Deborah Bass is a teacher."

I furrowed my brow in confusion, "I fail to see how that is significant, Holmes."

"Sleep on it and perhaps you'll see where I'm going."

The next morning, I awoke to find that Holmes had already gone out. His note asked me to await a response from Drake to a message that he had sent earlier, and that if he was not back by eleven, to meet him at the Sons of Isaac Club at noon. The Doctor's note came while I was eating breakfast. Coincidentally, it was a list of foods. What these had to do with the case, I'm sure I had no idea. But I slipped the reply in to my pocket to show Holmes when next I saw him.

He did not return by eleven, so at eleven-thirty, I put on my hat and coat and went out to hail a cab. The drive to St. James's Square was short and I arrived early, but I had reasoned it was better to be early than run the possibility of being late. Arriving at the club I asked if Sherlock Holmes was already there, but was advised that he was not and that I could wait until he did so.

The reception area was tastefully decorated. On one oak-panelled wall were photographs of the club's officers and below them was a photo of Abraham Loew draped in black silk. Other walls held paintings depicting scenes of Jewish history. The blessing of Jacob over Esau by Isaac, the parting of the Red Sea, the falling walls of Jericho, Samson swinging the jawbone of an ass amid bodies of Philistines, and David slaying Goliath with his sling; all familiar stories of the Old Testament.

I did not have to wait long. Holmes arrived just minutes after I did, and the reception clerk rang for an escort to take us to the club president's office. As we walked, I handed Holmes the message from Drake. He glanced at it, nodded, then stuffed it in to his coat pocket.

We were ushered into an office, where we were announced to an elderly gentleman with a long grey beard who was wearing a prayer shawl and a Hoiche hat. He stood from behind his desk and waved us to a seat. "Mr. Holmes, Dr. Watson, *shalom*. I am Rabbi Aaronson, current president of the club. I understand from your message that you wish to speak about Abraham Loew. How may I help you?"

"*Shalom*, Rabbi," said Holmes. "Thank you for seeing us. We have been engaged by the Loew family to assist the police in the matter of Mr. Loew's kidnapping and death. To that end, we are interviewing those who knew him to ascertain if he had any enemies. We are convinced that he was taken by someone that he knew."

The Rabbi's bushy grey eyebrows rose in surprise. "That is shocking! Abraham Loew was a well-respected member of our club and the Jewish community at large. Certainly, he was a good businessman but to have such an enemy among those he knew is difficult to fathom. Are you sure that it was not some random thug or racial prejudice?"

Holmes shook his head slowly. "I am afraid that the evidence is quite convincing. Do you know of anyone he was having disagreements with?"

The Rabbi held his palms up and replied, "Disagreements are a fact of life in Jewish culture, Mr. Holmes, especially in this club. Just as Isaac's sons, Jacob and Esau, argued over the birthright and Isaac's blessing, we have lively discussions of religion, philosophy, politics, and science ... just about anything where two or more sides can be taken is subject to debate amongst our members. But nothing rises to the level of violent threats or physical attacks. No, I cannot believe Abraham was kidnapped by any of our members. Did his family mention anyone?"

"Only some of his business competitors, but that has not led to any viable suspects." Holmes reached into his pocket and presented the list of foods to the Rabbi. "One more thing if I may. Can you verify that all of the foods on this list are kosher?

Rabbi Aaronson took up the paper and ran a gnarled finger down it, nodding as he did so. He handed it back to Holmes and replied, "Yes, Mr. Holmes. All of these would be accepted as part of a kosher meal. But, what are these ticks."

Holmes replaced the paper in his pocket. "These were the foods that were found at the scene of Loew's captivity. Whoever took him apparently knew his Jewish dietary restrictions. However, the ticks were made by the police surgeon who found these various ingredients in Loew's digestive tract and those particular items indicate a high sugar or carbohydrate content. Something which Loew was told to avoid by his doctor due to his diabetic condition."

Holmes stood at that point and said, "Thank you for seeing us, Rabbi. We hope to get to the bottom of this quickly."

Aaronson stood as well, raised his hand, separating the middle and ring finger, and replied, "*Shalom* and *mazal tov*, gentlemen."

155

Chapter Seven

"**W**hat now, Holmes?" I asked as we re-emerged on to the street and hailed a cab.

"I am still missing one vital piece, Doctor. We must speak with Korman regarding the Esterhaus connection."

Arriving at Scotland Yard, we found the Inspector in a perplexed state. He bade us to sit down and said, "I've gained some information connecting Gunther Esterhaus to Loew, but I fail to see how it could be relevant. He did work for Loew at one point, but he retired four years ago, after his parent's death in a fire, and moved to Sussex with his wife. He claims that he hasn't left that county since."

Holmes was all attention to this new information, "Do you know at which store he worked?"

Korman handed the document he was holding over to Holmes who read it and gave a quick smirk. Handing it back to the Inspector he said, "This may be just the data I need. With your permission, I will follow this lead and let you know if it proves significant."

We left Korman and again hailed a cab. Holmes declared, "My tapestry is almost complete, Watson. We need to take another trip for what I believe will be the last piece of evidence."

"Ah, you're going to visit the widow again?" I ventured.

"No, Doctor. We're going to pay a call to the Ealing branch of Loew's department store. It is not so large as the Oxford

Street or Richmond locations, but it may be of vital importance to our investigation."

"Holmes," I reminded him. "It's Sunday, the store won't be open.

He stopped short, uttered a rare curse, and reluctantly instructed the driver of the cab we eventually secured to make for Baker Street. On the way we stopped at one of the usual haunts of Joe Wiggins, the leader of what Holmes referred to as his Baker Street Irregulars. These were street urchins whom the detective would use to be his eyes and ears since, as Holmes pointed out, they could go anywhere unnoticed by the adults they were watching. He gave Wiggins instructions and some coins to spread amongst those he would need for the task. I had stayed in the cab and when my friend returned, I asked what arrangements he had made.

"The Irregulars will keep an eye on our suspect for the time being and inform me if he should take any steps towards leaving town. That is the only step I can take until I can confirm my suspicions tomorrow."

The next morning, we arrived early in Ealing by train, took a cab, and alighted at the aforementioned store. It was indeed smaller than the premises on Oxford Street but still well-appointed and had the same variety of departments. Holmes enquired of store manager if he could examine some old employment records.

As we left the establishment to hail a cab back to the railway station, I said to my friend, "I can't believe what this implies, Holmes. How could he have done such a thing? And how did he get a key to the mausoleum?"

"Greed, Doctor, and an anxiety to move faster towards his future. We must go to Kensal Green to look into the key situation, then we may lay our evidence before Inspector Korman."

"You don't wish to inform the family first and see how they want to handle the situation?"

"You forget, Doctor, it is not a simple matter of the kidnap as we have a second victim. The death of the cab driver Jones must be taken in to account."

"Yes, of course. I had quite forgotten that among all this talk of kosher diets, Jewish competitors, and the Esterhaus connection. There can be no leniency. The man must be arrested and charged."

At the cemetery we were met by the sexton, John Oldman. He was a short, stout fellow of perhaps fifty years of age. Holmes introduced us, and naturally he was shocked and highly concerned over this breach of the Esterhaus mausoleum. "I don't understand how they got in, Mr. Holmes."

"Obviously they somehow obtained a key," answered my friend. "Where do you keep them?"

"Oh, they hang in the cabinet over there. That way I can retrieve them for any family members who may have forgotten theirs. Many people come to visit the departed in remembrance on special occasions and holidays."

"May we see them?" asked Holmes.

"Certainly," said Oldman as he rose and walked over to the wall cabinet and unlocked it with the key on his pocket watch chain. There were dozens of keys on hooks labelled with family names.

"Does anyone other than you have a key to this cabinet?"

"Just my assistant, Jack Grier. Due to the ventilation slots the mausoleums get dusty and cobwebs can form, so he and his men will go through them occasionally and clean them."

Holmes stroked his jaw and asked, "I need you to think back over the last few weeks, Mr. Oldman. Was there ever an occasion when this cabinet was open while you had a visitor, one who maybe you left alone for a few minutes?"

Oldman pursed his lips in thought then brightened, "Why, yes! About two weeks ago a fellow came in to enquire about how to go about purchasing a mausoleum for his family. I showed him how we kept the keys safely locked away. While I was doing so, he suddenly had a coughing fit. He needed to sit and I left the room to fetch him some water, but I was only gone for a minute and he was still in the chair when I returned."

Holmes asked to see the key to the Esterhaus vault and examined it with his pocket lens. "As I thought," he said.

"What?" asked the proprietor.

"Wax," replied the detective, holding his lens and the key out for Oldman to see the minute traces of wax left behind. "Your visitor made a wax impression of this key so that he could have a duplicate made. Now we know how he got in. Do you remember this man's name, or what he looked like?"

The man described by Oldman generally fitted Holmes's primary suspect except that the prospective client bore a heavy beard and moustache. "Easily faked for an effective disguise, Watson. The evidence is too strong to ignore. We must inform the Inspector."

By the time we returned to the Yard, we did not find Korman at his desk. However, we did run into Inspector Lestrade. He listened to Holmes with great interest and agreed that we had enough evidence. He said that he could arrange matters but asked Holmes if we could wait for Korman to return and so ensure that the elderly Inspector would be the one to make the arrest.

"Korman is about to retire, Mr. Holmes. This would be a nice feather in his cap to go out with. You don't have any reason to suppose that our culprit is going anywhere today do you?"

Holmes agreed that would be fine as he was having the suspect watched. He also felt the entire Loew family should be in attendance to hear the news. To allow for all the members to be present, Holmes arranged for the meeting at the Loew residence to be held at six o'clock that evening and messages were sent to all the pertinent parties.

When the moment arrived, Holmes, Korman, and I were admitted to the Loew home. This time by the regular butler. To accommodate everyone, they were gathered in the dining room around a large table with the chair at the head notably vacant and draped in black.

Jethro greeted us as we were shown in. "All are assembled except Caleb, Mr. Holmes. Can you start without him as mother is most anxious to hear your report."

Holmes replied, "Yes, Inspector Korman has news that cannot wait any longer." We declined seats and remained standing as the Inspector stepped forward, cleared his throat, and addressed his remarks to Mrs. Loew.

"Madam, first let me state again that I am deeply sorry for your loss. Unfortunately, the news I bring today will be equally sorrowful." He hesitated before plunging forward with his announcement, "At five o'clock this afternoon, we arrested your son, Caleb, for the kidnapping of your husband and the murder of one Michael Jones, the cab driver that he paid to assist him."

An audible gasp went up from the family members. Rabbi Herschel Loew and his brother Kenan went to their sister-in-law's side while her daughter, Sarah, rose to go to her as well. Deborah Bass cried out, "No, he couldn't have!" Jethro sat stunned and Daniel, keeping his solicitor's head about him, demanded, "What proof do you have, Inspector?"

Korman took a deep breath and stepped back saying, "I will let Mr. Holmes explain."

My companion stepped forward, rubbed his palms together slowly, and began, "I have checked the records at your Ealing establishment and found that your son and Gunther Esterhaus worked there at the same time four years ago, which is likely how he knew of the mausoleum where Abraham's body was found. Interviews with employees at the Oxford Street store indicate that while they saw Caleb wish his father 'good afternoon' on the day of the kidnapping, that they were not aware of his presence again until the next morning when the store opened.

"Unfortunately, he did not know of his father's new diabetic dietary restrictions. He thought that he was being kind in providing a week's worth of supplies of kosher food and wine during his father's imprisonment, little knowing that he was contributing to his death by giving him food high in sugar and carbohydrates.

"He enlisted the services of the cab driver, Michael Jones, to be on hand on that rainy day to pick his father up for the trip to his club. Then to also delay departure just long enough for him to follow him into the cab, likely in disguise, and chloroform him. Finally, to help carry the unconscious victim into the mausoleum. Jones was a poor man, and Caleb promised him, a large sum of money. It was too tempting for Jones to resist. Afterwards Caleb came home and Jones went on his way, well-paid for his assistance. Unfortunately, when the newspapers reported your husband's death, Jones demanded more money and Caleb could not leave Jones around to tell what he knew."

"But why, Mr. Holmes!? Why would Caleb do such a thing?" cried out Mrs. Loew in her anguish.

Holmes gave a slight shake of his head. "Your son is remaining silent until he speaks to his barrister. However, if I may speculate, I believe it was two-fold. He was greedy and anxious to get out from under his father's thumb. He was also eager for his marriage to occur, but he knew that they could not afford it. With insufficient funds and the fact that Miss Bass would be forced to resign her position and lose her income, it became imperative that he raise more money. The relatively small amount of £2,000 compared to your vast fortune aroused my suspicions early on in that this was the work of an insider. Someone who knew the amount was easily obtainable and that it would not be damaging to the family fortune."

"Wait," said Jethro, shaking himself free from the shock of it. "Why would Deborah be forced to resign her position?"

Deborah herself chose to answer before Holmes could reply, "Under the ridiculous laws of England all female teachers must be unmarried. Apparently, the school administrators still believe that a married woman's duties to her husband and children would preclude her from having the proper time to be an effective teacher."

Turning back to Holmes, she implored with a tremulous voice, "You are certain that he has done this, Mr. Holmes?"

Holmes sadly nodded his head. "I am afraid so. His greed and love for you overrode his judgment, and it got out of hand when Abraham died from diabetic shock."

Korman broke the silence pervading the room by asking permission to search Caleb's room for the ransom money.

Daniel went with him, and they soon returned with a strongbox full of cash. They also presented two steamship tickets for New York later that month. Caleb had seemingly planned an escape to America where he could start his own business and where Miss Bass could obtain a teaching position despite being married.

"I'm afraid this settles it, Mrs. Loew," said Inspector Korman. "Again, I am very sorry for your troubles, madam. Your son is being held at Scotland Yard if you wish to see him."

Unable to speak, she waved us away with a handkerchief that was now wet with her tears. Her son's greed had exacted a terrible price, and she needed time to deal with it.

Several days later, Daniel Loew called upon us at 221B Baker Street. I invited him to sit and offered him a sherry but he declined. "I'll only be a minute, Doctor. Mr. Holmes, I have a cheque for your services. Painful as the results were, you did complete your task for the family."

He handed over a draught from a well-known bank, and Holmes set it upon the table. "An unpleasant one, I assure you," he replied. "Had it not been for the death of Jones, I would have confined my results to your family alone and let you decide how to deal with your brother."

Loew nodded. "Interesting that you should say so, Mr. Holmes. Mother is refusing to testify against Caleb in exchange for his disinheritance, and the removal of his presence from London."

"Pentonville prison will have to suffice. He must face the murder charge," answered the detective.

"He is fighting that murder charge, Mr. Holmes," replied the solicitor. "He was unaware of father's diabetes and wished him no physical harm. He says that he went to bribe Jones to leave London and keep quiet, but Jones demanded more than Caleb wanted to pay. They fought, and Caleb says that he killed Jones in self-defence."

Holmes shrugged his shoulders. "I was not hired to solve

Jones's murder so I will leave that affair to the crown prosecutor."

"What about Miss Bass?" I asked, concerned for the young lady's welfare now that her fiancé had been outcast by his family.

"She is going ahead with her teaching for this term. She is furious with Caleb for not discussing the future that he had planned with her. I doubt she will take him back even if he is acquitted."

Daniel left us, and Holmes placed the cheque in his pocketbook for later deposit. We sat back down with brandies in hand, and Holmes grew philosophical. "When you think of it, Watson, Caleb's greed is much like Jacob, the son of Isaac. They both committed their crimes to gain the family fortune and please the woman that they loved. In Jacob's case, he stole the birthright from his brother at the encouragement of his mother."

"It's hardly the same thing, Holmes," I responded. "Jacob didn't kidnap and kill his father, and Miss Bass had no idea what Caleb was planning as to their future in America."

"I was referring only to Jacob and Caleb's motivation," answered my friend. "Greed for money and love for women are often a recipe for catastrophe. I've seen it all too often."

"Well, I can tell you that I shall never marry a woman for her income, Holmes. In fact, I would avoid it to assure her my feelings were out of love and not mercenary."[1]

"Good for you, Watson. Good for you."

---

[1] See the Arthur Conan Doyle's *The Sign of Four* for the dilemma that this statement had upon Watson in this story.

Epilogue

It came out in the trial that Caleb Loew had used a Nealy Smoke Mask[1], which the store supplied to the local fire brigade, in order to hide his identity while getting into the cab. With the rain distracting what few pedestrians were out, and his collar turned up and hat pulled low, he was able to enter the vehicle after his father while Jones delayed departure. The mask also protected him from the chloroform fumes.

Loew was found guilty of kidnapping his father and also of murdering Jones. His self-defence plea did not sway the jury. Involuntary manslaughter charges for his father's death were not pursued. He was sentenced to death and as I write he is awaiting the outcome of an appeal.

Miss Bass maintained her teaching position and became highly involved in the woman's suffrage movement. She severed all ties with the Loew family.

Merriam Loew turned the administration of the stores over to Jethro Feldman assisted by Daniel Loew who continued to act as legal advisor.

---

[1] Invented for English firemen in 1877.

Lust

The Backstage Pirates

Chapter One

As we sat in our rooms at 221B Baker Street on that sweltering August day in 1882, Sherlock Holmes, the consulting detective, and I were not expecting any visitors. Thus, we were in our shirtsleeves *sans* collars and ties. The window was open, despite the sounds and smells of London in the summer, to allow whatever breeze might make its way in. Accordingly, I had placed paperweights appropriately on various papers on the writing desk. Without a case to occupy his mind, Holmes was engaged in chemical experiments, which fortunately did not include using his Bunsen burner.

A knock on our door and the voice of our landlady was a welcome interruption when she called out, "There's a young lady to see you, Mr. Holmes. She says you recently assisted her mother."

Holmes and I both rose, and as we made our way to our bedrooms to take up collars and ties, my companion called out, "Show her up, Mrs. Hudson!"

We re-entered our sitting room just as Mrs. Hudson escorted a familiar figure into our presence. I immediately strode forward to take her hand and show her to a chair while Holmes merely said, "Good morning, Miss Morrow."

Judith Morrow was a successful actress whom Holmes had been hired to investigate on behalf of a client, Donald Ellington, a banker, who was concerned over the relationship and feelings his son had developed towards her.[1] While my companion does not usually take on such cases, he was drawn in by the fact that he had detected something amiss during the initial interview. Ellington had described her as a 'raspberry tart' due to her long red hair and occupation. Today, she was as beautiful as I recalled from our first meeting just a few months prior. Due to the heat, she carried a parasol and wore a light linen dress of pale yellow which contrasted nicely with her red tresses. The case had not ended well for Miss Morrow, and there seemed to be a sadness to her countenance which her determined attitude could not conceal.

"Thank you, Dr. Watson," she said as she took her seat.

"How is your mother?" I asked, somewhat fearful of the answer.

She bit her lip, sighed, and replied, "She is slipping away. The cancer is growing, and the doctors believe that she only has a few days left."

"I am sorry."

Holmes spoke up. "You have my condolences as well, Miss Morrow. I perceive that you have taken time off from your career to care for her."

She looked at Holmes. "Yes, how did you know? Have you been to the theatre?"

Holmes shook his head. "There is a freshness to your face which brings out your natural beauty. An actress who is applying theatrical makeup six days a week could hardly compare to your current complexion. Now, how is it that we may help you?"

She shifted slightly, as if to reply with a preprepared statement, then spoke quietly, "First of all, Mr. Holmes, I need to get something off my conscience. I have mixed feelings where you are concerned. Your investigation into my life and relationship proved disastrous. On the other hand, had you not interfered the results would have been equally devastating."

She sat up a little straighter and continued, "So I suppose I should be grateful, but it is a bitter pill to swallow, Mr. Holmes,

---

[1] *The Case of the Raspberry Tart* in *A Sherlock Holmes Alphabet of Cases, Volume 4 (P-T)*

and if my temper should get the better of me during our future conversations, I trust that you will understand."

Holmes bowed his head. "My discovery gave me no pleasure, but it was essential that you were made aware of the truth."

"I know," she replied, then changed the subject. "My purpose today is to enlist your services to investigate a dangerous situation at the Criterion Theatre. There has been an attempted kidnapping of Cynthia Barlow, the actress who took over my role. Fortunately, it was thwarted by the stage door keeper and a couple of the cast. I have been calling at the theatre two or three evenings a week when father is home to watch over mother, and I believe that something more sinister is going on. The crowd of gentlemen who normally hang around the stage door after the shows has grown considerably and become rowdy. I've seen signs of what appears to be groups working in concert as if attempting to isolate certain women, and I believe that I've identified the ringleader."

Holmes, who was now sitting opposite the young lady, leaned forward with his elbows on his knees and asked, "Have the police become involved?"

"Yes, Inspector Lestrade has taken up the case. But all he's done is rearrange the beat of the constable on duty so that he is at the theatre stage door when the show finishes. The management has hired two guards, but it hardly seems enough against such a crowd if they become determined to do their worst."

At the mention of Lestrade's name, Holmes had leaned back in his chair and steepled his hands under his chin. The detective had once described Lestrade to me as 'the best of a bad lot'. I recalled that the man had the build and determination of a bulldog, but an unfortunate stubbornness for his own opinion and a lack of imagination towards other possibilities to the solution of a crime.

Holmes dropped his hands to his lap, fingers intertwined, and asked our guest, "What would you have me do?"

She leaned forward and declared, "When we first met, you were introduced to me as the actor, Will Scott. My mother has confirmed this from your early work with her, and it has obviously helped you in your current profession. I believe that you should infiltrate this gang in disguise and get to the bottom of what's going on, so that the police can gain the evidence that they need to put a stop to it."

Turning to me she added, "And Dr. Watson, since you are a chivalrous gentleman as you proved on our first meeting, you could be of great assistance as an additional guardian at the stage door, or in the passageway, escorting the actresses to their cabs."

I could hardly disagree I felt that we owed this young woman something for the pain we had caused her in the past. I could also not deny the fact that I was attracted to her beauty myself. Without waiting for Holmes's reply, I answered, "I would be happy to assist in any way I can, Miss Morrow."

We both turned to look at my companion, who raised one hand to his jaw in contemplation and then replied, "I will give your idea serious consideration. But no matter which method I choose, I shall certainly look into the situation and do whatever it requires to ensure the safety of these ladies."

The actress briefly bowed her head, and took a deep breath as she stood. "Thank you, gentlemen. If you need my help in arranging matters, you know where to find me."

I walked her to the stairs and watched until she exited our front door. Returning to our sitting room, I enquired of my friend, "Well, Holmes, what do you plan to do?"

"Our first order of business," said he, "is to call on our mutual friend Lestrade and see what steps he is taking so that we do not interfere with his efforts. Would you care to come along, Doctor?"

"Absolutely," I replied. "I should like first-hand knowledge of the police plans, and it's bound to be cooler down by the river at any rate."

Chapter Two

As our cab dropped us off at Great Scotland Yard, we found that being only a couple hundred yards from the Thames afforded us some slight breeze to assuage the stifling heat.

The Inspector was in his office behind a desk reading a report and there was a high stack of files to one side. Upon seeing us in his doorway, he set down the paper in hand and asked, "Well, if it isn't the theorist, Mr. Sherlock Holmes. And Dr. Watson as well! What sort of trouble have you fellows gotten yourselves into now?"

Considering how often Lestrade had dropped in on the detective for assistance in the year and a half that we had shared rooms, I thought this remark rather condescending. Holmes, however, ignored the Inspector's attitude and merely replied, "We have been engaged on a case that overlaps with one of yours, Inspector. Before proceeding, I would like to know what you are doing, so that we do not act at cross purposes."

Lestrade's brow furrowed, and he cocked his head at us curiously. "What case would that be?"

"The attempted kidnapping of Cynthia Barlow at the Criterion Theatre, and the growing aggressiveness of the stage door crowds," answered my companion.

The Inspector looked at us askance and replied, "There's hardly a case there, Mr. Holmes. We've got a description of the culprit, and our constables are on the lookout for him. I've arranged for the man on the beat to be in the vicinity when the theatre finishes, and the management has hired some guards for the stage door. That's all we're doing at this point unless it escalates, so whatever you have in mind, feel free to act."

I could stay silent no longer, "That is intolerable, Lestrade. The lives of those young girls may well be at risk!"

He looked at me, and with some little patience said, "Doctor, we see this sort of thing all the time. The more popular the show, especially if it features several beautiful ladies, the bigger the crowd afterward. I admit that this is the first kidnapping attempt I've had, but we're keeping an eye on Miss Barlow specifically."

"Has she given you any information regarding who tried to take her?" asked Holmes.

The Inspector shook his head, "She claims that she did not recognise him, though apparently he spoke with a foreign accent. He had dark hair, a thin moustache, and was at least three inches taller than she, for she had to look up to see into his brown eyes. She is tall at five foot seven inches, so I would venture our culprit to be about five foot ten inches or so. He was of a medium build with no other outstanding features that she noted, though she did say that his coat was damp as if he had come up from the river."

Holmes nodded at this statement and bade Lestrade good day. "We shall keep you posted if we make any progress, Inspector."

Then he turned and left. It took me a moment to fathom his departure, for I was sure that he would have other questions. When I caught up to him, I asked, "Why didn't you press him for the details of what happened? You might have discerned another clue."

He shook his head. "Lestrade's information is secondhand, Watson. We shall gather the true facts from Miss Barlow herself, and perhaps jog her memory for more. We will go to the theatre and speak with the manager, Charles Wyndham, and while there we will obtain Miss Barlow's home address."

Wyndham had gained notoriety on the stage in varying degrees as he acted occasionally while pursuing his medical degree. I knew that he had travelled to America and served as a doctor with the Union army between 1862 and 1865. During breaks in service, he had made two attempts on the Broadway stage in New York but failed both times. However, upon his return to England after the war, he had put what he had learned to good use and soon became known as an 'innate talent' and 'an accomplished actor' taking on several Shakespearean roles and other parts under the great playwrights of the time. He later went into management and took over the Criterion Theatre in 1876 while continuing to act in various productions. The Criterion with its Portland stone façade reminiscent of the French Renaissance style, includes a large restaurant with bar, dining rooms, a ballroom, and a theatre with a capacity of over five hundred.

When we arrived, Holmes and I found Wyndham in his office. It was a rather untidy oak-panelled space with papers scattered about the place and with posters of famous productions on the walls. But, like Holmes, he could always put his hand on what he needed. As he rose to greet us heartily, I judged him to be about forty-five years old, and perhaps five foot ten inches; solidly built, clean-shaven with wavy brown hair and a handsome face. "Mr. Holmes, and you must be Dr. Watson. Please come and sit down, gentlemen." Once we had all taken our chairs, he continued, "I do hope that you are here to help with our crowd control crisis. Miss Morrow advised me that she was going to call on you."

Holmes nodded. "The young lady can be very persuasive, and we do feel an obligation to her. What can you tell me about what has been happening and the steps that you have taken?"

Wyndham relayed all the incidents, and we learned that not only Miss Barlow but some of the other actresses had found themselves in uncomfortable situations. Fortunately, they had extricated themselves before a physical abduction could be attempted.

Holmes asked, "Do any of these ladies have anything in common? Do they live at the same boarding house, for example, or are their stage roles especially alluring?"

The manager pursed his lips and stroked his chin in thought, then replied, "There are seven ladies in the show, Mr. Holmes. Four have reported incidents. Two of them reside at the same boarding house. One still lives with her parents, and the other with her husband. As to roles, that's the odd part. The leading lady has not been bothered except by the usual autograph seekers and wealthy aristocrats. Miss Barlow has the secondary lead, of course, having taken over from Miss Morrow."

"When you say 'incidents', what exactly did they report?"

"In these cases, men would talk to them persuasively and gently take them by the arm, offering to escort them through the crowd. As a rule, stage door onlookers don't touch the actresses. They ask them for autographs or make offers to take them for drinks or late suppers, but they don't become physical unless the actress responds to their suggestion. After Cynthia's episode, the actresses have become more wary and decline all such offers. Now they travel in pairs, or arrange for a friend or relative to pick them up. I've taken on some guards at the stage door, but I still feel uneasy, Mr. Holmes. I've learned to trust women's intuition over the years, and from what I've seen with my own eyes, I agree with Miss Morrow's assessment. There appears to be some sort of gang awaiting their chance to snatch one or more of the girls."

Holmes asked for a list of the names of the ladies and also their addresses. He advised Wyndham that he would like to meet with all of them that evening after the show, and told him that our next stop would be to see Miss Barlow.

"Let me give you a letter of introduction, Mr. Holmes. Then she'll be inclined to let you in. With luck, you'll find her roommate, Katrina Rouseau, at home with her as they share accommodations. She was another one of the four."

Chapter Three

When we arrived at the Percival Street boarding house, we found an establishment that was tightly run by a cautious middle-aged couple, Charles and Adele Robinson. Mr. Robinson was at the front desk as we walked in. He was a large, muscular fellow with the look of a boxer about him. He stood up from his stool with the attitude of a former soldier. I noted that he kept one hand out of sight below the counter, and I could only imagine what sort of weapon that he might have concealed there.

"What be your business here, gentlemen?" he demanded in a strong baritone voice with a suspicious edge to his question.

Holmes, never intimidated, walked right up to the counter and introduced us, handing one of his cards to the gentleman. "I am Sherlock Holmes, and this is my colleague, Dr. John Watson. We have been hired by the Criterion management to look into the incidents that have occurred at the theatre recently, and we would like to speak with Miss Barlow or Miss Rouseau."

Robinson took the card, glanced at it, and replied, "I've never heard of either of you, and we don't allow our boarders to have gentlemen callers. These ladies are under our protection in this establishment. For all I know you two are part of the problem they're having. So, you can just be on your way. If you are who you say, then you can speak to them later at the theatre."

While initially insulted by his insinuation, I revised my opinion when I realised that this type of protection is exactly what I would have wanted for any female friend of mine in such a place. Holmes merely bowed his head with a brief nod, pulled the letter from Wyndham out of his breast pocket, and handed it to Robinson.

Even though it was on Criterion stationery, the manager was still guarded. He called out for his wife, who came from the dining room where she had been preparing the table for lunch. Adele Robinson was a sturdily built woman. Tall and somewhat muscular herself, she was more attractively handsome than beautiful. She did have kind eyes, and I could imagine a pleasant face, were she to allow herself a smile.

Mr. Robinson handed her the letter, and after she read it, he asked, "What do you think, dearie?"

She gave us a stare with searching eyes and finally replied, "Have them wait here. I'll take this letter up and see if either of the ladies are willing to come down and speak with them."

He gestured towards a sitting area off to one side of the reception, where we waited patiently. It did not take long, for both of the young ladies followed Mrs. Robinson down the stairs in less than a minute after she had gone up.

Miss Barlow immediately recognised me as being the doctor who had offered my services to Judith Morrow and put out her hand. As she shook it, she looked sideways at my companion and questioned, "I thought that you were the actor, William Scott?"

Holmes bowed and replied, "On occasion, I am he, Miss Barlow, but for now I am here in my capacity as a private consulting detective. Mr. Wyndham and Miss Morrow have asked for my assistance with this possible threat at the theatre. Won't you both sit down so that we may discuss it? I should like to hear the details from your own lips, and I may have questions that the police failed to ask."

As we all sat, Miss Barlow introduced her fellow lodger, Katrina Rouseau. In contrast to Miss Barlow's tall figure and long ginger hair, Miss Rouseau was a petite copper redhead, perhaps five foot two inches in height, with short curly locks surrounding a bright heart-shaped face. Both women appeared to be in their early twenties and quite beautiful.

I took copious notes as they related their experiences to Holmes. Miss Barlow did not have much to add to what Lestrade had already reported to us, except for the fact that the man who had accosted her kept looking around as if he were expecting assistance, which fortunately never came before she was rescued. She did say that he produced a knife to get her rescuers to step back so that he could turn and retreat.

The incident with Miss Rouseau took place two days later before the guards were in place. In her case, she was heading towards Piccadilly to hail a cab when two men came up on either side of her. Normally she wasn't the object of these stage door fellows as she had a very small part in the play. Admirers were primarily concentrated on the two leading women. She considered herself more endearing than beautifully alluring as her fellow actresses were. Thus, she was surprised at their attention. She was flattered at first, but then she noted at the end of the passageway that there was a carriage waiting and the driver leering in her direction. Recalling what had almost happened to Cynthia, she suddenly stopped. She checked her purse, pretended that she had forgotten something, and started to turn back. Fortunately, right behind her was Brian Regan, one of the stagehands, who had been asked to watch over the actresses. The two men 'escorting' Miss Rouseau started to reach for her but stopped at the appearance of this gargantuan fellow. Regan was six foot five inches tall and built like an ox. He held out his hand and said quietly, "Katrina, you are needed backstage."

She tilted her head back to look up into a face that was both gentle and commanding at the same time. She could see in his eyes that she should go with him and said over her shoulder, "Excuse me, gentlemen. Duty calls." Then she noted the glare Regan gave to the two men and gratefully began to march back to the stage door so that Regan could put himself between her and possible danger.

Holmes asked if she could describe her would-be assailants. Unfortunately, she was of little help. "I didn't get a good look at their faces, Mr. Holmes. They kept to either side of me. They were taller than me, perhaps five foot six inches in height. They each had a dark, short beard and one had a thick moustache." She stopped, then added, "It's funny now that I think back on it. Something gnawed at my thoughts at the time, and now I realise that their facial hair looked very similar to that which some of our actors use. It appeared too dark and too uniform in colour, as if it were meant to be seen only by a distant audience."

She also recalled that their speech seemed forced, as if English was not their primary language, though she could not discern what accent they might have had. She could remember no more but suggested that Regan probably had a better look at them head-on for a description. Holmes agreed and said that he would talk to the stagehand later that day.

We concluded our meeting, and Holmes encouraged them to continue to take all precautions. Miss Barlow assured him that Mr. Robinson was quite protective and even escorted them to their cabs when they went out, which at this point was only to the theatre.

Luncheon was upon us, but Holmes gave no thought to it. However, we did return to Baker Street, and he suggested that I remain to partake of Mrs. Hudson's cooking as he had places to go where it was best he go incognito. Still, I offered to come along, but he insisted that this part of his job was better done alone.

As I awaited Mrs. Hudson's fine food, Holmes disappeared into his bedroom only to emerge some ten minutes later unrecognisable. With unruly hair and a beard streaked with grey, the stoop-shouldered person before me wearing seaman's garb was the picture of an ancient mariner. The pipe in his yellow-stained teeth reeked of an inexpensive tobacco, and his clothes had the smell of fish and seaweed about them.

As he left, he said, "I shall return in time to accompany you to the theatre tonight, Watson, where we shall question the other ladies and Mr. Regan."

Chapter Four

That evening, I was just finishing dinner in preparation to leave for the theatre when Holmes returned. He made quick work to make himself presentable before we caught a cab to the Criterion, as he wanted to arrive prior to the opening act to examine the area where the stage door exited.

On the way, I asked Holmes what he had been doing dressed up in his sailor's attire. He replied, "I've spent some time down at the docks, Watson. I believe I've made some headway in our case, and I have put Wiggins and the Irregulars to work to gather more data. We shall see if this 'sailor' aspect is common among the other cases."

The alleyway that exited the rear of the theatre was wide and well-lit. Delivery vehicles could make their way from the street to the back door easily. However, during performances, it was closed off to traffic and people exiting that way had to walk to Jermyn Street to hail a cab.

We had been this way before, during Miss Morrow's case, but Holmes made detailed notes of all the niches and doorways that could be made use of by kidnappers. Then we entered and tracked down the stagehand, Brian Regan. The man was as large as Miss Rouseau had described. Taller than Holmes by a few inches and with broad shoulders, he took up nearly a whole doorway when he passed through. We were able to pull him aside for a few moments into an empty dressing room where we could question him.

Holmes began, "I take it that you have not been here long, Mr. Regan. I did not notice you during the case we had here just a few months ago, and I am certain I could not have missed so large a specimen as yourself. What brought you to employment here, and what ship did you work on before?"

The fellow was taken aback at Holmes's declaration of his being a sailor. "I started two months ago, and like many stagehands I used to work on a ship. Was my appearance that obvious?"

Holmes brushed his question away with a quick explanation. "The sway to your walk, the callouses on your hands, and the knots you tie when raising a backdrop all speak of some years at sea. What brought you ashore into this line of work?"

Regan glanced at the door to ensure that it was shut and that we would not be overheard, then replied, "I got tired of the lonely life at sea for months at a time. I wanted to settle down and start a family. One day on shore leave I came to this theatre to see a show. Afterward, I thought maybe I could make a go of it using my size and strength as a stagehand. They hired me on the spot. I resigned from my post and took a room here in town. The pay's decent, the work is a lot easier than on board a ship, and I get to work indoors out of the cold, wind, and rain."

"What ship were you on?" asked my companion.

"The Indian Princess. A three-master of the India-Burma Line."

"Miss Rouseau said that you were facing the men who accosted her the other night and may have gotten a better look at them than she. Can you describe them?"

I had my paper and pencil out to ensure I got every word and found Regan to be quite observant. He gave an excellent description of the men as well as their clothing and the way they moved. "They were sailors, sir. No doubt about it. Like old-fashioned pirates if you ask me. They had that sort of look about them."

Holmes thanked him for the thoroughness of his statement and then asked one more question, "Why were you following

Miss Rouseau? There wasn't really any reason for her to return to the theatre that night."

I hardly believed it possible that a man of Regan's bearing could look sheepish, but that is the best word that comes to mind to describe his reaction to my friend's question.

He quietly looked at each of us and asked, "May I have your word, gentlemen, that you'll not repeat what I am about to say?"

Holmes replied, "If I have no legal reason to reveal it to solve the case, then your secret will remain in this room, sir."

The stagehand nodded his massive head twice. A large curl, like the forelock of a wild stallion, fell and dangled between his eyes. He swept it back and answered, "I've rather taken a fancy to Miss Rouseau, but I've not mustered the courage to tell her so. Since the troubles began though, I've made it a point to keep an eye on her to make sure that she gets to a cab safely each night."

I smiled at the thought of this giant feeling so intimidated by the petite Katrina Rouseau, who was more than a foot shorter and probably ten stones lighter. Yet, even having just reached the age of thirty, I had to admit that I could also be made timid by the power of a beautiful lady no matter her physical size.

Holmes, whose opinion of women seemed to be more clinical and scientific when not downright frustrated by their 'illogical thinking' as he puts it, seemed surprised at his attitude. "I thought as much," he stated. "I will keep your secret, but, if I may, I would advise you that it is foolish for you to do so. Why waste your time admiring someone in secret? Life is not a Miguel de Cervantes novel[1]. Loving pure and chaste from afar only leads to false hope and despair. You must seize the moment, Regan! If she declines your feelings then you can grieve and move on. Life is too short to waste time on pursuits that you fail to pursue."

It was typical of Holmes to make such a remark. In the year and a half that we had shared a flat, I had never known him to see any woman socially. I do not know if the emotion of love

---

[1] Holmes is referring to Cervantes's tale of Don Quixote.

even existed in that mechanical brain of his. Being somewhat more experienced with the fair sex, I offered the fellow some different advice.

"I agree with my friend to some extent, Mr. Regan. However, under the current circumstances when tensions and emotions are running high, I would suggest that you wait until the case is closed and things are back to normal. You would not want to risk her accepting your friendship out of her fear of attack. When the time comes, it would be better for you to be seen as a gentleman with honourable intentions rather than a mere bodyguard in extreme circumstances."

Regan thanked us for our advice, and we asked him to introduce us to Miss Viola and Miss Haynes, the other two ladies thus far accosted. Virginia Viola (a stage name no doubt) was a tall woman whom I would call attractive but not a stunning beauty. Her strawberry blonde, shoulder-length hair was her most outstanding feature for its unusual colour. Otherwise, she was of a slim figure but with a vivacious personality and was all too willing to speak with us regarding her experience. Her case was similar to Miss Rouseau's, and the description of the men who had approached her was identical to that Regan had given us. The two gentlemen approached her on either side and began philandering with her. Fortunately, her husband arrived at that moment, apologised for being late, and 'encouraged' the rascals to leave.

Linda Haynes was a young actress who still lived with her parents. She was but eighteen years old with chestnut hair that fell in coils down the sides of her round face to her shoulders. She still exhibited vestiges of her baby fat and had a very minor role in the play. She seemed a little anxious of Holmes, and I stepped in to put her at ease. "Miss Morrow and Mr. Wyndham have asked us to look into the matter of the women who've been aggressively bothered by men after the performance. We would just like you to describe your incident and tell us what the man or men looked like, so that we can attempt to stop them."

My soft tone and the fact that I was a doctor seemed to put her at ease. She sat demurely, hands folded in her lap, and in her soft voice responded, "There was just one man, Doctor. A husky fellow about five foot six inches tall. He had brown hair and a beard but no moustache. He had one gold tooth in front and his clothes smelt like the sea. You know, a musty dampness? Anyway, he offered to walk me to a cab, but I told him that my father would be waiting with our carriage. That seemed to put him off. He seemed somewhat skittish after that, as if he didn't quite know what he should do. He stayed with me step for step, until we got to the end of the alley where I spotted my dad and waved to him. That really seemed to bother the fellow, for he immediately left my side without a word. Almost like he was afraid of being seen with me."

"When was this and have you seen him since?" asked Holmes.

She gave us the date and told us that she had seen him one other time since then, sitting up in the driver's seat of a van near the end of the alley.

"Thank you, Miss Haynes. I would suggest that you allow one of the men Mr. Wyndham has hired to escort you to your father's carriage each night until we get this matter sorted out."

"Thank you, Mr. Holmes. I have been doing just that and, thank God, nothing else has happened. Do you think it's really a gang of kidnappers like the other girls are saying?"

Holmes took a moment before replying, then he answered, "I'm still gathering data, Miss Haynes. But be assured, I will not rest until we have made things safe for all of you again."

We watched the show from the wings until the penultimate act, when Holmes told me to escort Miss Barlow and Miss Rouseau to their boarding house afterwards and to keep my revolver handy. He went outside to take up a spot in the alley where he could observe the behaviour of the crowd and take action if needed.

After the show, as we left the theatre, a guard handed me a note saying, "From Mr. Holmes, Doctor." I gave it a quick read and put it in my pocket. Holmes had heard from one of his Irregulars and was off to observe for himself. He asked that I join him after my task of being a guardian was complete. Then I escorted Miss Barlow and Miss Rouseau, with Brian Regan close behind, to a cab and on to Percival Street. Dropping the ladies there, I instructed the cabbie to the destination where Holmes had desired me to meet him.

Chapter Five

Despite the heat of the summer days, night time by the river was chilly, and I was glad for my top coat when the cab dropped me off at a hotel near Tower Bridge.

Even though I was not in formal dress, Holmes invited me up to a room and had me change into the clothes of a common workman. "We're going to take a walk down by the docks, Watson, and I'm afraid your gentleman's tailoring would not fit into that environment and we don't want you to get robbed."

Now suitably attired, Holmes and I made our way into St. Katharine's dock where scores of boats were berthed.

A little further down river towards Wapping and anchored in mid-channel was the ship that he wanted to observe. We soon came across young Wiggins hiding in the shadows of a warehouse. "Those men who left when you was here before came back, Mr. Holmes, about a half hour ago. Just the four of 'em, no other passengers in the van," he whispered.

"Thank you, Wiggins. You may take the rest of the night off," answered the detective, handing some coins to the boy, who clutched them gratefully. "Just be sure that you, or one of the other Irregulars, are here by noon tomorrow to keep track of their comings and goings."

"Thank you, Mr. Holmes," replied the eager boy, who then added, "One other thing, when they came back and rowed out to the ship, there was a lot of yelling and shouting. I couldn't understand most of it 'cause it weren't English, but somebody was awful mad."

"Yes, I expect so," replied the detective, who thought a moment and then gave an additional instruction. "Tomorrow, make sure there are at least two of you and have someone follow the van. If it goes anywhere other than the Criterion theatre, have them report to me or Dr. Watson at Baker Street to let us know where they've gone."

"Aye, sir," answered the lad.

After the boy took off, Holmes and I manoeuvred into position to view the vessel in question. It appeared rather opulent and I could see the name 'Havets Konge' on the stern. I asked Holmes. "Whose ship is that?"

"I enquired at the dock master's office earlier today, Watson," he replied. "That is 'The King of the Sea', owned by Vilmar Fredericksen. A prince of the Isle of Agurk."

"Danish royalty?" I asked quizzically.

"Not precisely. The Isle of Agurk lies off the west coast of northern Europe where Germany borders Denmark. Both countries have attempted to lay claim to it but the population there continues to assert independence. The ruling family claims kinship to the former King Frederick VII of Denmark by way of a nephew or cousin, I believe. At any rate, they will not accept German rule and assert that they declared independence from Denmark when Frederick died. Vilmar is the only son of their Queen Sorena, who has ruled there since her father died without a male heir some eighteen years ago. He is therefore the prince and heir-apparent. He is young and wealthy. His ship has been moored here for nearly a month. He is apparently on holiday and has been taking in the various night time attractions London has to offer, including our theatres."

I shook my head to be sure that the lateness of the hour was not affecting my thought process. "You mean to say this Agurk prince has sent his men out to kidnap British actresses? That's outrageous! Have you informed Lestrade?"

My friend shook his head. "One does not accuse foreign royalty without proof, Doctor. That is why we're here tonight.

I am going to sneak aboard that vessel and learn what I can. You will remain here and act only if I am caught or have not returned within an hour. In such a case, you must go to the Yard and fetch the police."

Holmes started to go, but I grabbed his arm. "Wait! Won't he have diplomatic immunity?"

The detective shook his head. "Agurk is not recognised as a separate country by Great Britain. We consider him a citizen of Denmark and so he is not covered by a diplomatic treaty. But should it become necessary, you should advise the police that his men will likely be armed."

Before I could protest further, he had slipped beyond my reach and out of whisper range. Following the shadows, he took a roundabout route, and I lost sight of him for a few minutes before I spotted him again making his way towards the vessel in a rowing boat that he had purloined. He soon disappeared behind the hull. All was quiet now aboard the ship, as it was nearly midnight. Only a single lantern lit the deck, and the portholes along the side were all dark except for two which appeared to be flickering with candlelight.

I kept a sharp eye out for any movements aboard ship as well as listening for any sounds that might indicate that Holmes had been spotted. Fortunately, I had brought my opera glasses to the theatre that evening and had slipped them into my workman's coat along with my Webley revolver. This gave me a closer view of the vessel, but in the inky night, there was still not much to make out. Then I saw what appeared to be a shadow on the starboard side. I watched in consternation as it inched its way along toward the candlelit portholes, hanging by some sort of strap from the deck rail. I knew that it must be Holmes and feared for his discovery at any moment.

Somehow, he managed to peek into the first window, then slide past it to spy into the second. Suddenly, he dropped into the water, keeping his body straight to minimise the splash. My heart leapt to my throat when he did not immediately come up again, but this was then replaced by fear that he might, as the porthole opened and the silhouette of a fierce-looking head popped out. It was a man with unruly hair looking as if he had just jumped out of bed. He rubbed his eyes and peered all around the water, looking for signs of some swimmer. Finally, he shook his head, yawned, and closed the porthole again.

Well over a minute had passed, and I wondered just how long Holmes could hold his breath. As two minutes approached, I started to panic and wondered how I should go about searching for him.

I scanned the water with my glasses and at last spotted a figure climbing up onto a jetty. Again, taking a circuitous route, Holmes made his way back to my position, soaking wet but with a look of satisfaction on his face. As a doctor, I was more concerned for his health at that moment and insisted that we get back to the hotel so he could change into dry clothes. On the way, I asked, "I thought surely you were about to be caught, Holmes. Was it worth the midnight swim?"

He flashed a brief smile. "Indeed, Watson. Let us settle before a warm fire and some brandy, and I will tell you what I have discovered."

Chapter Six

Now into dry clothes in front of a roaring fire with brandy in hand, we took advantage of the hotel room Holmes had procured for the evening, and he advised me of the details of his nocturnal adventure.

"There was a night watchman on the bridge," he said. "Even though he was asleep, I felt I could not chance boarding the vessel so boldly. I had noted the dimly lit portholes and presumed that there was some sort of nightlight for whoever was sleeping in those quarters. I had formed a hypothesis and needed to confirm it before involving the authorities. I formed a loop with my belt, and, using the lowest deck rail, I edged my way along the side to get a look into those windows."

His countenance grew grave, and he leaned forward with his next remark. "The first room I viewed was a large space with several beds and lavishly appointed. Only two of the beds were occupied, though a third appeared to have been recently in use. The sleeping forms were two women, both red-haired and comely. They did not appear to be in distress, although I recognised that the lock on the door was of a type that could only be opened from the outside."

"They were prisoners then?" I exclaimed with outrage.

"I would assume so, Doctor. I then moved on to the next porthole. This cabin was smaller but luxurious, and I noted two naked people asleep in the bed. One, whom I supposed to be the Prince, and the other an attractive, fair-skinned redhead who could not have been more than sixteen years old. Unfortunately, my silhouette upon the window had cast a shadow which somehow stirred the Prince. I dropped into the water as quietly as I could, swam underneath the boat, and came up by the jetty."

"So, we go to Lestrade now?" I said eagerly.

"Yes," replied my friend. "What we have is still circumstantial. We don't know that the ladies's cabin was actually locked or that any of them were aboard involuntarily. What we need Scotland Yard for is to help us set up a trap to catch them in the act, and I believe that I have the perfect bait."

The next morning back at Baker Street Holmes had left early while I slept in, tired from our exertions the night before. When my companion is hot on the scent he can go with minimal sleep and food for days, so this did not surprise me. While I breakfasted, I also kept an eye out for any news from Wiggins or one of the other Irregulars. I assumed Holmes was concerned that the kidnappers would move on to another theatre after so many failed attempts at the Criterion.

Just after I had finished and was settling down with the morning paper, Holmes came bursting in and cried out, "Ah, Watson, good. You have eaten, I see. I must implore you to slip into your coat, for the heat wave has lessened its attack upon the city today. I have a cab waiting, and we must be off to the Yard."

I threw aside the paper and rushed to grab my coat, hat, and stick. Following my companion down the steps and out to the street, I was pleasantly surprised to find the four-wheeler already occupied by our client, Miss Judith Morrow.

I tipped my bowler as I sat down and said, "A pleasure to see you again, Miss Morrow. How is your mother?"

She bit her lip and replied, "Her time grows short, Doctor. Dr. Talmadge says any time now."

I placed my hand upon her forearm and nodded my condolences.

"Time to mourn later, Doctor," she said bravely. "There are other lives that we can save, and I am grateful to you and Mr. Holmes for your assistance in doing so."

I had to admit that I was somewhat concerned at Holmes using Miss Morrow as his 'perfect bait'. Her recent separation from her lover and the health issue with her mother must have been weighing heavily upon her. Holmes's answer to me the night before was based solely upon his logical mind and, though plausible, not always true for every personality. Yet, Miss Morrow was a strong young woman, and I hoped this distraction would be of good use to her.

Arriving at the Yard, we again found Lestrade in his office. As soon as he saw us in his doorway with Miss Morrow, he groaned. "Not again. I've told you we're doing all we can."

Miss Morrow barged in and strode swiftly up to the desk in preparation for berating the man, but Holmes placed a hand upon her shoulder and spoke out first. "We have new information, Inspector. We know who is behind the kidnapping attempts and believe that he has already snatched up three other women."

The Inspector threw down his pencil and demanded, "You have proof of this, Mr. Holmes?"

"I have substantial circumstantial evidence and will be able to provide you with positive proof tonight if you will assist us."

The sceptical police official waved us to be seated. As there were only two chairs, I held one for Miss Morrow. Holmes insisted I take the other in deference to my old war-wounded leg. He then outlined what we had learned, including the fact that he was fairly certain that the bridge watchman of the previous evening had been Miss Barlow's assailant. After laying this groundwork, he proposed his plan to the Inspector. Lestrade frowned and asked Miss Morrow, "You are willing to go along with this? It could be dangerous."

"It could be fatal to these other women if we do not act!" she exclaimed.

The Inspector reluctantly agreed and our plans for the evening were arranged in great detail. When we left, our companion turned to Holmes and asked, "You are sure this will work? How do we know this Prince's henchmen won't grab a different girl?"

"Do not be so modest, Miss Morrow. You have the three features these men have been ordered to find."

"Being an actress?" she guessed.

Holmes shook his head. "The theatre is what attracted the Prince in the first place, and the Criterion has exactly the type of woman he is seeking. Young, attractive, and red-haired."

I spoke out at that. "He has a fetish for specific hair colour?"

"Think of our four victims, Watson. Not a true blonde, brunette nor raven-haired beauty among them. Barlow is ginger-haired, Viola is strawberry blonde, Rouseau is a copper redhead, and Haynes has chestnut coils. The women on the ship were three redheads of varying shades. If we dangle Miss Morrow's raspberry locks in front of them, if you will forgive me, Miss, in addition to her age and beauty, they will salivate at the opportunity to obtain what their employer is looking for. Plus, I will ensure that she is the one they pick up tonight."

"That appears to be the most dangerous part of the plan, Holmes," I argued. "You will certainly be outnumbered."

"I have a contingency for that, Doctor, that will make me more than a match for them."

That evening, while I was accompanying Inspector Lestrade and a contingent of constables to St. Katharine's dock, Holmes put his plan into action. He later described it to me thus:

After the show ended, all actors and other personnel were held back so that Holmes and Miss Morrow would be the first to leave. The guards had kept the crowd back at a reasonable distance in the alley but could only spread themselves so far. Just as Holmes and the actress had gotten beyond them, Regan came out escorting Miss Barlow and Miss Rouseau, thus being about fifty feet behind. They timed it to reach the guard's perimeter just as Holmes was gaining the exit to the street. A man came up to Miss Morrow just as Holmes had turned to look back to make sure that there was no danger behind them.

The stranger grabbed Morrow's arm and attempted to drag her to a waiting van. Holmes, having already recognised the individual before he turned, pulled his gun from his pocket and pointed it at the fellow as he snatched up her other arm. In a dialect common along the river, he demanded, "Not so fast, m'fine fellow. I know what you're up to and who you work for, and I've decided to grab a reward for m'self. You just take us to that van and get in the back with us without any trouble and tell your driver I've got the prize your Prince wants."

At the sight of Holmes pulling his gun, Regan ordered the ladies back inside and rushed to aid the detective, while the crowd parted as he ran towards the street. This had all been pre-arranged to establish Holmes's *bona fides* as a kidnapper himself. What went awry was that the true kidnapper, having manoeuvred Miss Morrow between them, pulled a gun of his own behind her and attempted to fire at Holmes. The detective was forced to shoot the fellow, but the kidnapper's gun went off and Regan went down. The constable on duty who was cognizant of the plan knew that he was supposed to back off in the face of Holmes's gun, but instinctively he raced up to Holmes, who pointed the gun at him and said, "Don't do it! Go take care of that other fellow and leave us be, or you'll be next!"

The constable remembered his role and ran to Regan's aid while Holmes dragged Miss Morrow, who was doing a fine acting job of trying to get away, to the van and pointed his gun at the driver. "You! Take us to your master's ship and be quick about it!"

Seeing that he was about to deliver such a prize to his employer, he gave no thought to his comrade, set his whip to his horse, and drove furiously away with Holmes and Miss Morrow in the back.

Well-hidden, Lestrade and I, along with six policemen, anxiously awaited the arrival of Holmes. As time dragged on, I could only hope that my friend's scheme had not gone awry.

Confident as I was in him, there are always unknowns that can interfere with the best-laid plans. However, at about the time we would have expected a vehicle to arrive from the theatre after the show's end, the same van we had seen the previous evening pulled up. The driver hopped down, opened up the back, and ordered Holmes and Miss Morrow onto a rowing boat. The detective played his part as a ruffian thoroughly, however. He pointed his gun at the driver and told him, "We ain't goin' nowhere. You go tell your Prince that I've got a prize female just to his liking, and he can have her as soon as he pays me for her. Otherwise, I've got other buyers who'll give a handsome fee for this pretty one."

Hesitating because he knew the Prince did not like to be forced to do anything, but afraid to face this gunman, the driver chose the better part of valour and rowed across to the ship, then retreated onto the deck, and disappeared below where even from that distance shouting was soon heard. Holmes held Miss Morrow at the corner of the van, in case they needed to duck behind it for cover.

Finally, the Prince emerged with the driver from below deck. The latter rowed them both back to where Holmes and Miss Morrow were waiting on the quayside. Wearing a brightly coloured dressing gown of red and gold over white trousers, he gazed upon this prize female he was expected to buy. He looked younger than I expected. I had only glimpsed his head in the dark the previous night and thought of him as a lustful man in his thirties. Now he appeared little more than twenty. His youthful smile leered lecherously at Miss Morrow. Unfortunately for him, it was as unattractive as it was unwelcome. I could just make out that the left side of his face was significantly covered by a large purple birthmark. It was triangular in shape, running from under his eye down to his jaw and back to his ear. I understood now why he felt he had to have women brought to him.

In heavily accented English, he demanded what price this rude sailor wanted for his wench. Not wanting to be turned down, yet still pretending to be greedy, Holmes had decided that at this stage he would ask for £20. A hefty sum for a street thug, but a pittance for a prince with his own vessel. He had guessed correctly. Vilmar Fredericksen reached into an inner pocket of his garment and pulled out a pocketbook, at which point Holmes raised his weapon to aim at the man's head and said, "No quick moves! You bring the money over here, hand it to the lady, and back off. I'll take it from her and leave you to your pleasure. If anyone tries to follow, I'll be trading lead for gold."

The Prince smiled at this English fool and started to hand the money to the driver, but Holmes said, "No! I said *you* bring it yourself! I want you between me and your men in case somebody gets an itchy trigger finger."

The Prince frowned but reluctantly stepped forward, stroking his moustache ever more appreciatively as he got a closer look at this beautiful redhead. He counted out the money and held it out to Miss Morrow. Holmes nudged her from behind, and she grudgingly took the notes in her left hand.

Once she had it, she held her hand high, pulled a gun from behind her back where it had been hidden in her bustle, and joined Holmes in covering the Prince. Her hand raising was our signal to charge in. Lestrade blew his police whistle, and we all rushed to the scene. I had my Webley in hand pointing at the men on deck just in case, and the Inspector quickly cuffed the protesting Prince. Later the ship was boarded with one of the constables freeing the three women from below deck. Once back on land they ran crying to Miss Morrow as the only other female in sight. Once she explained what was happening, they all descended upon Holmes with hugs and kisses until he was finally able to extricate himself.

Epilogue

Being caught in the act, Prince Vilmar Fredericksen was charged with kidnapping and enforced servitude, among other crimes. During interviews while awaiting trial, it came to light that he deeply resented his mother, the amber-haired Queen Sorena whose very name meant 'stern' in English and which was apparently the way she had raised him. In turn he had stolen funds from the Agurk treasury, confiscated the ship and ordered its crew to do his bidding upon the threat of death. He had learned English from one of his tutors growing up and therefore chose to sail to London. Adhering to the misconception that English women were sexless and prudish, he assumed them to be so like his mother that forcing them to serve his every lustful whim, would somehow satisfy his yearning for the deep pain he wished to inflict upon her.

When she was informed of his actions and arrest she made no effort for his return to face justice in his own country. As far as she was concerned, he had disgraced himself and was no longer fit to be a citizen of Agurk, let alone its future ruler. Instead, she issued a proclamation that her younger sister would now be the heir-apparent.

Vilmar was sentenced to twenty years imprisonment but was killed by another prisoner after just eight months – it seems that they did not appreciate his superior attitude towards them.

The women we had freed were two waitresses and a singer, and they all managed to overcome their ordeal, though I have

199

heard that the youngest moved to America to get away from the memory of her imprisonment and sexual abuse. Hopefully, a fresh start will assist her recovery.

Brian Regan only suffered a bullet grazing his ribs. Being the big man that he is, it merely threw him off balance without serious injury. But before he could get back up to go to Holmes's aid, Katrina Rouseau had rushed to him and thrown herself upon his chest, crying out his name and imploring him to not be hurt. It transpired that she had been just as infatuated with him as he was with her, and they were married at the end of that theatrical season.

Miss Morrow was grateful to Holmes for listening to her and acting upon her request, but he would take no payment from her, considering it his civic duty. After her mother had succumbed to her long fight with breast cancer, the actress returned to the theatre the following season and maintained a successful career on the London stage.

Gluttony

The Case of the Final Morsel

Chapter One

The 31st October is All Hallow's Eve – the day dedicated to remembering the dead. By strange coincidence, it was on this day in 1886 that marked the beginning of a deadly case for my friend, Sherlock Holmes. We had just finished lunch when our landlady, Mrs. Hudson, announced that we had a visitor and gave his calling card to the detective.

After reading it, Holmes told Mrs. Hudson to show the man up and handed the card over to me. I read the following: 'Marvin Armitage, *The London Trident*'. It also included the address of the popular thrice-weekly newspaper. I handed it back to my friend saying, "I don't recall the name, Holmes. Do you know him?"

"Only by reputation, Doctor. He is the food editor and restaurant reviewer. You will recall the Giuseppe Rivano case?"[1]

"Of course, you saved him from a murder charge against a food critic who was blackmailed into writing a bad review of Rivano's Ristorante."

"Exactly, and when we solved the case and the retractions were written, Armitage was one of those who came to the rescue and wrote a true and positive review to help bring people back to Rivano's."

---

[1] *The Adventure of the Italian Gourmet* in *A Sherlock Holmes Alphabet of Cases* (Volume 2) by Roger Riccard.

"And I'm glad I did!" came a voice from the doorway. "The meals I've had there have been among the most excellent I've ever reviewed."

I turned towards the door and beheld a massive human being. He was not tall, perhaps five foot seven, but his bulk was enormous. Even with my doctor's eye I could not guess his weight but presumed it to be well over twenty stone. Unfortunately for his health, it was not spread throughout his shoulders and chest muscles, but had settled into his stomach which brushed both sides of the door frame as he entered.

"Mr. Armitage!" cried Holmes with sincere warmth. "Welcome, sir. Please have a seat there on the sofa."

Armitage smiled, and said in self-deprecation, "Where else would I sit? You don't have a chair in here that would fit me."

Holmes smiled and introduced me, "This is my colleague, Dr. John Watson who is good enough to assist me so anything that you have to say can be declared in front of him."

"Good afternoon, Doctor. I am glad to make your acquaintance. But please, do not mention the word diet to me. I've heard it all."

"As you wish, sir," I replied with a sardonic smile.

Once we were all seated, Holmes asked, "What brings you to my door, Mr. Armitage? It cannot be urgent, for you took time to enjoy a lunch of mushroom-smothered steak at The Humpty Dumpling."

Armitage, like so many others before him, looked startled at Holmes's statement of facts about his recent whereabouts. "Oh no you don't, Mr. Holmes," he cried. "I've heard about these pronouncements of yours. You could not possibly know that. You must have seen me there presently and just beat me to your address by mere minutes!"

Holmes shook his head, "I have been here all morning, sir, as Watson and Mrs. Hudson will attest."

"Then how ..."

Holmes gestured with his hand towards the writer, "The sawdust clinging to your shoes and trouser cuffs is from the wood used on the floor of that establishment. There is a slight drip of mushroom sauce on your lapel, and your breath, despite your best intentions, gives off the odour of that unique dish. That particular combination adds up to the restaurant I have named. Now, I repeat, what brings you to Baker Street?"

Armitage just shook his head, "Well your reputation is certainly well-earned, Mr. Holmes. As to my seeking you out, it is at the insistence of my editor. The newspaper keeps getting threats directed at me on account of my columns. Especially my restaurant reviews."

He reached into his inner breast pocket, pulled out a folded paper, and handed it to Holmes. "This is my reason for today's visit."

Holmes took the message as he observed, "You do not seem particularly concerned about this threat, Mr. Armitage."

The critic held up a podgy hand in a backhanded wave, "Bah! I've been getting threats of one sort or another ever since I took this job. The person who held the position before me did as well. Different people have different tastes. Just as beauty is in the eye of the beholder, so taste is in the tip of the palate. I have never been physically attacked. Though I have been the victim of verbal abuse from time to time as well as these written complaints. My editor is overreacting but insisted that I bring this to you for your opinion."

Holmes glimpsed at it and handed it over to me, "Watson, be so good as to use your narrative skills and read this aloud as if you were the author."

I took up the typewritten page and, after a brief glance to evaluate the tone, cleared my throat and read as follows:

To Fatty Armitage,

You, sir, are a fraud and a fake. You obviously have no talent for taste as your bulbous size shows you will eat anything without regard for quality, so long as there is sufficient quantity for your gross appetite. How you can dare to write critical reviews of London's restaurants is an affront to responsible journalism. But restaurateurs

```
will  soon  be  able  to  taste  victory,  all
because your palate is so warped, you won't
even  taste  your  demise  when  it  comes.  Enjoy
your  meals  this  week,  one  of  them  will  be
your last.

  A True Connoisseur
```

"This was dated two days ago," I declared.

Armitage added, "The newspaper received it yesterday afternoon. It was addressed to both the editor and myself so the office boy delivered it to him first. It triggered a level of concern in him above others that I have received and so my editor insisted that I bring it to you."

Holmes nodded as he took the document back from me. He studied the paper, held it to the light to discern its watermark, and ran his finger along each written line. I knew from experience that he was not reading the words, but studying the typed letters for any unique characteristics.

He finally lowered it to his lap and addressed Armitage, "Your editor was correct to have cause to be concerned. These are not the rantings of some upset restaurant patron. This was written by a highly intelligent person as indicated by the vocabulary. The paper is good quality as suggested by the watermark. The fact that this person has access to, and possibly owns, this typewriter indicates someone of at least moderate means, or working in a professional occupation again implying that they are well-educated. The neatness of the typing demonstrates that it was not typed in haste but was carefully thought out. There are implications of passion, prejudice, and a deep-seated anger in the tone. The fact that it is typewritten could also indicate that it is someone whose handwriting you, or your editor, might recognise and therefore knows you and your habits. All this makes for a clever and dangerous adversary. Someone who could conceivably devise a method to poison your food in such a fashion as to not be perceived. In my opinion, you are in extreme danger, sir."

Armitage looked abashed, and suddenly concerned "You really think so, Mr. Holmes?"

My friend stared at the man gravely and said, "I would not bet your life on my being wrong."

Chapter Two

The reporter took out a large red handkerchief and wiped his brow as nervous fear began to sink in. "What shall I do, Mr. Holmes? Eating is my livelihood I cannot just stop."

"As I recall you write more than just restaurant reviews," answered Holmes. "You also publish recipes and make recommendations as to local markets for various types of foodstuffs. I suggest that you stick to those tasks for the time being, until we have had a chance to investigate who this enemy of yours might be. Do you have any thoughts on the matter as to whom hates you enough to threaten your life?"

Armitage folded his hands across the top of his ample stomach and pursed his lips in thought. At last, he said, "My last bad review was nearly a fortnight ago. I lambasted Alexander the Grate's café in Lamberly for their small portions, bland sauces, and their cheese dishes which they advertise so blatantly, yet provide so limitedly. Although I did not condemn them altogether, I did suggest that there were better alternatives for those seeking a wide variety of cheese dishes from the continent. The last time I advised the public to avoid a restaurant completely was nearly a month ago. I suggested *The Meat and Greet Steakhouse* in Soho used inferior and questionable meat, and that pet owners in the area should make sure that their dogs and cats were locked in the house every night. It was quite disgusting, Mr. Holmes."

"Was there any immediate repercussions from the owner?" asked the detective.

"I believe that he threatened to sue the paper for libel but his correspondence to the editor only called me some vile names. There was no threat of violence."

Holmes nodded, "And you can think of no other possibilities?"

"No, Mr. Holmes no one else comes to mind."

"Very well. We shall look into the matter. Do you have a trustworthy cook at home?"

"Oh, yes, Mrs. Carver. She's a widow and has been with me for three years. She knows my tastes exactly. She comes in on days when I'm not out reviewing restaurants. I'm fortunate that she does not leave me to run her own establishment for she's as good a cook as anyone I've ever reviewed."

"I suggest that you advise her of your situation and that she double-checks all her ingredients. Also, she should not accept any deliveries from any person that she doesn't know, even if they claim to be from the shops where she usually orders. Also you should not eat out for the time being."

"I will take your advice to heart, Mr. Holmes. I hope you can solve the matter quickly. I have several restaurants that I should review over the next few weeks. I will naturally postpone them though my editor will only be patient for so long."

"I am currently able to devote myself exclusively to your case, Mr. Armitage. I will be in contact directly I have news."

Armitage left us, waddling his way out of the door and down the stairs. My medical curiosity made me watch him until he had exited our domicile. I then turned to my companion. "Whoever is threatening him must be impatient, Holmes. In his obese condition it's a wonder that he's still alive. How do you propose investigating?"

"As always, Watson, we must first look to motives."

"That seems rather apparent from the tone of this letter," I said, holding up the document Armitage had left with us. Someone wants revenge for a bad review."

"Not necessarily, Doctor. As you recall from previous discussions we have had, there are many motives for murder. The tone of that letter could be interpreted in more than one

210

way. It could also be a misdirection. Pointing us towards one motive when there is another in play."

"How do you mean, Holmes?"

He raised a forefinger, much like a lecturer, "Just for argument's sake, suppose that there is someone in love with his cook, Mrs. Carver, but he can't entice her to leave Armitage's employment. Eliminate Armitage and she becomes more susceptible to remarry. All the while the suitor is throwing suspicions in another direction so as not to become a suspect."

"You think that revenge is not the motive?" I enquired with surprise."

"I am always wary of situations that appear too obvious, Watson. The review of Alexander's restaurant does not seem to rise to this level of provocation, and the time lapse since the steakhouse review seems too long for someone with the level of vehemence intoned in that letter. I shall not eliminate those suspects, but I intend to look at a variety of possibilities as to whom might wish Armitage dead or scared and out of the way."

"So where will you start?"

"First, I shall meet with the editor who sent Armitage in our direction. I want to get his unbiased opinion on why he was so concerned about this letter over the other threats that have been received in the past. I know that you have patients this afternoon, Doctor, so I will keep you appraised of my findings when I return."

"It's Sunday, Holmes," I pointed out. "Will the editor be in his office?"

"Editors have no set hours, Watson. The news dictates their work. *The London Trident* publishes an evening edition on Monday, Wednesday, and Friday. If he's not available I have other sources that I can talk to. I may take dinner at The Meat and Greet tonight, just to ascertain whether Armitage's review was justified. If I do not return by five o'clock, please advise Mrs. Hudson that I'll be eating out."

With that, he threw on his overcoat against the Autumn chill and ventured out to begin his investigation. A half hour later I also left to visit the first of two patients that I had that afternoon. Little did I know that I was to have another that evening.

Chapter Three

My patients that day were not especially challenging. A broken wrist which I was merely examining to ensure that no complications had set in and that it was healing correctly, and a severe cold which I was endeavouring to keep from turning into something worse through medication and strict routine of warm blankets and hot soup.

Returning home, I had plenty of time before dinner to catch up on the day's post, and as five o'clock came and went I advised Mrs. Hudson that Holmes would not be returning for the evening meal. Thus, she served up my dinner early, at five-thirty, for I had missed afternoon tea while with my patient. Afterwards, I decided to look at some back issues of *The London Trident* to see what other reviews Armitage had written recently. Fortunately, Holmes keeps stacks of various newspapers dating back several weeks in the event something may be of import to a case. I noted a few columns that were unfavourable, but nothing so scathing as those Armitage had already mentioned. However, I felt that I should inform Holmes, as some people are more sensitive than others when it comes to criticism.

Just after seven, Holmes returned. At first, I thought that we had a visitor for the sound of footsteps on our stairs was nothing like his usual pattern. It was more trudging and unsteady. He opened the door with a swift burst, cast his hat onto the rack, and started to remove his overcoat but let it fall to the floor as he made a dash for the water closet. No words can reproduce the sounds that emitted from behind that door. Suffice it to say, it must have been a full two minutes before I could even get in a word to ask if there was anything I could get for him. He choked out 'bottled water!' and I retrieved a glass of the same for him from our sideboard. I entered the enclosure to find him leaning over the sink with the sounds of flushing water draining the toilet. I thought how fortunate we were that Mrs. Hudson had modernised her home with indoor plumbing just months before we had moved in. I handed Holmes the glass and he took it gratefully and washed out his mouth.

When he felt steady enough, we retreated to the sitting room. I had rarely seen Holmes ill before, and on those occasions that he was it was usually from either a relapsing cold, or fatigue from overwork and lack of sleep. Otherwise, his only incapacitations, not counting his occasional usage of drugs, had been contusions or lacerations from his amateur boxing bouts or criminal encounters.

Back in the sitting room, Holmes sat on the sofa. Once he caught his breath, he declared, "Armitage's review of The Meat and Greet Steakhouse was unfortunately accurate, Doctor. I believe that they are in violation of the sale of Food and Drugs Act of 1875. I shall have to report them to the authorities."

I poured him a glass of medicinal ginger ale and advised him to drink it slowly. As he did so I asked, "Did you learn anything else while you were there?"

He set down his glass, closed his eyes while pinching the top of his nose, then took a deep breath and replied, "The owner, Angus Roarke, could not possibly be the writer of the letter to Armitage. He's a lower-class braggart with too hot a temper and too little education to have been so articulate an author of that threat."

"Could he not have had someone write it for him?"

Holmes shook his head and immediately regretted it. Holding his hands to his temples he replied, "His personality is too volatile and also conceited to associate with anyone smarter than himself, and he certainly has no patience to learn how to use a typewriter. No, I'm afraid he's not our man, as criminal as his cuisine may be."

I shrugged and replied, "Well, while you were out, I went through back issues of *The London Trident* and found a few more critical reviews that Armitage has written recently. None as bad as those he mentioned to us, but still, a more sensitive soul could have taken affront."

I held up three issues of the newspaper opened to the appropriate page, "Shall I read them to you or would you prefer to wait until your stomach is more settled and you can concentrate?"

He took another sip of ginger ale and laid down on the sofa, hugging a pillow to his abdomen he closed his eyes and requested, "Read them please, Watson. I need the distraction."

I was about halfway through Armitage's review of the Torts and Tarts bakery when I was interrupted by the sound of footsteps on the stairs. The sound was too heavy to be Mrs. Hudson, who would normally announce a visitor, especially at this hour. I shifted in my chair, ready to spring in case our visitor had confrontation in mind, but just before the top step was reached Holmes called out, "Come in, Lestrade!"

The weasel-faced Scotland Yard inspector opened our door and stopped, momentarily confused at the sight of Holmes on the sofa and me in the opposite chair, when habitually those positions were reversed. Holmes calling out his name before he opened the door didn't help his expectations either.

"How did you know it was me, Holmes?" he enquired with a tilt of his head and furrowed brow.

Holmes, still without looking up from his prone position, replied, "Your frequent visits here have ingrained the cadence of your footsteps into my memory, Inspector."

My companion finally sat up and took another sip of ginger ale, "Forgive me," he said. "I was temporarily incapacitated by some meat, the mystery of which I have yet to solve. Have a chair and tell us what we can do for you."

The Inspector removed his bowler and sat in the chair next to mine across from Holmes. "Interesting. You are the second case of food poisoning I've come across tonight, Mr. Holmes.

Unfortunately, the first was fatal and we are fairly certain that it was deliberate. I understand that Marvin Armitage, now the late Marvin Armitage, visited you today?"

Holmes leaned forward, elbows on his knees as he anticipated Lestrade's next statement by enquiring, "How was it done?"

"According to his housekeeper, when he arrived home for the evening, he was eating a baked potato purchased from a street vendor. This was not unusual. You are aware that he is a large man with a prodigious appetite and such an item would be a mere snack for him before his dinner."

Holmes shook his head and leaned back on the sofa "The fool! I had just warned him this afternoon about not eating out until his case was resolved!"

"That's why I've come to you, Mr. Holmes. His cook, Mrs. Carver, told us that he had planned to see you today regarding some threats that he had received. I need any information he may have told you to further my investigation."

Holmes waved to me, "Watson, be so good as to show the Inspector the letter which prompted Armitage's visit to us."

I retrieved the piece of paper in question and handed it over to Lestrade. He read it and remarked, "Well, that seems plain enough. What did you tell Armitage?"

"I advised him to refrain from any further restaurant reviews for the time being, not to eat out, and to stick to the meals prepared by Mrs. Carver. Also, to have her inspect her ingredients and deliveries thoroughly, and not to accept anything supplied by anybody that she didn't know."

"Sound advice," agreed Lestrade. "Too bad he didn't take it. The doctor is still conducting tests but we feel it's likely that the potato was poisoned. He had eaten about half of it and suddenly keeled over as he sat at his desk. We've attempted to track down the street vendor, but he has disappeared. Other hawkers in the area didn't recognise him and said that he was new to that location. Rather an unusual fellow. He wheeled about a cart with the potatoes on a bed of hot coals. When he sold one, they say he wrapped it up and handed it to the customer. I've never known a potato vendor to do that before as usually they just give you the potato unwrapped so as to warm your hands. It is also singular that this one did not pitch his stand where crowds come by but in residential side roads. We found his cart abandoned a few streets away. All the potatoes were gone and the cash box was empty."

Holmes thought for a moment then asked, "What was the potato wrapped in?"

Lestrade had to think as it was not a detail that he had written down. Finally, he snapped his fingers and said, "It was an old newspaper. I remember now. It was doubled over to protect a person's hands from the heat."

"Did you save it?" asked the detective.

The Inspector looked confused, "Why no, Mr. Holmes. What would be the point of that?"

"It may contain evidence," scolded Holmes. "The publisher, the date, which section of the newspaper. Any or all of these things could prove useful."

Lestrade, a little perturbed at being upbraided by this amateur, answered defensively, "And what good would all those things be? It's not as if this fellow would write his name and address or his confession on the newspaper is it! No, you're barking up the wrong tree there. We're looking into the known vendors to try and find the owner, but as he left his cart behind, he has probably fled town having done his deed. If that's all you have to offer, Mr. Holmes, I'll just take my leave and continue my investigation in the morning."

He stood and bade us a good evening. After he left Holmes attempted to stand, then thought better of it. "Watson, I need you to be my legs tonight."

"Anything I can do to help, Holmes," I replied, always anxious to share his adventures.

"You need to go to Armitage's house and retrieve that newspaper before Mrs. Carver disposes of it. While you're there, see if any of the staff noticed the potato vendor and if you can get a description of him. If you can enquire of the neighbours too that would be even better."

I threw on my overcoat and Derby, took up my walking stick, and immediately proceeded to the house of Marvin Armitage, hoping that I would be in time.

Chapter Four

Armitage's home was a modest affair. The two-storey house was just large enough for him and his files. With his bulk, the upstairs was impractical to use daily so it was reserved for his papers and storage. Armitage used a bedroom on the ground floor where he also had an office and there was a dining room next to the kitchen.

It was a young maid, who opened the door, though I noted an older woman in the background who must have been Mrs. Carver, obviously on guard against a late evening visitor.

"Good evening," I said, presenting my card. "I am Dr. John Watson. Sherlock Holmes and I are working on the case of your late employer, Mr. Armitage. I would like to ask a few questions if I may. I promise to be brief. I know this must be quite a shock to you both."

The maid introduced herself as Miss Barret. She was a petite young girl. No more than twenty. Blonde curls escaped from under her mop cap and I imagined that she was quite pretty when not dressed for housework.

Mrs. Carver came forward and took the card from the younger woman. She, in contrast, was a comely widow of perhaps forty with a no-nonsense air about her. Her brown hair was pulled back from her round face into a tight bun and her stout body appeared formidable in its attitude.

She looked at me with a mixture of suspicion and disappointment. Inviting me in she stated, "You and Mr. Holmes are a bit late. What good can you do now?"

Understanding her anger but refusing to accept blame, I replied, "The last thing that Holmes told Mr. Armitage was to not accept food from anyone but you. I can only say that presently we wish only to bring his killer to justice."

Somewhat mollified she asked, "The police have already been here. What more can you do?"

"We have met with Inspector Lestrade. Holmes is concerned that he may have left some evidence behind. Do you still have the newspaper that the potato was wrapped in?"

The two women looked at each other. Miss Barret said, "I picked it up from the floor and threw it into the rubbish bin in the kitchen."

Mrs. Carver replied, "I set it aside with the firewood for the stove to use as kindling. I haven't lit the stove since then."

"May I have it please?"

She nodded, "Follow me, Doctor."

We all walked single file to the kitchen where Mrs. Carver bent to retrieve the newspaper sheet from the firewood box. She handed it over, however, its condition was not promising, It was smudged from the heat of the potato and being handled by Armitage and the vendor. I could only hope that the publication information would be of some use for my friend. I was suddenly struck by the story it was open upon. It was Armitage's review of The Meat and Greet Steakhouse.

My thoughts were interrupted by Mrs. Carver asking, "If you don't mind my saying so, what good will that do you, Doctor?"

I shrugged, "Mr. Holmes has unique methods for deducing facts from observations. This may give him some clues about the potato vendor. Did either of you happen to see him by chance?"

Mrs. Carver had been busy preparing dinner but Miss Barret had been washing windows and noticed him on the street. She remembered that he seemed tall, but was hunched over as if crippled, he had a red beard and moustache, a brown jacket and Derby, and he was wearing gloves to handle the hot potatoes.

I asked Miss Barret what time the peddler had appeared and she said that it was just a little before five o'clock. I asked a few more questions about him, and I also learned that she had only been employed by Armitage for a month. She had replaced the previous housemaid who had got married.

I was about to leave, then remembered Holmes's example of an alternative theory and asked, "Do either of you have a suitor?"

Scowling at the seeming impertinence of the query, Mrs. Carver grumbled, "What sort of question is that to ask at a time like this?"

Realising what she must be thinking I quickly explained, "You misunderstand, madam. Holmes is considering multiple theories and one of them is that someone wishes to entice one of you away from your employment so that you would be free to marry."

"Hmph, not likely," declared the widow with a huff. But Miss Barret lowered her head and shyly stated, "I have a beau, Doctor, and he and I are engaged, but he certainly would not have killed Mr. Armitage. We need my income to afford to get married."

I thanked the ladies and took this information and the newspaper back to Baker Street. I found Holmes asleep on the sofa. Even a man of his unique constitution will succumb to the exhaustion brought on by food poisoning. However, quiet as I was, Holmes awoke as I was placing my hat and coat on the rack by the door.

In a scratchy voice, undoubtedly due to the sore throat from his earlier episode, he said, "Watson, would you be so good as to fetch me another ginger ale and tell me what transpired at Armitage's house?"

I poured out another glass for him and set it and the newspaper on the table where he could reach them at his leisure. "I'm afraid it's not in good shape. But it does contain Armitage's review of the steakhouse. That cannot be coincidental. The housemaid said that she saw the vendor while she was washing the windows and gave me a description of him."

Holmes cocked his head at that, "Armitage failed to mention he had a housemaid. Tell me about her. Does she live in?"

"She's a pretty little thing of perhaps twenty years of age. Petite, blonde, shy. She only comes in every other day to do the cleaning and just started a month ago. She is engaged and needs the income from her work to afford to get married. Mrs. Carver laughed at the thought of re-marrying. Both of the ladies are quite upset at this tragedy and I am concerned for their future employment."

Holmes picked up his pipe, then thought better of it with his throat so raw, so he merely chewed on the stem without lighting it. "So, the scenario I proposed in the example of Mrs. Carver does not apply to either of them. Had Barret ever seen this potato hawker before?"

"She had not, but then she only washes those windows irregularly. I still cannot believe Armitage would buy food from a stranger after you having warned him."

Holmes shook his head, "Very likely he took the note literally when it said 'last meal' and felt that a snack was safe. He also probably thought that a street trader could not poison his entire stock of food on the off chance that he should wish to purchase a single potato. I am surprised that Armitage was not suspicious of this unusual vendor. No one else sells potatoes in that area, or in the way he does."

"Perhaps he thought it was some new contrivance that the man was trying out," I offered.

"Foolish in light of the threat that he'd received," barked Holmes. "I'm sure that the vendor kept aside one specific potato for Armitage, likely the largest one he had, knowing Armitage's propensity for large portions."

Holmes put down his pipe and reached for the paper I had set down, "Now let us see what this newspaper tells us."

He unfolded it and, seeing how crinkled it was, frowned, but he smoothed it out enough so that he could read it. Noticing the review of the steakhouse he commented, "Our culprit certainly has a macabre sense of humour, Doctor."

Chapter Five

"Holmes," I said with concern, "Don't you find it coincidental that you are poisoned by The Meat and Greet Steakhouse on the same day that Armitage is poisoned by food wrapped in their review? Could the killer have seen Armitage come here and then decided to follow you, poison you, and then poison Armitage? Perhaps he felt that you were too big a threat to risk, and so put his plan into action today."

Holmes shook his head, "You know how I loathe coincidences, Watson. But in this case, I am afraid it is just that. Unless the killer has an accomplice, it would have been impossible for him to be at the restaurant and in front of Armitage's house in the time frame that these events occurred."

Then I remembered Holmes's intention to visit the newspaper office, "Was Armitage's editor of any use to you?"

"Robert Forbes? No, he was not in the office," replied my companion. "I did get to talk to one of the reporters who was finishing a story for tomorrow's edition. He said that most of the staff were indifferent towards Armitage. Some were disgusted at his appearance but no one was actively angry with him. I also verified that no one has come into the office lately to complain about any of the reporters, just the usual flow of letters to the editor in disagreement with various items that had appeared in recent editions. My revelation of the letter Armitage had received was news to him and the food columnist's death was a shock."

Then Holmes asked me to retrieve a sheaf of papers from his overcoat pocket as well as his magnifying glass. I had hung his coat up while he was indisposed and now went to the rack where took out his lens and several sheets of paper from his inner breast pocket. I noted the top sheet had three odd phrases typed onto it.

```
bright vixens jump, dozy fowls quack.

BRIGHT VIXENS JUMP: DOZY FOWLS QUACK?

1234567890!();
```

I handed it to Holmes asking, "What is this, Holmes?"

He gave a slight grin as he took up the threatening letter again, placed it on his lap, and gathered the stack of papers I had handed him. He held them up to me and said, "This is a typewriter test, Watson. These three lines contain all the upper and lower case letters, the numbers, and the most frequently used punctuation on a standard typewriter. I typed these out on every typewriter at the newspaper office."

I nodded, "I see, and you're going to compare them to the threatening letter to see if any of them match." I tilted my head and enquired, "You think that it may be somebody at the newspaper that is responsible then?"

"I am still discerning the motive, Doctor. Despite what the reporter told me, there could be someone in that office with a grudge against Armitage. Remember our old list of motives for murder? Revenge, jealousy, fear of exposure, greed, protection of a loved one, or even a mental disorder. Any of these could apply to Armitage. We do not have enough data to eliminate a cause as yet. Therefore, I imagine possible hypotheses, gather facts, and test the data. After I eliminate the impossible …"

"Whatever is left must be the truth," I replied, finishing his old maxim.

Holmes pointed the lens at me, nodded, and said, "Exactly. Another thing to consider is, why the killer sent the letter at all.

Why give a warning that could cause Armitage to take precautions and therefore not become a victim?"

"Perhaps he wanted the pleasure of seeing Armitage fearful and cowering before his demise?" I postulated.

"That would fit the personality we've assigned to the writer of that letter," agreed Holmes. "He is calculating and not quick-tempered. His intelligence and ego could be such that he was certain of his method. He may have even had an alternate plan in case his original scheme did not work. All things for us to keep in mind during our investigation."

He then bent over to begin examining the documents for comparison. He kept moving the paper back and forth as if trying to bring it into focus. Finally, he slammed the sheet down on the sofa next to him, "It's no use. My eyes are still blurry. How long does the effect of food poisoning last, Doctor?"

"Depending on the severity it could be days," I stepped forward and felt his forehead. "No more fever so you seem to be passing through the other symptoms fairly quickly. I imagine you'll be all right to see in the morning."

Holmes pinched the bridge of his nose and slowly shook his head, "Very well, Doctor. Fortunately, I only ate a few bites of that meal. Obviously, the best option for me at this point is to go to bed and get a fresh start tomorrow. In the meantime, if you care to assist, you can take over and see if there are any unusual characteristics of any letters or punctuation marks that show up in both the threatening letter and in one of the typewriters from the newspaper office. Make any notes of your findings and leave them for me in the likely event I wake up before you."

He trudged off to bed while I gathered up the papers and took them to the dining table where I had better light and could spread them out. I noted some handwritten numbers at the top right corner of each page but could only assume it was Holmes's shorthand for which typewriter the sheet had come from since they had no meaning to me.

As I went through the sheets of paper, I started to notice an anomaly with the threatening letter. I made a note of it and resolved to see if any of the papers Holmes had typed had the same condition.

Three sheets into the stack I found one with the identical fault as the original threat. I set it aside along with Armitage's letter and my note of the discrepancy. I finished checking the last of them but only the one complied with my findings. Then I took myself to bed, though I doubted I would fall asleep anytime soon for I was anxious for the morrow to see what Holmes would do with this information.

The next morning, I was surprised that Holmes was still at home when I entered our sitting room. He was in his dressing gown and drinking tea at the dining table where he was reading my notes and examining the pages with his lens.

He greeted me with what appeared to be perplexity, "Watson, you did an excellent job with your examination of these papers. The lack of serifs on the letter 'f' is quite clear and only shows up on one other sheet."

"Yet you seem concerned, Holmes," I replied as I poured a cup of tea for myself.

He set down the magnifying glass and sat back in his chair, folding his hands across his abdomen. "I had calculated the odds of this threat being from one of his co-workers at roughly twenty-five percent. Like you, I thought it more likely that it would be from a disgruntled restaurant owner. Yet there were still reasons a fellow employee might be involved. What concerns me is which typewriter this offending paper is from."

"Whose is it?"

"His editor, Robert Forbes."

Chapter Six

I gulped the sip of tea that I had taken and set the cup down quickly before it fell from my hand at this news. "But he's the one who sent Armitage to you with the letter in the first instance. Surely, he would not have wished to call your attention to the threat if he was the one making it!"

"That is what puzzles me, Watson." He picked up the unlit pipe from the table next to his saucer, this time a long-stemmed churchwarden, and began chewing on it as he stood and walked to his chair by the fire. "I beg you not to speak to me for the next hour, Watson. I need to process this new data."

I decided, rather than tiptoe about the room for the next sixty minutes, that I would step down the street and treat myself to breakfast at a café, relieving Mrs. Hudson of that task for the morning. After stuffing myself with bacon, sausage, eggs, a slice of tomato, fresh toast with marmalade, and tea, I returned to Baker Street in time to see Holmes emerge from his bedroom fully dressed.

"Where are you off to, Holmes?" I asked as he was obviously leaving to confront someone or to seek more information.

"We, if you will be so kind to join me, Doctor, are off to the offices of *The London Trident.*"

He led the way and hailed a cab, explaining to me the part that he needed me to play in the action he was about to take. Thirty minutes later we entered the newspaper building and made our way to Forbes's office.

As we walked through the large area of desks, tables, and cabinets, I took note of multiple pairs of eyes turned our way. As this was Monday, a publication day, the entire staff was in and busily working away on that evening's edition.

Forbes's office was open and he was poring over a typewritten sheet on his desk, marking it up with a thick pencil to indicate corrections. When Holmes and I arrived at his door he looked up and waved us in, indicating that we should close it and sit down. Holmes did so, however, I remained standing and glanced about at the various desks and workers as Holmes had instructed – I was to observe any adverse reactions to our presence.

"What happened, Holmes?" demanded the editor with his jowly face scowling at the detective.

"That is still to be determined by the post mortem which is our next stop. It appears that Armitage ignored my advice and purchased a poisoned baked potato from a street vendor."

"What was your advice?"

Holmes repeated what he had told Lestrade and at this Forbes seemed satisfied that it was Armitage's own fault for not obeying Holmes's precautions. Holmes then asked a question of his own. "May I see the timetable for your employees for last Tuesday and Wednesday? I am particularly interested in anyone who works late."

Forbes hesitated but decided to comply and pulled out a ledger opening it to the previous week. Holmes viewed the contents carefully, then asked, "This Benson fellow, what does he do?"

"William Benson? He's my obituary writer, Mr. Holmes. It would surprise you how many people die in London each week. It's pretty much a full-time job for him. Oddly enough, he sent a message to say that he was sick today. I had to write Armitage's obituary myself."

"Would he have access to your office after you left for the day?"

"Anyone would if they stayed late enough, but he generally leaves on time as you can see there in the log. What does this have to do with your case?"

"Could he have left and come back after you were gone?"

"I suppose that he could," agreed Forbes.

"Is he a red-headed fellow with a beard and rather tall?"

"He is somewhat tall, Mr. Holmes, but he's clean-shaven and has brown hair." Holmes nodded then pulled the papers from his pocket and set the threatening letter and the typing test from Forbes's typewriter next to each other in front of the editor. "Note the letter 'f' in each document."

The editor leaned over, adjusted his bifocals, and studied the two documents, "They match, so what? Wait, you're not accusing me of Armitage's death? That's crazy!"

"I agree," said the detective. "But that threat was typed on your typewriter. Why did you not notice that?"

Forbes gestured with open palms as if to indicate that he did not know, then said, "I suppose that I'm so used to the broken serif in the documents I type every day that it did not register that this wasn't normal."

Holmes nodded, "A reasonable explanation for now. But tell me about Benson. Has he expressed interest in Armitage's job?"

Forbes thought back, "A few months ago, around the beginning of summer, he approached me about getting off the obituary desk. He wanted to do some 'real' reporting. He did not mention any particular position. I think that he was just tired of the tedium of his job and the lack of variety."

"Would you provide me with his address and then point out his desk to me?" asked Holmes. The editor did so, saying, "I can't believe William Benson would kill for a promotion."

"We shall see, Mr. Forbes," said Holmes. We went to the desk that he had pointed out. Everything atop of it was neat and orderly, as were the drawer contents. Whatever else Benson was, he was a methodical man.

We left, instructing Forbes not to mention our visit with anyone, and drove to the police surgeon's office. Dr. Donald Drake greeted Holmes and I cordially, and answered Holmes's question before my friend had even time to ask it.

"Marvin Armitage did not die of food poisoning."

Chapter Seven

Holmes and I both registered surprise. I found my voice while Holmes pondered and said, "But the threatening letter, the strange potato vendor, the timing of his death after eating the potato ..."

Drake handed me his chemical analysis report, blood and gastric juices did indeed indicate no trace of any poisonous substance. I handed the document back to him and asked, "What killed him then?"

"Angina pectoris. His obesity finally got the better of him."

"That seems awfully coincidental," I stated with scepticism.

My companion finally spoke up, "Not necessarily, Watson."

Turning to Drake he said, "Thank you, Doctor. Your opinion is valued as always. Have you informed Lestrade?"

"I was just about to send him my report."

"I know that you must follow protocol and use official channels, but would you mind if we shared your news with him on our way to our next stop?"

"Certainly not, Holmes," replied the elder physician. "Tell him I'm sending the paperwork along presently."

"Come, Watson," cried my friend. "We shall enlighten the good Inspector and then proceed to our final destination to ascertain the truth."

Drake said, "You know the truth then?"

"I am fairly certain, Doctor, but this cause of death has caused me to reconsider my original theory so I must dig a little deeper."

Lestrade was in his office and greeted us rather enthusiastically, "We have found the owner of the potato cart, gentlemen. One of our constables recognised it and we were able to trace the fellow to a public house where he was celebrating. He's locked up now and as soon as he sobers up, we'll get the truth out of him."

If Holmes was surprised at this, he did not show it. In fact, he congratulated the Inspector, "Well done, Lestrade! Your persistence has paid off. May I ask, have you determined a motive as to why this street vendor would wish to do Armitage harm?"

The smile on Lestrade's face turned into a frown, but he recovered and said, "We'll get that out of him when he can speak. Likely it was over some bad review Armitage gave him."

Holmes shook his head slowly, "Our victim did not review street tradesmen, only restaurants and food markets."

Lestrade's face turned even more weaselly than usual as he appeared to concentrate. After a few moments, he said, "Perhaps he lost his job due to a bad restaurant review and was reduced to selling on the streets and wanted revenge for his lost position."

Holmes nodded in approval, "Excellent, Inspector. Your imagination improves. That is indeed a viable theory except for one thing."

The Inspector's eyes narrowed, "What's that?"

"We've just come from Dr. Drake. The potato was not poisoned. Armitage died of a heart attack."

Leaving Lestrade to ponder that puzzle, Holmes and I soon found ourselves exiting from a cab in front of a neat little flat on Bedford Row in Clerkenwell. Holmes's knock on the door was answered by a young woman, looking to be several months with child and having a small waif tagging along behind her who could not have been more than three years old himself.

Holmes politely removed his hat and asked, "Excuse me, Mrs. Benson? My name is Sherlock Holmes and this is my associate, Dr. Watson. We've come from *The London Trident* offices and would like to speak to your husband regarding a story that he is working on. It is rather urgent."

She invited us into the sitting room while she went to fetch the reporter. I looked about the place as we waited. It was modestly decorated with barely usable furniture. The carpet was getting a little threadbare and the curtains had seen better days. It was obvious why Bill Benson needed a promotion to a higher-paying job.

When she came back, she said, "If you've been to the office, you know that my husband is not feeling well today. But he has agreed to see you if you don't mind meeting with him in the bedroom."

Holmes nodded and she led the way to a small room with barely space to stand between the bed, the chest of drawers, and the wardrobe. She closed the door and left us to our business.

Benson could not look at us. He lay under the blankets which barely covered his long lean frame, with the signs of a fever gleaming on his brow. His brown hair was matted with sweat. His clean-shaven face was pale, and his eyes were bloodshot from lack of sleep. He kept staring out of the window. Finally, he said, "I didn't kill him, Mr. Holmes. I swear it! There was no poison in that potato!"

Holmes and I looked at each other. This spontaneous confession was not the result to which we were accustomed. I could only assume that the man's guilt was eating at his soul.

"Where did you get the cart?" asked Holmes.

"A fellow let me rent it in return for my telling him that I wanted to do a story about street vendors in London, and would make sure his name would appear favourably in the newspaper. I lied about which paper I worked for and wore a disguise so that he couldn't point the finger at me if Armitage confronted him later. But then some roughs stole the cart from me as I was taking it back."

Holmes nodded, pointing his cane at the prone figure on the bed, "It's true you did not poison him, Mr. Benson. But I am afraid that you might be held responsible for his death."

"But I was only trying to scare him into quitting, Mr. Holmes! When I stopped by the police station this morning to see if there had been any new obituaries for me to work on and found that he was dead I was mortified. That was not my plan at all."

The detective shook his head, "You admit then that you used Forbes's typewriter to create your threatening letter. You dressed as a potato peddler and gave him the potato wrapped in his bad review. Although you did not intend to kill Armitage, your action in scaring him might be considered in a court of law as a factor in his demise."

"Are you here to arrest me, Mr. Holmes?" he asked with a quivering voice as his hands clenched the covers under his chin.

The detective shook his head slowly, "I do not have that authority, and seeing your living circumstances and your wife's condition, I understand your motivation. I shall, however, have to report what I know to the police. I suggest that you prepare your wife for what lies ahead and pray for leniency."

We left that humble abode with Holmes ordering the cab to take us to Scotland Yard. During the journey my thoughts turned to what Benson would be charged with.

"He didn't actually kill him, Holmes. Armitage did that to himself through his unhealthy habits," I said. "Won't his crime be merely that of menacing behaviour?"

"Technically you are right, Doctor. Armitage's own gluttony had weakened his heart, as you predicted when he left our initial consultation. However, when he saw that the baked potato Benson had given him was wrapped in his own scathing review, the shock was too much for him. He remembered the threat in the letter and his overtaxed heart gave out from fear."

"So that extra morsel of food at just the right moment was fatal for him," I commented.

"A lesson to be learned, Doctor. I believe it was Benjamin Franklin who said, 'To lengthen thy life, lessen thy meals'."

Epilogue

Benson was indeed charged with menacing behaviour contributing to involuntary manslaughter. However, as there was no intent to kill, he received a mere six-month sentence. He lost his job at *The London Trident*, but was able to secure a better position at a newspaper in Liverpool where he became a successful journalist.

Holmes reported The Meat and Greet Steakhouse to the authorities and it was closed down following multiple testimonies from former patrons, food critics and even its staff. It was later reopened under new ownership and has since become a destination for fine food and drink.

Mrs. Carver found new employment as a cook at one of the better restaurants in London. Miss Barret married her beau and continued her work as a housemaid, and later a housekeeper, for an affluent family in Holland Park thanks to a recommendation from Sherlock Holmes.

Sloth

The Case of the
Writer's Block

Chapter One

It was early May 1897 when a caller came to 221B Baker Street seeking the services of my flatmate, Mr. Sherlock Holmes, the consulting detective. She was a comely young lady of perhaps twenty years of age and five feet two inches tall with an hourglass figure of perfect proportions. Her olive skin and gleaming eyes like tiger-eye jewels were striking. Her beautiful face was surrounded by jet-black luxurious hair which fell to her shoulders and curled upward again at the ends.

She was introduced to us by our landlady, Mrs. Hudson, who had shown her upstairs due to her distraught demeanour. "This is Miss Aviana Morini, gentlemen. Miss Morini, this is Dr. John Watson, and the detective, Mr. Sherlock Holmes."

The lady stepped forward and offered her hand to me, which I courteously bowed over, unable to take my eyes from hers, and merely saying "Enchanté" so dumbstruck was I by her allure.

Holmes, less affected by the charms of a beautiful woman, gave her a quick handshake and waved her to a chair. "Pray take a seat, Signorina Morini, and tell us what brings a Sicilian actress to our fair capital."

The young lady froze for a moment, then stepped gracefully across to the chair Holmes had indicated. Once settled in she asked in a charming accent, "You have been to Palermo and seen me perform, Mr. Holmes?"

"I have not," he answered.

"Then how do you know these things about me?" she queried with a suspicious look.

"Your accent, colouring, and facial features are a pleasant combination of the Italian, Greek, and other Mediterranean cultures that inhabit that cosmopolitan isle. Your movement to catch the light and glide smoothly as you walk is habitual among actresses, as is the trace of your theatrical makeup still present behind your left ear. All of this gives away your origins and profession. Now how can we help you?"

"I see I was well advised to come to you," she replied, then continued. "I believe my fiancé was murdered, Mr. Holmes."

The detective nodded, "Who advised you to seek me out?"

"I have been to this Scotland Yard that is supposed to be so famous. But they say I have no evidence so they can do nothing. An Inspector Hopkins suggested I come to you."

She hesitated, as if not wishing to speak her next words. At last, with trembling lip, she uttered, "Mr. Holmes, I fear my Anthony may be dead, and, if so, I know who killed him!"

I was surprised at this statement but Holmes seemed to take it in his stride. I immediately reached for a pencil and paper to take notes. Something I would normally have already done were I not so distracted by her beauty.

Holmes said "Let us do this in the proper sequence, Signorina. First of all, what is your fiancé's full name and description?"

She raised herself up with pride, "Anthony Pietro Apollo. He is twenty-two and built much like Dr. Watson. He has brown hair, brown eyes, and what you call handlebar moustachios. He was born in Palermo but came to study classics at Oxford. He had ambitions to become a writer, Mr. Holmes. In his last letter to me, he told me he had finished the script for the drama he was working on. He hoped to find a theatre or publisher who would take a chance on a new author. That was three months ago."

"Do you have that letter?" asked Holmes.

She pulled the envelope with its contents from her purse and handed it to the detective. "Do you read Italian, Mr. Holmes?"

"I have made a study of Latin in researching language roots as a hobby of mine," answered my friend. "And as a consequence, I am somewhat proficient in Italian."

He glanced over the letter and handed it across to me. My Latin was restricted to that needed in my profession as a doctor so I could not read it word for word but understood the gist of the text. As I was doing so, he continued his questioning.

"You say that you know who killed him. What makes you think that he is dead, and who do you suspect?"

She hesitated, realising that her answer may sound bizarre, but was sure enough of herself to proclaim it anyway, "The playwright, Bertram Hagerty."

"Hagerty?" I questioned. "The one with the new hit play in Drury Lane?"

"*Si*, yes, Dr. Watson. That is the man and that play, I am sure, is Anthony's."

Chapter Two

Holmes, unperturbed, asked the young lady, "What makes you think these things?"

"I came to England to look for Anthony. My brother, Mario, is with me as an escort and is waiting downstairs. I wished to speak to you alone, Mr. Holmes as Mario is very protective and I have not told him my suspicions of Mr. Hagerty for fear of his reaction in case I am wrong.

"But I am not wrong, Mr. Holmes. I was reading the review of that play in a newspaper and it sounded much like Anthony's. I went to see it and now, I am sure."

"Many plays have similar plots," replied Holmes. "How can you be so certain?"

She raised her chin with pride, "The name of the character played by the lead actress is Avianna. Anthony had told me he named that character after me."

Holmes steepled his long fingers under his chin and stared at this potential client. I, who knew him so well, could tell he was evaluating her character, intelligence, sincerity, and possibly her sanity. The idea of a successful playwright such as Bertram Hagerty stealing another writer's work was hard to imagine. That he would kill to do so seemed beyond the realm of possibility. Yet his use of the unusual name, Avianna, seemed far too coincidental to dismiss her claim out of hand.

At last, he lowered his hands and stated, "I will look into the matter for you, Signorina. I cannot promise results, but if there is anything to be found I will exhaust my resources to do so. Did Anthony have any friends in London?"

"He knew no one here except my uncle's family on Saffron Hill near Farringdon."

"Is that where you are staying?"

She answered in the affirmative and gave an address in the largely Italian community within the city. Any word we had would reach her there. She also gave us the address where her fiancé had been staying. It was up in Islington just down the street from what used to be the Almeida Theatre. She had been there, but the landlord was a most disagreeable man who would not let her in, nor turn over Anthony's things to her, stating, "He owes me rent and I'm keeping his goods until he comes back and pays his arrears. If he ain't back by the end of the month I'll sell his stuff to get my money. You can bid on it then!"

Holmes frowned and said, "Well, we'll see what can be done about that. In the meantime, I would advise you not to confront Mr. Hagerty. If he is guilty of some crime, we do not wish to put him on his guard against our efforts to prove it. Dr. Watson and I will make discreet inquiries and see what evidence we may uncover. May I keep this letter for now? I promise I will return it when my investigation is complete."

She hesitated, but then agreed, "If it will help you find my Anthony do what you must."

She stood, reached into her purse, retrieved a small money pouch, and held it out to Holmes. He waved it aside, "Save your money until we have something to report."

She thanked us with a look of hope, replaced the money pouch, and retreated down the stairs. Holmes and I both went to the window and observed her and her brother, a large, barrel-chested fellow, get into a cab and drive off. As we returned to our chairs, Holmes withdrew his volume of indexes containing the letter 'H'. While he turned the pages he asked me, "Do you know anything of this Hagerty fellow, Watson?"

I was lighting my pipe and took a draw to ensure that the match had succeeded, then replied to my friend. "He had two successful plays while you were off on your hiatus, Holmes. Mary and I saw one." I choked back a breath as I heard myself say the name of my dear departed wife. After a beat, I spoke on, "It was called something like *After Sunset at the Seminary*. It was a comedy about young seminarians. It was rather funny, but also quite scandalous and the church protested against it vigorously, but that just drew in more crowds. However, I believe his last two efforts were 'flops' as they say in the theatre. This new play is being heralded as his great comeback."

A thought struck me. I shook my head and sniffed at the coincidence.

Holmes enquired, "What amuses you so, Doctor?"

I blew out a puff of smoke and replied, "His new play is called *Look for Me When I'm Dead*."

Chapter Three

Holmes shook his head at my statement. While my friend's logical brain prefers to ignore anything supernatural, I occasionally am in wonder about the tricks the Fates play upon us mortals. Likely it was a coincidence that Hagerty's play title should be exactly what we were attempting. Yet the remarkability of it struck me as a chance at poetic justice if what Signorina Morini suspected turned out to be true.

Meanwhile, Holmes had found very little in his index for Bertram Hagerty. A rare occurrence indeed, but then again, Hagerty had come into the public eye during Holmes's absence abroad.

"All I have on this playwright fellow is his occupation, address, and an article regarding his last failure which also mentions the previous one, plus some early successes. Do you know anything about the man, Watson?"

"Very little beyond what I've told you," I replied. "I know nothing of his family, but I believe that I read somewhere that he is a visiting lecturer at Oxford. That may mean he attended there as well."

Holmes snapped the book shut, stood, and replaced it on the shelf. "I shall have to go out then. Care to come along, Watson?"

"Certainly. Where to, Holmes?"

"First the offices of *The Daily Telegraph*, then to the Garrick Club. After that, we shall see."

At *The Daily Telegraph* Holmes enquired after the reporter, Thomas Kent. I remembered the fellow from a previous case. His position as a theatre critic for the newspaper should certainly be beneficial to Holmes now.

The tall, lean, and lanky fellow was summoned and welcomed us enthusiastically, shaking our hands as he said, "Holmes, it's good to see you, and you as well, Dr. Watson. Come in there's an office back here we can use."

Kent led the way through the room of scattered desks and reporters typing away. At last, we came to an office where he closed the door as we sat. Jovially he asked, "Well, what can I do for the world's greatest consulting detective?"

Holmes, as was his wont, came straight to the point, "I need to know whatever you can tell me about the playwright, Bertram Hagerty."

"Bert?" said Kent with a raised eyebrow. "Is he in some sort of trouble?"

Holmes raised an index finger to his lips and gave the reporter a look. Kent inhaled a deep breath and nodded, "Ah, I understand. The usual terms, Holmes?"

"Yes," agreed the detective.

I knew that this meant that, should a story arise out of this investigation, Kent would be given first access to it. He occasionally strayed outside the bounds of theatrical reviews, just for the variety of doing some more meaningful reporting, and Holmes was one of his best sources for that.

"Well, let's see. He is from moderate means. His father owns a carriage-building company. He attended Oxford, though I don't believe he graduated. As I recall there were rumours of some sort of a scandal. Nothing salacious, mind you. I think that there was a question regarding plagiarism on a paper he had written. He was not expelled, he left voluntarily. Supposedly it was to spend more time working on his first play, a comedy called *My Horse for a Kingdom*. It turned out to be successful and he was hailed as a brilliant new playwright with a fresh perspective for what modern audiences sought."

Holmes nodded, "I understand that after some initial success, he had some failures."

Kent nodded, "Yes, two absolute 'bombs'. He hasn't gotten anyone to underwrite a play of his for the last couple of seasons. This new drama is a big hit, however, so he must have gotten his old magic back."

"You've seen the play of course?"

Kent looked askance at Holmes "You know I never miss an opening night. I wrote a favourable review weeks ago."

"Tell me, if you are familiar with his works, does this one appear to be in his usual style?"

The reporter tilted his head in thought before replying, "That's hard to say, Holmes. His successes were all comedies. He has only written one drama that was produced and it was one of his 'flops'. This new one has excellent character development, a clever plot, and a twist at the end that no one would have ever seen coming. It is really very good ..." he hesitated. "Now that you mention it, it is better than I would have expected of him."

Kent's face brightened and he leaned forward, whispering, "Is that what this is about? You believe that he stole the play?"

Holmes, also keeping his voice low replied, "It has been suggested."

Kent pressed for more, "So your client is claiming to be the original author. How will you prove that?"

Holmes shook his head, "My client is concerned for the original author's health and whereabouts. As to proof of the play's authorship, I still have work to do. Your insights into Hagerty's past and talents have been helpful. At least now I have reason to believe that my client may be on to something."

Chapter Four

After a few more questions regarding the play's producer and any other personal information Kent had about Hagerty, we left the reporter and took to the streets again. When we hailed a cab, Holmes instructed the driver to take us to the theatre in Drury Lane.

"Are you going to interview the producer, Holmes?" I asked, logically I thought.

"No, no, Watson," he replied. "I do not wish to tip our hand too soon. Voicing our suspicions to the producer would very likely result in his saying something to Hagerty and we cannot have him know that we are on his trail."

"Then why the theatre, Holmes?"

"We are going to purchase tickets for tonight's performance. I need to become familiar with the play and the artistic style before I can make any judgements about our quarry."

Fortunately, being mid-week, the play was not sold out, though we did have to settle for circle seats. From the box office, we walked to The Garrick Club. Membership at The Garrick is limited to actors, playwrights, lawyers, and other men of letters. Fortunately, Holmes, being a former actor, retained his membership as an aid to his work as a detective. I had become a member based on my journalistic efforts in recording Holmes's cases. We were thus welcomed and made our way to the downstairs dining room where lunch was being served.

Holmes decided that we should split up and he made the rounds of his theatrical friends while I mingled with the journalistic members.

Of course, I was inundated with questions regarding Holmes and when I was going to publish more of his adventures. I was so busy answering questions that I was barely able to ask any. I did manage to mention that I was going to see Hagerty's play that night and was advised as to its unique plot, though given no details. I was also spared the revelation of the surprise ending only being told, 'Do not dare to leave early'.

I ate a light meal during our time there and noted that Holmes had departed upstairs to the bar where I later found him amidst a crowd of his theatrical friends. He could barely keep away the myriad of people desiring the true story of his three-year absence.

When we finally left the club, I felt exhausted from the ordeal. Holmes seemed quite satisfied, however, and I asked him what he had learned as our cab headed north.

"It appears our dear Mr. Hagerty has undergone quite a transformation in personality in recent months," said my friend.

"In the past, he was quite adamant in his arguments regarding changes made by the director, or the way actors portrayed his lines, and he attended every performance. Now he is withdrawn, morose, much more amiable to suggested changes and only comes to the theatre at weekends."

I nodded and contributed my own observations, "I heard he rarely comes to the Club since his new play opened, whereas, during his previous plays, he was there nearly daily to receive the accolades of his fellows. What do you make of it, Holmes?"

"I believe it is further evidence that the play is not his," stated the detective. "His not caring when changes are made indicates a lack of possessiveness. Think how upset you have been when Doyle, or the editors at *The Strand*, made changes to your manuscripts after all your careful crafting. From all accounts, Hagerty's ego is, or used to be, far greater than yours. His lack of attendance at the theatre and his Club tells me that he is likely feeling guilty about receiving credit for a work that is not his own creation."

"But how do we prove it?"

"I am hoping that we can find some evidence at our next destination."

"I was lost in thought when you spoke to the cabbie, Holmes. Where are we going?"

"To Islington. I need to examine Apollo's personal possessions."

The peculiarity of that statement caught my imagination. I suppose it was due to my earlier idea of the Fates being involved in our case, and I pictured us invading the realm of the gods on Mount Olympus. Apparently, the slight grin on my face gave away my thoughts as Holmes turned to me and said, somewhat mockingly, "I trust that his landlord will be less formidable an obstacle than Zeus."

On Almeida Street, with its long rows of brown brick over white block houses, we found the number Avianna Morini had given us. The door was opened to us by a coarse-looking gentleman of approximately forty years. He was in shirtsleeves and appeared to have neglected his razor that morning for there was at least a day's growth of beard upon his face. When he spoke, the alcohol that he had consumed with his lunch was quite evident upon his breath, but he did not appear inebriated.

"Who be you and what do you want?" he asked in his rough accent.

"My name is Sherlock Holmes and this is my associate, Dr. Watson, and you are?"

He looked us up and down as if deciding we were who we said we were.

"My name's Duffy, I own this building but I got no rooms for rent right now." He suddenly stopped and looked closely at my friend. "Sherlock Holmes you say? I thought you was dead. Fell off a mountain over in Switzerland they say."

Holmes gave a slight shake of his head and gave a glance in my direction, "They were wrong. Here is my card."

Duffy took the card, looked at it, and then asked, "Well, what is it you want then?"

253

"We've come to enquire after Mr. Anthony Apollo."

"He ain't here. Disappeared awhile back owing me money."

"I am aware. I should like to examine his belongings to see if I can determine where he went."

Duffy shook his head, "Like I told that fiancée of his, I'm keeping his goods until month end then selling 'em off."

"If I can find him, wouldn't you rather have him pay your money than the sorry price his meagre belongings would bring?" asked Holmes in his most persuasive tone.

Duffy thought about that for a few seconds. "Well, 'tis true he didn't have much." Making a decision he said, "All right you can come upstairs and look through his things, but you can't take nothing."

We followed him up the stairs and he unlocked the room once occupied by the young Sicilian. I examined the wardrobe and checked the pockets of his clothing while Holmes made a circuit of the room observing the window which he noted had recent damage to the sill, and finally concentrating on his desk, whereupon a typewriter sat gathering dust. Duffy stood in the doorway, keeping a close watch to make sure that we took nothing.

Holmes examined the typewriter with his lens but shook his head at the results. He checked the drawers and found a half ream of foolscap and several sheets of carbon paper. He became animated at this discovery and again used his lens to inspect the black sheets closely.

I walked up behind him and said, "There's nothing but clothes in the wardrobe, Holmes, and the same for the chest of drawers. Whatever valuables Apollo had, he must have had on him when he left. What did you find here?"

He held a black sheet up over his shoulder and I took it from him. Even with my naked eye, I could see what had excited Holmes. "Well, here's one piece of the puzzle solved," I stated, handing the page back to him.

My companion turned towards the landlord, who had walked up behind us to see what Holmes had found.

"Mr. Duffy, we believe these pages will lead us to Mr. Apollo, but I need to take them with me."

The landlord started to protest but Holmes held up his hand, "I will give you two guineas for these sheets now, and at the end of the month I will guarantee that you will receive no less than the same again for the rest of his goods."

Duffy scratched his stubbled jaw as he thought, "Four guineas, eh? Well, Mr. Sherlock Holmes, you've got a deal if you'll put it in writin'."

Holmes took two sheets of paper, placed a carbon between them and typed out his agreement with Duffy. He then removed the sheets, signed through both copies and handed the original to the eager landlord. His copy, plus the stack of carbon paper, went into a large envelope, of which there were several in the drawer.

As we were bidding the man *adieu*, I put a question to him. "You seem to have been more accustomed to manual labour than being a landlord, Mr. Duffy. How did you come to own this place?"

"Aye, Doctor," he said. "I was a wheelwright since I was a lad, but me widowed aunt died last year and left this place to me. Income is a sight better and the work blessed easier."

I smiled, "You are a fortunate man, sir. Thank you and good day."

Regaining a cab once more, Holmes ordered the driver to Baker Street then turned to me, "I could have told you Duffy was a wheelwright, Watson. He has all the physical characteristics, even after several months away from the work. I had thus also deduced the building was an inheritance, though it would have taken a little more examination to determine who the unfortunate relative was."

"I have no doubt, Holmes," I responded. "But I also knew that you would not bother with it as it has no bearing on our case, and I was curious as to how an individual of his type could afford such a dwelling in that neighbourhood."

"You are correct in that it has no bearing. But these," he held up the envelope, "are assurance that Signorina Morini is correct about the play being stolen."

"Does that mean Apollo is dead?"

"It does not prove it, but there is a high probability and now we have the proof we need to confront Hagerty."

Chapter Five

Back in our rooms at 221B, Holmes hung up his coat and went straight to the dining table where he could more closely examine the carbon pages. I went to the sideboard and poured each of us a whisky and soda.

"Watson, be a good fellow and bring me a pencil and several blank sheets of paper," he asked as I set his drink next to him. I noted that he had spread out the black sheets of carbon paper.

"Holmes," I said, handing the paper and pencil over. "I've used carbon paper myself and it seems highly unusual that Apollo would leave behind so many readable sheets. I always use the same sheet over and over again until it has sufficiently worn out its copying properties."

Holmes was starting to write and even as he did so, answered my question, "It appears our young friend wanted a superbly clean and sharp second copy of his work. He was not such a spendthrift as to use only one carbon sheet per page. But note that the verbiage only makes sense if you read every other line. What he has done is type out a page in double space, then, for the next page he has offset the carbon paper so that his new text falls between the lines already there. With fresh carbon, his second copy will come out virtually identical to the original."

"I see," I said. "So, you are copying out what the actual document said by writing every other line. Will you then take it to Inspector Hopkins so he can arrest Hagerty?"

"Not just yet, Watson. We can tell from these pages that the title is the same as that of Hagerty's play, but that may only mean that he used the title after it was mentioned to him by Apollo. I propose to copy out the text and then take it with us tonight and then compare it to the actual play Hagerty claims to have written. If that is verbatim, we have our man for plagiarism at least. With that threat hanging over him, we shall have leverage to learn the true facts."

The task took Holmes much of the afternoon. He would not accept my assistance, but he did allow me to read the pages as he finished them, so as to familiarise myself with the drama before we saw it that evening. At last, just as Mrs. Hudson was serving our tea, he set down his pencil and declared, "Finished!"

I took up that final sheet and read it. With raised eyebrows, I declared, "It really is rather clever, Holmes. My friends at The Garrick were right. The ending is indeed a surprise."

He took a sip of the whisky I had replenished, "Another point in favour of it being identical," he said. "But we must be certain. Let us down our fair landlady's repast and be off to Drury Lane."

Having copied the sheets himself, Holmes felt he knew the play well enough that he had me hold on to the pages to check them as the play progressed. Fortunately, even with the lights dimmed for the performance, I could just make out the documents.

From the very first scene, the location description and the dialogue were just as noted in Apollo's script. Scene after scene confirmed that we were seeing the play Apollo had typed and put his name to as author on the title page.

At the play's end, I asked Holmes what steps he would now take. "First," he replied, "I propose that we go to Saffron Hill and inform Avianna Morini of our findings. Then we shall arrange to go together to Scotland Yard first thing in the morning to inform Hopkins of the proofs we have. My suggestion to him shall be that we confront Hagerty and demand the truth in consideration for some slight leniency in his sentencing. Perhaps life in prison as opposed to the death penalty, if he, in fact, killed Apollo."

"You think there is a chance he did not?" I asked, surprised.

"We only know that the young man is missing, Doctor. The state of his health has yet to be ascertained. It is a serious fault to jump to conclusions too soon."

Our client's address on Saffron Hill was less than a mile and a half from the theatre and on a pleasant spring day it would have been an easy walk. Being late at night, however, we took a cab and were deposited at the lady's steps by eleven o'clock.

The door was opened to us by a middle-aged man of stocky build, thinning black hair, and a slightly greying moustache with the classic Roman nose of so many Italians. "What is you want?" he said in accented English and with suspicion.

My friend replied, "We have come with news for Signorina Morini. I am Sherlock Holmes and this is my colleague, Dr. Watson."

The gentleman twisted his large bulk into the house and called out, "Avianna! *Vieni qui!*"

When she arrived, he took a slight step back so she could see around him and she assured him that it was all right to let us enter. She led us to a sitting room where she formally introduced us to her brother, Mario, who proved to be even more imposing than the glimpse that we had had of him through our window. A Herculean figure of a man who stuck by his sister's side as if they were conjoined twins. Also to her Uncle Tomaso who had answered the door, Cecilia, his wife, and his son, Enrico.

Almost fearfully she asked, "What news have you, Mr. Holmes? Is Anthony ..."

She could not say the word and Holmes immediately assured her that we had not found her fiancé, but had discovered proof that Hagerty had stolen his play. "It is enough to take to Scotland Yard and open an investigation towards Hagerty's arrest. Once we confront him, I am sure that we will learn more about Mr. Apollo. I would like you to come with us in the morning to see Inspector Hopkins."

Enrico, a handsome youth roughly the same age as our client, asked, "What proof have you found?"

Holmes gazed upon the young man briefly, then answered, "A copy of his play was left in his rooms. We compared it to the performance we saw tonight. It is definitely the same work."

The young man nodded thoughtfully, then turned to his cousin, reaching out for her hand, "If they have this proof you must go with them, Avi. The matter must be settled for your peace of mind."

Avianna had been holding her other hand to her breast to try and still her beating heart, she now formed a fist and hit the arm of her chair, "Yes! I will go with you, Mr. Holmes. This man must pay! What time in the morning?"

Holmes suggested that we would pick her and her brother up at eight so as to be at the Yard before nine. Arrangements having been made, we excused ourselves and left for Baker Street. I felt secure in the knowledge and evidence that we had gained and that the case was as good as solved.

However, I had forgotten another of Holmes's adages, 'Never presume when only an assumption is warranted. Especially when still lacking data'.

Chapter Six

The next morning we invaded Inspector Stanley Hopkins's office like a thundering herd. As angry as Avianna Morini was, Holmes had convinced her to let him do the talking. Hopkins had stood in a defensive posture upon the arrival of so many people at his office at once, even though escorted by a constable. When he recognised Holmes he breathed a sigh of relief, sat back down, and waved us all to be comfortable.

As there were only two chairs for guests, Holmes and I stood and let Avianna and her brother take the seats across the desk from the Inspector. If their proximity intimidated the young official, he did not let it show. He looked over their heads and asked, "I presume you have discovered new facts in the Apollo case, Mr. Holmes. I gather it is something that now makes it possible for me to act in an official capacity?"

"Yes, indeed, Hopkins," replied my companion. "We searched Apollo's rooms and were able to reconstruct a copy of his play from his papers. We compared it to the one Hagerty has performing in Drury Lane and they are identical. It is certainly proof that they knew each other and provides you reasonable grounds to question him."

"You say that you *reconstructed* a copy of his play?" asked Hopkins. "What exactly does that mean?"

Holmes explained his process as he turned over the evidence to the Inspector. Hopkins examined the carbons and the copy

261

Holmes had handwritten and nodded in agreement. "And you are quite sure that this is exactly the play you witnessed at the theatre?"

Holmes gave the young man a look that made the Scotland Yard Inspector feel foolish for even asking such a question. Hopkins merely said "Ahem, very well. Let's go and see what Hagerty has to say about it."

Bertram Hagerty occupied a brick house that had been rendered and painted white on Stamford Road in Dalston. He was a bachelor of roughly thirty years of age, living alone. He had a housekeeper who came in during the day to clean and prepare meals that he could heat up whenever he felt like eating. She was the one who answered the door upon our arrival.

Hopkins advised her that we were there to call upon Mr. Hagerty regarding a police matter, and that she should fetch him without delay. We were shown into the front room where in the thirty seconds or so it took him to appear, I noted that it was a spartan affair. It was habitable, but there was little in the way of furniture, and that which was present was inexpensive. There were no paintings on the drab plaster walls. For someone who was supposed to be a creative genius, it was dreary and uninspiring.

When Hagerty entered the room his countenance matched the environment. Hopkins made introductions and, being so many of us, Hagerty invited us into the dining room. The only place with sufficient seating for the small crowd.

Before Hopkins could speak again, the playwright made an extraordinary statement, "Apollo's dead, isn't he?"

Avianna Morini gasped and her brother took her hand, whether to comfort or to prevent her from attacking our suspect, I could not be sure. Holmes had his elbows on the table, hands interlocked beneath his chin and steepled index fingers reaching nearly to his lips as he stared at the man, not wishing to interrupt a possible confession.

Hagerty's eyes narrowed in confusion and his lips trembled as he attempted to digest this statement, "Are you arresting me, Inspector? I haven't committed a crime!"

Avianna could hold back no longer. She rose from her chair, slamming her fist on the table, and shouted "Liar! You killed my Anthony and stole his play!"

Mario pulled her back down and Holmes said to her sternly, "Wait until we hear what the man has to say, Signorina."

Hagerty had thrown himself back in his chair, ready to spring to his feet in defence against this sudden outburst. Hopkins had stood to keep himself between Avianna and Hagerty but now re-took his seat and turned toward our suspect and said, "Mr. Hagerty, we have proof that Anthony Apollo wrote the play which is now performing in Drury Lane under your name. Apollo has been missing for weeks. You must see how this looks, sir. Can you give us an explanation other than what the young lady has accused you of?"

Hagerty tugged at his collar and then leaned forward, forearms on the table. "First let me say that I am sorry Anthony is missing. This has been of great concern to me as well. He shows great promise and I was going to make him my protégé and possibly a partner. He came to me with his play months ago, asking me to read it and advise him. As I was in a period devoid of ideas, I had the time and agreed to do so. It was quite good for a first effort. I made some suggestions and he did the rewrites and came back with two copies. We read through them together and I said it was good enough to submit to a producer. He told me that he had previously presented some works to a couple of producers and had been ignored as an unproven newcomer. It was *his* idea that we submit the play under my name so that it would at least garner some attention.

"That may sound like a slothful way for me to get back into the theatre, using another man's work, but I was as desperate as he to do so. We came to an agreement that I would take the credit for this one but share the proceeds with him equally, and then we would collaborate on a new play wherein he would be listed as co-author. I have it in writing and can show you the document that he signed."

"We'll get to that," said Hopkins, "Go on."

"Well, as you know the play was accepted. Once it went into rehearsals it was in the hands of the director. Anthony and I met weekly to discuss new ideas for our next work. Then I received a letter from him stating that he needed to travel out of town for a month, but that his weekly cheques against the play's profits should be sent to a certain post office where he would have them collected for deposit until he returned. That was two months ago and I've not heard from him since."

Holmes spoke up and asked, "Would you please show us the agreement that you signed as well as the letter from him regarding where to send his money?"

Hagerty, followed by Hopkins, stepped into the next room, retrieved some papers from his desk drawer, and returned, handing them to the policeman. The Inspector read over the agreement and handed it in turn to Holmes saying, "This looks pretty straightforward. It confirms the story that Hagerty did not steal the play but was given the right to use it by Apollo in return for consideration."

Holmes perused the typewritten document, paying special attention to the signatures. Then he asked to see the letter Hopkins had just read regarding where to send Apollo's share of the profits. It was also typed with a handwritten signature. Holmes placed one page atop the other, offset just enough so that the signatures were in close proximity. He turned the papers towards me and instantly I knew what he was observing. He then set the papers on the table in front of Avianna Morini. "Are these both your fiancés's signature?

She took up the agreement first, to see if Anthony had indeed signed over his author's rights. Shaking her head in disappointment she then took up the letter. She looked up sharply at Holmes, then at Hagerty. "This is *not* Anthony's signature! It is a forgery! What have you done with him?"

Hagerty was stricken with fear, "Nothing, I swear! Look, here is the envelope it came in." Holmes snatched the envelope from the playwright's hand and studied it with his lens. "It is a genuine postmark. But that does not mean you couldn't have posted it yourself and forged the lad's signature."

"I did no such thing! I have nothing to do with his disappearance. I need him alive to help me with our next play!"

Hopkins remarked, "With the success of this current one your reputation is restored. You have no need to tie yourself to an amateur."

The writer shook his head, "I've been having a hard time coming up with new ideas. Anthony's fresh outlook on life and his foreign cultural background are the spark I need to reignite my creative flame. I've no desire that any harm should come to him!"

"I am afraid that the evidence lies against you for now, Mr. Hagerty," declared the Inspector. "You'll need to come with me."

As Hopkins prepared to take his prisoner away, Holmes made one last request.

"Inspector, I should like to satisfy myself on one point before you depart."

Hopkins, who has always trusted Holmes, rubbed his jaw and replied, "Anything within reason, Mr. Holmes."

The detective turned to the playwright and asked, "Where is your typewriter, sir?"

Hagerty pointed to the room from which he had retrieved the papers and said, "In there, why?"

Holmes, instead of answering, strode off immediately to the other room, sat at the machine, inserted a blank sheet of paper, and typed out a copy of the letter instructing Hagerty where to send the money. He plucked the sheet from the roller and placed the two documents side by side. Even looking over his shoulder without a magnifying lens, I could see the difference. Hopkins caught it as well. The open space of the letter 'e' was half filled in with ink. Obviously due to a dirty typeface on the type head. The letter was not typed on Hagerty's machine

"Still, Mr. Holmes," said the Inspector. "He could have used another typewriter to forge that document."

"From my examination of the carbon copies from Apollo's desk, I believe that this agreement was typed on *his* machine. As to who typed it, we shall have to investigate further."

265

Chapter Seven

We split up into two four-wheelers for the ride back to Scotland Yard. Holmes had me accompany Hopkins and his prisoner while he rode with Avianna and her brother. Hagerty eventually accepted the situation; that he was not going to be set free while the investigation was ongoing.

Holmes was hatching a plot with Avianna based upon an observation that he had made. She was shocked at the suggestion and Mario seethed with anger at the possibility that Holmes's idea might be true. He dropped them at their uncle's home and proceeded to catch up with us at Scotland Yard. He informed Hopkins of his plot but the Inspector hesitated, "You know we can't use that as evidence, Holmes."

"I believe that the threat of what I have proposed will bring the culprit to us, Hopkins. All we have to do is lay in wait."

Hopkins finally agreed that it was the only course of action he could see at the moment, and so we set a time to meet later that evening. Holmes and I returned to Baker Street for a late lunch. As he prepared his chemicals I asked, "Do you really think this is going to work, Holmes? Won't the fact that two people used it obscure the findings?"

"Very likely, doctor," he admitted. "I confess that I am counting much more on our quarry coming to destroy the evidence that he thinks we are collecting so we can catch him in the act and secure a confession."

Hopkins came by at seven o'clock as we had agreed then we proceeded on to Apollo's rooms in Islington. Duffy was not happy to see us since we had not found his missing tenant, but the presence of the Inspector secured us entrance, and we advised the landlord that we would be occupying the room for the evening.

Holmes turned down the gas and we were forced to sit in darkness as any light would warn off our prey.

The Inspector asked my friend, "How did this fellow get past the landlord?"

"The window has been forced," replied Holmes in a soft voice. "I noted that the first time we were here. It is within arm's reach of the drainpipe and there is a convenient ledge between the lower floor and this one. A common feature of the time when these houses were built. Our enterprising fellow likely tried but was unable to get past the landlord. Thus he resorted to breaking and entering. He used Apollo's typewriter to create the message about where to send the money."

Holmes and I took up positions either side of the chest of drawers near the window while Hopkins stepped into the wardrobe with the door slightly ajar.

I looked to my friend and asked, "Speaking of the money, why not just stake out the post office where it is being sent and grab the man when he picks it up?"

"It is an option we may have to fall back on," admitted Holmes. "But he could always claim that Apollo asked him to pick up his envelopes or some such story. This way we'll have proof that Apollo did not write those instructions."

We sat in silence after that, the only sound being a church clock in the distance tolling the hours. A few minutes after they had struck eleven, we heard a scuffling sound outside. Then a dark shadow appeared against the curtains at the window. We heard the sharp snick of metal on metal as some tool was used to force back the latch. Then a leg stepped through the curtains and landed on the floor. It was quickly followed by a torso and head, and finally the other leg. The burglar carried a dark lantern which he opened just a crack and set on the table next to the typewriter which he then proceeded to place into a large carpetbag that had been strapped to his back. When his hands were full of the machine, Holmes stepped out of his hiding place, his bulldog firearm at the ready, and ordered, "Stay where you are, you're surrounded!"

To emphasise the fact, Hopkins left the wardrobe and turned up the room lights while I emerged from beside the chest of drawers, my army revolver in hand. The look on our quarry's face was sheer panic as he turned ashen in fear. At first, I thought that he was going to faint, but then he dropped the typewriter on the desk and made a rush for the door. Neither Holmes nor I wished to shoot an unarmed man. I was about to fire a warning shot when Hopkins, using the rugby skills that had served him well in school, executed a superb tackle and came up with his knee in the fellow's back as he placed handcuffs on him.

"Is this the man you expected, Holmes?" he asked as he stood the burglar up onto his feet.

"Yes, Inspector," answered the detective.

"Enrico Morini," declared Hopkins. "I am arresting you for burglary, fraud, and possibly kidnapping and murder. Do you wish to make a statement?"

The lad shook his head vehemently in silence and we escorted him out of the building. I took up the carpetbag with the typewriter as evidence and we bundled into a four-wheeler off to Scotland Yard.

Chapter Eight

Our prisoner refused to speak to anyone until we sent for his father. While he waited in a cell, Hopkins made some hot coffee for the three of us in his office.

"What made you suspect this fellow, Holmes?" asked the Inspector, when we had settled in to await Tomaso Morini's arrival. "All the evidence seemed to be against Hagerty."

Holmes took a sip from his cup and then replied, "Hagerty may be guilty of sloth, being willing to take another man's work as his own rather than working harder himself, but his demeanour was all wrong when we confronted him. A writer should be able to come up with a better story than the one he related to us. It would have been much easier on his part to merely say that he bought the rights to the story from Apollo and never heard from him again. Instead, I believe, he told us the truth which required much more detail for him to remember.

"Also, when we were at the Morini house informing young Avianna of what we had found, Enrico's attitude towards her and his reaching out for her hand were such that seemed to be more than that of concern for a cousin. I believe the fellow is in love with her, and that he took advantage of the situation to remove his rival."

I spoke up and asked, "You believe Apollo is dead then?"

"I think it highly likely, Watson. Otherwise, he is being held captive somewhere, but that may require an accomplice which increases the danger to Enrico as it would open him up to blackmail in the future.

"However, it is possible that he has done it alone and is keeping Apollo alive in some out-of-the-way secure location in case he needs him, or until he could find a way to make it look like Hagerty killed him. But eventually, he would have to eliminate him as a witness."

It was approaching one o'clock in the morning when a constable came to inform Hopkins that the Morini family had arrived. When the Inspector ordered them to be shown in, we found Tomaso was accompanied by Avianna and Mario.

The father demanded, "What is going on? Why have you arrested my son?"

We had all stood at his entrance and the Inspector replied, "Enrico Morini has been caught in the act of burglary and is believed to be responsible for the disappearance of Anthony Apollo."

"No!" cried Avianna in surprise. "Enrico would not do this to me!"

"Even if he loved you?" stated Holmes.

Her hand went to her throat. "Love …"

Hopkins spoke up, "I think that we had all better go and let Enrico speak for himself." He led the way to the cell and opened the door where Enrico lay curled on the bed in a foetal position. When he looked up at the sound and saw not only his father but Avianna there as well, he sat up and pressed his back to the wall. The defiance was gone from his face, replaced by panic.

Looking straight at his beautiful cousin he cried, "Avi! What are you doing here? I only asked for my father. You can't be here!"

Hopkins spoke up, "As an injured party she has the right to confront you as you were stealing her fiance's property when we arrested you. Now tell us the whole story and where Anthony Apollo is."

Avianna spoke up, tears welling in her eyes, "Enrico, what did you do? Where is my Anthony?"

The effect of her presence loosened the young man's tongue. He could not, would not lie to her. But her statement put a vehemence into his voice. He jumped to his feet and cried, "*Your* Anthony? That dreamer who sat around all day thinking that he could make a living telling stories? *I* love you. *I* can take care of you. Have you forgotten the summer that we had three years ago when we came to Palermo to visit your family?"

Avianna seemed taken aback, then replied, "We went on excursions, had picnics and saw plays. No more than I would do with any friend. You cannot seriously think that meant I loved you. Besides, you know what happens when first cousins in our family marry. I would never risk having a child with such deformities."

Her statement put a stricken look upon him. Finally, Tomaso spoke up, "Enough! Enrico, say what you have done. *Parlare!*"

Despite his earlier bravado, the boy could not stand up to his father. He sank back to a sitting position on the bed and buried his face in his hands for a moment. Then, without looking up he told his story.

"Anthony visited us often and told us of his progress in his work. I had been to his rooms a few times at his invitation to go for a meal or a drink. He told me of his meeting with that playwright fellow and how well things were going. When he mentioned how much he was paid for his play and the share of profits he was making I knew that he would soon send for you. In fact, he had a letter telling you the good news and I offered to post it for him on my way home so that he would not have to go out. As soon as I was out of sight of the house, I tore it open and read it. My worst fears had come true. He was writing to tell you of his success and asking you to set a wedding date.

"I could *not* let that happen! The next night I took him out to celebrate, got him drunk, and turned him over to some sailors who were looking for seaman for their voyage. He's halfway to China by now, impressed aboard an American ship.[1]

---

[1] Impressment, or to use the colloquial crimping or shanghaiing, died out with the end of sailing ships and was illegal in the United Kingdom at this time but was still an acceptable practice aboard American ships up until 1915.

"I wrote the letter to Hagerty and have been collecting the money ever since so that I could save it up for you and me to get married now that I had made it look like Anthony had deserted you. I could not believe that this detective had found a copy of his play, and when you told us at dinner tonight that he was going to test Anthony's typewriter to find out if it was I who typed those payment instructions, I was going to steal the machine and destroy it. It would look suspicious, but I thought it would be blamed on the landlord trying to sell Anthony's chattel's to recover the rent arrears owed to him."

He rolled back onto the bed, refusing to look in our direction and merely said, "Now you know it all."

Mario started forward with murderous intent, but Tomaso, who is no small man himself, stepped between them and Avianna's brother grudgingly submitted to his elder and returned to his sister's side. She had listened intently to this tale and grasping the fact that Anthony was still alive cried out, "What ship is he on?"

"All I know is that they were Americans bound for China." He replied weakly without looking at her.

Holmes spoke up, "What was the date you committed this act?"

Enrico spat out an answer of "I don't recall," but gave an approximation.

The detective nodded and said to our client, "I believe I can trace it, Signorina. Give me a day or two."

We all left the prisoner to contemplate his sins and, on the way back to Hopkins's office, he stopped and released Bertram Hagerty who received a sincere apology.

Epilogue

I awoke late after our long night and found Holmes already gone out which did not surprise me. He returned just before lunch and advised me of his morning activities.

"I've been to the docks, Watson, and found the name of the vessel that left port for China on the date suggested by Enrico. The American ship *The Lariat*, a twenty-four hundred ton, three-masted merchant vessel out of New York, bound for Hong Kong is the only one that fits the criteria. It has currently cleared Suez and is sailing around India. My brother, Mycroft is using his influence with his military contacts and is arranging for it to be met by a British warship where they will retrieve Mr. Apollo and return him to his choice of either London or Palermo."

"Well, thank God for that!" I said, then added, "You know, harrowing as it was, his story might make for a good play."

Holmes nodded, "They do say it is best to write about what you know. Perhaps Hagerty should try it."

www.ingramcontent.com/pod-product-compliance
Lightning Source LLC
Chambersburg PA
CBHW070326260626
47160CB00003B/963